catching Saradove

catching

by Bertha Harris

Saradove

HARCOURT, BRACE & WORLD, INC.

New York

for Jennifer Harris Wyland

contents

catching Saradove

yellow pollen

The park is the city's ugliest. It nestles in the dirty hands of the Lower East Side beside the baby and me. We squeeze ourselves in here trying to grow trees in unhealthy dirt, trying to work my tongue through the sounds of sure-fire Spanish. I wait through each night listening to the park expecting me with the morning. After the night, there is no other place to go. Baby needs babies, I need mothers to pantomime motherhood for me.

We follow the sun's path to the sandbox. The baby is hugging her tin pail and gathering her nerve and anger to explode it in the faces of children who will snatch her toys from her.

3

Excepting me, the whole human race is her giant, natural enemy. I alone give everything to her, she does not hate me; this little power keeps me proud. We hurry through what's left of the morning; afternoon is becoming too cold and dark for us to meet it alone on the street. The weather is entering the war of the pavements against us. At every corner, a bomb of cold explodes in my face. The weather is waiting now behind the sun, lifting its arm to give the final blow.

We thread our way through the ruins of neighborhoods that are slimy with the grease from meat packers' carcasses and decorated with bright humps of broken, abandoned automobiles. The young Puerto Rican boys, their minds always on turning a penny and making drama in the dark, have stripped the cars of their valuables and set the dross on fire. The innards of the seat cushions smoke the air for days.

I turn the stroller into Avenue B. There are the trees waving country colors through the city's haze at me. A tiny red sweater glints back and forth against the steel of a swing. There is only one more red light; the baby bounces up and down in her seat because she is nearly where the balls bounce. I begin to weave my anxiety around her. Every day one child desires the death of another for the prize of an oatmeal box; the children make violence look like sand castles. They hide and seek to murder. Each time I prevent a death, I feel the real knives inside me fight to slice through my brow, to be free to kill my own. Her life is the lock and key on my freedom to die. We are almost there. I shake myself and shiver in the sun: no freedom is worth even one of her shining eyes. I must be alert. Today the tall boy whose splendid fat cushions an infant mind will try again to force mine or another to swallow a piece of glass from the park's infinite supply. A blood- and urine-soaked bum will shuffle over from his newspaper bed to kiss my baby. His fury and my guilt will be enormous when I stop him.

4

The day hangs over us like a big flower on a summer bush, but it is autumn. Nature and magic conspire to grow good in me with roots that will choke my need to sleep until I die. The baby's hair turns to copper in the light. She is pretty in her yellow jacket. I am soaring up and away with *hubris* or like Superman. I will land with glamour in my hand, and the godmother will be waiting with her wand. In a minute now, I will be happy. The ragged pensioners lining the winding walk to the playground see my flight and ready their hard smiles to catch my fall. Meanwhile, they quarrel over memories of their youth to pass the time. Only a few men are here and they sit alone staring into the invisible pages of the *Daily News* and the Polish newspapers. The women huddle together, nodding their dirty braids at each other. Their coats are stuffed with strength and held together with crooked safety pins. Most of the legs are bandaged up with wide strips of gray elastic, but some gory veins still overflow into shoes. The women kiss and hug obese, has-been dogs who lie still and look pained. The pigeons circle and occasionally make a direct hit on the greasy braids, exciting a burst of American obscenities and foreign abuse from the crowd. Little boys, as assured and elegant as the pigeons, pedal up on their bicycles and yell "Ha Ha!" as if they themselves had arranged the defilement. The boys know that the old women hate them, hate all children except the ones that their daughters bear.

I'm taking too long going by these crones. All my hope's energy is being spent in a test of strength against these witches' curses. It is hopeless—the day must stand still, the moon wait on the other side for my spells to work. The baby grows impatient for the children. The old women stop waiting, start murmuring, stare me past their danger.

I nearly run the short distance to the sandbox, sending smiles ahead of me to all the mothers, who know me now. One rises to greet me. She is a Negro, a Northerner, as foreign and fascinating to me as an Egyptian, amazing in her grace and sure action. She is draped in something that looks Parisian, with a hat to match. She ran it up on a treadle sewing machine yesterday between breakfast and lunch. I come near, and her little boys fly like deer away from her for popsicles. I am the only person she is telling, it must be secret, but one of her friendly young men is leaving Third Avenue for Tangier with a protector and will sell, to the right people, his remaining Tiffany lamps for only forty dollars apiece. Instantly, I need one. I need three of them. All through the summer, the mothers and I, coated with sweat and soot, have talked of nothing but the ways and means of elegance. Like little white lambs, we have been led by the Negro through talk of silk and wood and fashion. She has loaded us with sacks of marble chips, with fifteen pretty Sunday-school chairs gouged out from the back of a thrift shop. We pester the young men for bargains, exchanging love-secrets with them, desiring the young men most of all because they are the prettiest of the elegant things we burn for. One mother wants nothing but a velvet love seat; when Truman Capote comes to tea, she says, it will be his. One mother swears the rug she found on a garbage can is genuine Aubusson. She has rescued an Aubusson and made it hers.

I want everything. I want to sit beneath three Tiffany lamps with Truman Capote in my hands until I have everything and shine with everything that is man-made and beautiful. I prod the mothers, maliciously, with memories of our winter and watch their faces dull. Then, we were living peacefully with our cracking plaster and linoleum floors. We were rabid over nothing but sit-ins at the mayor's office because a mad dog was loose in the playground and the jaded park attendant gave us nothing but lip.

The conversation is beginning to die; the sun is being

6

slashed to ribbons by a new, cold wind that won't wait today on sunset. We look at each other and at our children, wondering if it will be worthwhile to outwait the wind. There is no place to go but home, and it is still too early. My friend and I see new weather gather around our children's heads. Clouds the color of steel are gathering, like giant birds coming together from prehistory. If they swooped down, I think, and carried off our babies, what would we do. Sit quietly, I think, and consider this new start in life.

Two mothers, suddenly anxious for home's burlap curtains, leap up and chase a pair of children through the trees. They silence the wailing with promises of four-for-a-dollar toys from John's Bargain Store. Still, my friend and I sit together, thinking separately of the danger being prepared over the children's heads, wondering whether harm will fall from the sky or from our own loving arms. We watch their sunless heads fill with sand, their faces grimace, smile, scream with joy and fury in the ritual of their years.

I switch off all thought of that Tiffany lamp, and tell my friend so. I begin to welcome the darkening morning. I tell my friend that Con Edison would turn off the light inside such a thing if I gave their money to the young man. My friend has already forgotten her bright piece of luck; she tells me it's all right, another time, Saradove. She knows we should wait and be silent.

The weak old trees are beginning to creak in the wind, clawing at each other, fighting to hold their dear leaves. I feel myself shrinking on the bench, and my eyes go wrong.

Before me, there is nothing but a scrim of yellow pollen; pine cones rattle against the ground and scatter across the August yard. It is just after drenching rain, the moment before the dusk is going to fall, quick, and earlier than ever before.

7

The light and the air have been dredged from below a warm sea to shake and quiver above all the little white houses and gaping children waiting on their porches. Olympia, my mother, and I sit on the steps waiting for something to come to us. She pours Mercurochrome over my feet, which have been torn by sandspurs in my race home to see my family dive into this new, deep world. My bare foot is amazing, as red as roses, in the new light. Olympia's face glistens like frost. We are waiting for my father to come, and we are very quiet about it.

A car is coming! Bringing him, it is like the weather, more brilliant than it was meant to be. It could be the coach getting Cinderella home late. Two men, red-nosed, happier than they should be, lift my father from the car and leave him on the edge of his own grass. They laugh and call out to Olympia and me, but the sound is drowned in waves of light. Duncan's face, brighter than my foot, opens up wide with smiles, and his arms stretch out for our support. We fail him, and he falls like a big duck with pounds of shot in its body. He falls into a clump of rosebushes that do not resist, but wrap him tightly in their branches. They take him so easily they might have grown Duncan instead of thorns. In a flash, my mother abandons me to him. She is in the dark behind her screen door, out of the light in an instant. I start through the grass, like a cat toward its first mouse. The light puzzles my brain. All across the yard I creep and wonder why he thinks he can lie in the roses and wait for me to snare him. My birthright is the privilege of being the victim, and he has taken it back to himself without a warning. Of all the things I can do, the gentlest act is the easiest. Soundlessly, I stretch out on my belly and lay my head down beside his. Through the thorns, I see Duncan's eyes open and wink at me.

8

"You go on across the street and play, or whatever you're supposed to do."

His words drench my face in the pure smell of Jack Daniels. Modified by his breath, my face sinks down in the grass.

"Your steak's ready; the coffee's perked," I whisper to the damp earth.

"Who th'hell cares . . . listen, Sa'dove, here's what you do: pull down some more those roses, throw'm round us, pull down pine boughs, stake'm all round, we'll have something, a rosy little house right here, won't even need a top. Do that. Get up, do that."

I lift my head and look. A second before darkness comes, the light is again white and normal. A breeze starts on its usual course. On Duncan's lip, a dark petal sticks and flutters back and forth with his breathing. He's fallen asleep. Olympia stands above us, her head ringed with dark sky, and she pokes her arms through the thorns to unravel him. She drags him, moaning, to his house.

My friend wakes from her stare through the clouds.

"Look!" she whispers. I start to my feet.

"The children—has it happened already?"

She frowns. "What do you mean? I said, Look. There."

Into her afternoon, around the path, come two little waifs of men. By the turnings of their wrists, the lifts of their smiles, certain bendings of their knees, I am convinced, quick as a wink, that they are made of oil and canvas. They have escaped from a painting by Watteau to delight the park mothers. But, as they come closer, their trousers turn from pink satin into blue chino. Their only rosettes are pinned inside their whirling, luminous eyes. Their boots are high-heeled and polished; but they are efficient, unlovely. In them they sway to secret music coming from little transistors plugged into their ears—not minuets, I know—but still music far from this century, far into the twenty-first century. Like black icing, their hair is swirled and stuck into place above their pale brown faces. With the slightest effort, they sink like feathers onto a bench near us; they incline their heads barely an inch toward our dirty children, favoring them with two little rosebuds of smiles.

My baby sees the smiles and is dumbstruck: these creatures might be two Bobby Shaftoes come back to marry her. Untangling herself from the dumpcart, she rises from the sand and totters to a human being who, for the first time, is not her mother. She sees the flashing hands cranking conversation out of the air, and she yearns for the hands to lift her and toss her into that air. I hold my breath and loss inside me and watch her face make jokes at the pretty gods. She tosses her hair and holds out her arms, stumbling to court someone who, for the first time, is not her mother.

She nearly has them when they see her. The conversation—of Lila, Chickie, Maria, 'bella—stops. Their hands drop, silent, to their knees. They draw their shining boots beneath the bench and turn eyes on me, demanding rescue. Their little smiles are clenched into lean lines, and I am there in a flash. The baby screams and kicks in my arms, covering my face with her dirt. Only her need for someone else surpasses her hatred of mother. It's no ordinary fury: she hates me and all the warm milk from my breast, my spoons of applesauce, my rock-rocking songs of the evening. Alone with her every night in the cavernous, tilted bedroom of our crumbling apartment, I have filled her ears with the old tunes and words, my voice inching through the clamors of the street's summer twilights until she is asleep. Her brain is wrinkled over with brutal messages and sweet, sweet melodies.

10

Into her screams I whisper, "I dreamed my hall was filled with wild swine, my true love a-swimming in his blood."

The baby and her mother pull and struggle beneath clouds that are flapping closer and closer to smother them in their wings.

Like a fool, I chatter, "Say bye-bye, say bye-bye to your friends—maybe tomorrow, maybe tomorrow."

My words only stiffen her rage, her scream enters my head like a long needle to join the battle with my own knives. She unstoppers her lungs and, with a deep breath of the gray, heavy air, spews all the worn-out dreams I have bundled in long letters to her heart. She gags, and she vomits the songs I have fed her on. *Old mother, old mother, lie down and die with your roses, roll in pain in your August grasses. Stop this loving!* I cannot let go. We shudder together from the goose on my grave, and her final tears make clean new streams down my own cheeks as she lets her wish go and drops into sleep, defeated.

Our silence shreds the clouds and scatters the feathers to the north and south. The sun lifts its face and chooses to shine first on the returning smiles of the pretty gods, who have forgotten the beginning, but are glad to see the end. They turn to gold from the light spreading across them. They disconnect the music from their ears. Ignoring our looks, they begin to roll reefers with tiny slivers of cigarette paper, pressing and twirling with the dexterity of a master rolling Mozart from a clavichord. A flicker of the tongue, and they are finished. Marijuana's fancies snuggle in the air with all the dreams my baby has sent for a public hanging.

My friend looks off into my face. Her arms are full of sandy toys, her children hold her long legs and rub their eyes.

My place, she is saying, they can watch television, I'll scramble eggs, you can see my old coffee-grinder.

11

The baby's head is like a stone around my neck, and I say no, not this time. But she walks with me to the gate, past the empty benches where the old women have perhaps melted through the cracks and are greasing the sidewalk to break my back. The baby's feet dangle and bounce against my stomach; with my free hand, I pull the stroller behind us. Her body and children in motion again, my friend is pleased to indulge her speech and laughter with more rides on her mind's happy hobbyhorses. There will be lace tablecloths hanging at the windows next, she says, with salons on winter Sundays, she laughs.

She asks, "Saradove, do you know what a doll's house is?"

I answer, "We're not serious enough. Those Norwegians took themselves seriously—do you know what we are? Just a gaggle of girls, a gaggle of girls, then women, then girls again. And this is an ordinary day."

We part at the corner in the midst of lunchtime school children dodging cars and stuffing themselves on cigarettes before the next bell. I look ahead, at the way I am going. My friend's legs and children have pulled her far from me before I have moved, but her kindness overwhelms the distance.

She calls, "Wait! Have you considered how *they* would look hanging on a chain from the ceiling, with pink bulbs instead of fancy cigarettes stuck in their mouths, lighting up all those colors?"

I shake my head.

"Well, you consider!" And she is gone.

The way home is warmer; the pizza smells run before the man with the sweet-potato wagon. My arm aches with the sleeping baby who will wake when we reach our dark rooms and will begin again to look beyond me. I stumble on the broken pavement, and a wooden pulltoy slips from the stroller and drags behind us, tinkling its tune, falling-down,

12

falling-down, 'don Bridge falling down. I rub the baby's fresh-bread thighs, and finish my song into her ear, her ear that's vulnerable to the whole human race but me: And out of her grave there sprung a red rose/And out of his a brier;/And out of her grave there sprung a red rose/And out of his a brier.

the ferris wheel

Saradove and the man got off the bus at Fourteenth Street. She wept, as soundlessly as she could; he went forward, as fast as his boots could shuffle him, faster than her tears could fall. His hands were in his pockets, his chin on his chest. Passing the Con Edison buildings, they felt they were entering prison under gunpoint.

The Lower East Side, built to fall, was falling: the Puerto Ricans were brushing the pieces off themselves and onto the Jewish shopkeepers. The Negro women eyed the week-old lettuce in the bins and kept on moving. They jollied it up among themselves and thought, their hips knocking against each other's, about how Thunderbird could get them so drunk they'd never feel the knife slice their skins in the projects tonight. They all looked at Saradove cry like a baby, and knew why she cried, while Johnson rolled her down Avenue D through the dirt and pachanga music like the thinnest-shelled egg.

He doesn't dare, Saradove thought, he doesn't dare take my hand because he knows already that it would mean he must marry me; and he knows that then I'll snatch him out of his cowboy boots and pull him off his big horse. With me, Saradove thought, he won't be able to ride to the rescue any longer; with me, he won't have the chance to die a hero. Remember Leon Trotsky! he shouts at the romantic, candlelit anarchist meetings. Remember Mahatma Gandhi! he shouts at the electrified pacifist meetings. Saradove sobbed, loud enough to be heard, and Johnson spat furiously into the street; and the women around the lettuce bins snickered behind their hands.

Saradove thought, I know what he really wants, but he's stubborn as a mule, bull-headed as a baby: he wants me to do what Mama did, what Mama made me do, make a man from something else or something else from a man. He wants me to show him to his place on earth, the place that woman owns. Somewhere between her throat and nostrils, the tears choked Saradove. Angrily, she jerked Johnson's hand from his pocket, put it to her eyes and wiped them with its rough palm. Johnson made a fist with his hidden hand and bit down hard on his mustache. He made her walk faster, too fast for her to cry in earnest.

She ran behind. "I know," she shouted at his hunching shoulders, "I know what it is! Pacifism . . . anarchy . . . Mahatma Gandhi . . . Leon Trotsky . . . it's all a bunch of Teddy bears, one-eyed Teddy bears, in a big playhouse made just **for you!**"

15

She screamed, "It's just a big playhouse!" The butcher came out and waited for an instant in the doorway of his shop, but he lowered his meat cleaver and turned his back when he saw it was only a girl trying to catch a husband.

"Those big beautiful spirits who lead you—the ones with beards and buttons and the world's suffering, the ones who don't support their wives and don't buy milk for their babies —you know what they give *you*, Johnson? You know?" She hung on, breathless.

"What, for Christsake, what!" he yelled. He blushed with a terrible shame: a slim, very black man was standing at the candy store, sucking on an egg cream and shouting, "Go, baby, Go!" at Saradove. Johnson had to face that same black man every other week to buy a nickel bag of pot off him. That black man never had crazy girls wiping their noses on his hand and demanding, demanding. That black man just had beautiful chicks.

"One-eyed Teddy bears!" Saradove had her breath back. A wire from an orange crate tore into her leg, and she screamed it again, in pain: "One-eyed Teddy bears!"

The black man finished his egg cream, smiled at it all, and went back inside. Johnson made the heels of his engineer boots thud against the pavement. She had to run again. She had to hang on and pant the words.

"Toys! Your peace walks are toys . . . your red-eyed revolutionaries, bomb-throwing . . . toys! You get all dressed up in your mustache and leather jacket and engineer boots . . . you get to carry a sign. You get to look a cop straight in the eye and lie down flat at his feet. You want to hear what you see in the sky, Johnson? You want to hear?" She gasped, "You watch the clouds become dragons . . . and three pigs . . . and three bears with porridge . . . and a big

16

white boat to carry you off to China through the blue! Wait for me! Listen, Johnson!"

And she ran after him. At the doorway to his house, she sang; in a broken-breath voice, she sang, "Then take the key and lock him up, lock him up, lock him. . . ." Her voice broke entirely; she fell against him. He leaned, and let her rest.

She said, with a new breath, into his chest, "Don't you see, Johnson, if you don't love me and marry me and go get a job and make me a mother, don't you see, everything you do is a waste . . . because freedom and nonviolence and poor, rickety Puerto Rican children, all you love—" A five-year old Puerto Rican who had been quietly giving her his attention felt the insult, threw a stone, fled around the corner—"and all those Nagasakians are nothing but true love! *True love*, Johnson, that's what they are." She lifted her face and spoke into the mustache. "And here I am," she ended, "your true love, all the world's wrong rolled into me. Love me."

Johnson led her up the stairs. He knew it was wrong to use violence against anyone, even her.

Even in the mousy dark there was light enough for her to understand that his bed took up the entire room. There was space left only for a narrow cupboard built into the wall where the engineer boots could relax for a few hours every night, where the cashmere zoot suit, following Johnson from adolescence, could hang forever. Even as they breathed into each other's faces, even as he undid even her shoes, her mind told him, I will never let that awful suit down off its hook again. No woman ever had sheets this dirty; but when she lay down on them, she smelled camellia bushes, back home, beginning to bloom. And something pushed her out of her

17

glistening home yard forever, into the dark. She understood that all along camellia blooms and porch swings, exercise books and Olympia's rocking lap had smelled of barbaric male, of tenement dirt, of foreign faces eating *cuchifritos*.

She kept on crying. Her crying mouth opened and gobbled the pine-tree boughs leaning over the high porch steps where she stamped her feet and saw the petted girl next door peeking to see the whipping.

Mama wades right into the tiger lilies, she wants to whip me so bad she's mashing their heads down. Always, she goes right for the peony bushes for the best whips. I cry; I won't stop.

Olympia calls, "Open that door and get on in there! I'll teach you to talk like that to *anybody* again! Or me either!"

I slide across the kitchen floor and smash the potato vine into the sink with my waving arms. Red, yellow, and green splashes are in the brown linoleum: the Shadow and the Lone Ranger have been here fighting it out again. They've bled their peculiar veins onto our floor again. I leap from the switch and into the dark hall and scar the wax on the floor, scar even the smell of the wax. My roller skates are waiting here, and they will beat her face in . . . I will beat her bosom away. Last night I sat in the kitchen eating a bowl of delicious black-eye peas and knew, all at once, that their crushed, hot taste was the taste of Mama's breasts. I'll never touch black-eyes again. The skates are too far to reach; but this whole house is too small to contain my dancing feet. Her swinging hand makes me dance. Duncan's big radio lunges from the wall, and the tiny, carved figures of Comedy and Tragedy, who guard the mesh hole the world speaks from, sneer: You will never hear the Shadow speak to you again.

Before the switch drives me into the bathroom, where the first real lash and the last will be given, I get my last look at Duncan. He lies in the cavern of their bedroom, frowning and growing purple from the sight of me. His shoes are laced tight on his feet, are propped, as always, on *The Saturday Evening Post* to protect the white chenille. His body is sagging with the mattress, worn out with only one child to show for it. His hands elevate his head so that he can see.

"You hush that goddamned yelling. A man can't get no rest."

"But Mama . . . she's switching me . . . look at me, I have to cry!"

"Work like a dog all day then listen to this! For God's sake, Olympia! Can't you take her nowhere else, can't you remember my heart!"

Mama drives me in, her arm nearly broken already from slashing. Duncan slams his feet to his floor and hurls the alarm clock after us before he charges forward and bangs the door shut against us. He isn't going to get me this time! Mama calls out, afraid and worried, through the door that still trembles from its slam, "Duncan, Duncan! Remember the blood pressure, what the doctor said; remember the heart!"

The whipping commences.

"Stop that crying, stop that crying . . . if you don't stop that crying I'm going to kill you really!" She slashes, faster and faster. "Stop that crying . . . won't do you no good. . . ." Her words whisper against the stroke. "Look what you've done to your daddy, nearly killed him; then what will we eat? Hush that yelling, can't the poor man get no rest at all?" Her whip sings. The sweat rolls down her beautiful face, and at each stroke her elbow strikes hard against the sink.

Mama is beginning the potatoes; their smell slides beneath

19

the bathroom door and seeps through the wicker of the laundry hamper where I am still just small enough to hide.

She sat, as still as possible, on his kitchen chair, watching her tears splash one by one onto the pink-and-gold formica tabletop. It makes a stormy sunset, she thought, and the salt shaker is a lighthouse, mooing at it. Waiting to drown, resigned about it, Johnson sat on a four-foot stack of the New York *Times* Sunday editions.

For the tenth time he said, "Stop that crying." The words choke each other on his tongue and fall out mangled. What did he say?

"I said stop crying. Did I ever say I loved you? I said sex— love, I guess—is one thing, freedom another. If I let you stay with me it would be—it would be kicking Miss Freedom down the stairs and making you Mrs. Safety!"

He was very pleased with the way he had said it. But still he looked at her, saw how much she looked like the Statue of Liberty—carved, torch-lighted flesh and blood; and little enough. But they were all little enough. A pack of them danced to any beat he named at every party; they rushed to walk beside him on the marches to the U.N. There was Lorraine, for instance, just next door, content to come to bed, go out for beer, then get back home to her kids; and Lorraine had big breasts, a job, enough kids. Why Saradove? Because she cried? Because, sometimes from the corner of his eye, she did not seem there, real? Sometimes he could see the shadows of furniture and things slip through her flesh in ghostly outline; the light behind her crossed and shone through her body. Her tears were real enough, sliding across his tabletop; they interested him. He lit another cigarette and stretched out against the icebox.

He said, "Don't think it makes so much difference. You

can have freedom too. You should want it. Why do you want love from me, why do you insist on getting love, all of it they have, from everybody so that . . ."

"What?" Saradove whispered. The tears froze in her eyes. "So that what?"

The look she gave him paralyzed Johnson, stuck to him like ice; but he was brave enough to answer.

"So that you can eat up all that love and thrive, grow stronger, then run away. I think that when you run away it is on four feet. You leave us helpless and mad, with nothing but a memory of light that gets paler and paler."

There was silence, and she outwaited him. Johnson was near the truth; when he reached it, she would have him.

"I think I know who you are," he said.

The cigarette burned his hand; pain startled him back to life and away from her. Happily, he leapt and landed with his heel against the cigarette, grinding out its light meant to hurt him and her ways meant to trap him.

"You have to go," he said. "I have to get my laundry today."

To give him a noise to look for while she looked at him, Saradove twirled a tin teaspoon in her cup's last drop of coffee. Johnson's thoughts of laundry made his face stubborn and gleeful. At any moment, he could escape. It would be harmless now, to listen to her; so he listened, his body stiff with thought. Instantly, Saradove's tears stopped; calm and reason crept out of her voice, poured over Johnson, smothering his hopes half to death.

She moved her hands strangely, her mouth precisely, as though she were casting a harmful spell over him.

"Listen," she said. "Johnson, why do you think you can look at me without loving me? I run away only when it's time . . . but I came ready to stay this time . . . and look at you, too dumb to see the light. You're perfect, Johnson. You

21

don't adore me, you don't fit my body like a good duplicate of mine, you don't worry your head about my hundred-carat brain, you don't try to improve my appearance with bites off fairy tales . . . and listen to me. . . ." She spoke cautiously, making him sweat over every word. "Yet, I'm ready to be the nothing *you* want to be so that you can be—" she stopped, waiting to get his gaze straight in her face; she moved so that the light from the window would strike him—"so that you can be something else." She dropped the final straw. "Let *me* be the one to get the laundry every week!"

Something else, something extraordinary while *she* gets the laundry. Johnson's mind reeled, unreeled; instantly, he fell in love with the lie. The world began to roll again.

Below them, in the street, a miniature ferris wheel on the back of a truck was cranked up. The Italian at the wheel turned up his radio full blast. Waves of heat lifted up the rock-and-roll and threw it against Saradove. She frowned, stiffened, waiting for the sympathy that would make her suffering worthwhile.

The noise returned Johnson's powers to him. Life was for him again. He hitched up his shiny Levis; and when he ran to lean out the window, he rubbed against her without knowing it.

"I'm gonna shake, rattle and roll!" Johnson yelled to the ferris-wheel crowd. A boy leapt from the spouting fire hydrant and became a shiny brown fish hooked by Johnson's string and bent safety pin. Johnson beamed at his catch, and the boy shot him in the face with his water pistol.

"Hey mister, you gimme a dime to ride, huh?" The boy lifted his hands up for his reward. Johnson glowed with the heat of brotherhood, neighborliness, universal love. Asking for love, Johnson threw two nickels down to the boy.

"It's not the welfare state yet, son!" Johnson laughed. "Soon!"

The disc jockey from the truck's radio babbled like a tobacco auctioneer, screaming for the teens. Johnson's hips wiggled with the voice, tried to enfold, with his smile, all the sweating happy circus before him. It had arrived, like George for the maiden, to save his virtue at the last moment.

Alone, behind him, Saradove heard the music barrel through Johnson, saw the colors of the ferris wheel shift through Johnson's skin. Johnson, she imagined, was a thin curtain through which the world blew its breezes, shot its colors. He is not real, thought Saradove. I need to make him real.

Johnson leaned farther out the window. The block's own witch, fat, ill, a notorious hater of the PR's who were invading her community with their smelly *bodegas*, was being blasted with a perfectly aimed spray from the water hydrant.

"You bastids! You bastids!" she screamed from her little puddle. "You black foreigners you oughta be in jail. . . . I'm gonna tell the cops. . . . Yuh will be in jail!" But the cops, sweltering with ill temper on the edge of their domain, were fearfully girding their loins for the fight to the finish that the Intrepid Warriors and the Diamond Men had scheduled for the East River Park playground that night. They listened to the old woman rant every summer and wished that the PR's would hurry up and do her in.

A black cloud passing over the face of the block made Johnson remember that someone was still in his house. Smelling the rain before it came near him, the Italian slammed the gate of his ferris wheel shut. Despite the money left to be made, he choked off the disc jockey and swung onto Avenue D, seeking drier pastures. The riders, cheated out of their complete circle, cursed the fair-weather Italian, planned ob-

23

scene futures for him. Johnson, leaning above them, longed to soothe them all with ice-cream cones.

Enough, thought Saradove. She slipped her grandmother's silver bracelets from her arm, rattled them in the table's sunset to make Johnson turn around.

Johnson turned, his face weak with woe, his heart down on the street with the riders without a ride. He felt no better than Harry S. Truman or Joe McCarthy or Edward Teller ought to feel: as rotten as a landlord.

"You'd better hurry," he muttered, "before the rain gets worse."

Saradove thought. Will he remember a kiss? Or will the bracelets, if I forget and leave them on the table, hurt him more in the long run?

"Here's a bag. Here," he said. He pushed brown paper in her lap. "You can get everything in this."

She thought, I'm going to jam the bag over his head, punch him in the stomach, swiftly kick him in the balls. But she didn't; she meant to win. She wanted him to die happy, breathing fresh air, the toes of his boots turned up. Her hands moved, useless, shaking with impatience to pull him to her feet. There was nothing to do but take everything he had of hers and close the wrinkled bag over it all: sneakers, toothbrush, a dress. The bracelets lay quiet, dulled and hidden by her wish, in the drying sunset.

Johnson waited for her in his open doorway, at the end of a short, dark hall. Still in the kitchen, Saradove wondered at the perfect target his black silhouette made: with my tiny, pearl-handled solid-gold revolver, I shot him full of six bullets. All that nasty innocence ran out of him and ruined the floor. I have a magic potion that turns me invisible. Invisible, I will float above justice as it blunders through its search for me. She imagined some day materializing at a lectern, to tell the

24

thrilling tale to an audience filled with the awed faces of the Shadow, the Lone Ranger, Olympia, Duncan, the Young Adults' Sunday-School Class.

"Please go on, Saradove," he said. His hand clutched his doorknob. He thinks, Saradove thought, that the door is a life buoy, that I mean to drown him again. She found her legs, left him dry, began to speak as she moved through the darkness, casting the last spell left in her hat. He leaned toward her, trying to pull her forward and out, as though his wish to have her gone were a rope. The shape of him in the doorway could have been a cloud's or a rock's, both of them good things.

Saradove began talking; she began pulling the short flock of her hair about, as though she could reach through her scalp and handle the words waiting there, give them to Johnson, let their disastrous weight convince him as they sank into his palm.

She said, "Do you know what our trouble is, Johnson? Our ceremonies, our fantasies, are so different you think they could never live together in peace. You refuse to let your plan for world brotherhood include a woman, or let it get as small as a room with just the two of us in it. Take, for instance, our ceremonies."

Saradove watched his dark face, garnished the darkness between them with the witty smile, the brilliant eyes that had delighted him (something old-fashioned, something worn-out, untough, encastled in tradition there; something violent and unbrotherly), the brilliant eyes that had delighted him in the artists' bar two days ago for the first time.

"For instance," she said, "if it were me throwing somebody out—Miss Freedom, for instance—it would be from a room shining with flowers—anemones, I think—and a room with floors I'd polished for hours beforehand. I would have her

25

juiced on the thickest, most maudlin wine; I would have filled and refilled the thinnest goblets for her. I would have had her stumbling backward down my stairs, blowing kisses all the way. And she would have been down in my street for hours, staring up at my heavy, drawn curtains, hoping for a last look. She'd be weeping in her hankie over my great sacrifice. And where would I be, Johnson?"

"Where?" He wanted the story to go on forever.

"Sobering up in the bathtub with the best detective story."

Night was coming. The fluorescent tube above the stairs flickered on and touched them with a wrong color. Johnson's eyes, she saw, were suddenly a brighter blue; his eyes were washing his face away. Saradove tried to stop herself, but the story, suddenly, meant more than Johnson did to her.

"I forgot something," she said. "I forgot to say I'd have 'Jesu, Joy of Man's Desiring' playing softly on the phonograph all the while. That tune, like no other, destroys suspicion in your victim, makes selfish words sound noble."

Johnson's tears stopped; now tenderness dissolved his face; then admiration broke over it and drowned everything but itself. He watched her, for a moment shaken with the same guilty pleasure that took him when he found himself preferring his photograph of a hummingbird sucking at honeysuckle to a canvas by Jackson Pollock. She could see Johnson wishing he could have her again, there and then. He began twirling the doorknob to give her something to look at while he sorted out his wishes.

Saradove, undistracted, clearly heard him give her the victory. Buttercups and onion-grass were going to grow through the chinks in Johnson's firm, pure foundation; Saradove's soft, slight flowers were going to cut through Johnson's fortress. Birds were going to nest in his towers. On the other hand

26

. . . perhaps Johnson was not a structure ready for her ornament and decay; perhaps Johnson was the most innocent of beasts, ready to be trapped. She imagined, with pity, how he would look with a horn spiraling from his forehead's middle. She chose Johnson the unicorn; she would lead him with a rope of flowers. The scented rope, she decided, would be her wedding gift to him.

His face dried, his eyes paled.

"I'll go now," she said.

"Wait!"

Saradove stopped still, fearing, convinced that he'd noticed the bracelets; they were to be his wedding gift to her. But it was only his impatience to begin having her again.

"You didn't finish, Saradove." He stumbled behind her. Directly above them, the fluorescent light smeared their faces and made them seem old. "Tell me, what else would you do, I mean, after you started the music?"

She thought, It's as easy as dropping a net over him.

"I've forgotten," she said. She shook the bagful of clothes at him. "I've plumb forgotten, Johnson. You'd better hurry and get your laundry. The rain's stopped." She ran halfway down the first flight of stairs.

"But the fantasies," he called, "what were you going to say about that?"

Saradove leaned on the greasy banister, exhausted by her art, giggling. "Didn't I say—'not to mention our fantasies'?" Johnson laughed back at her. "What will you do, Johnson?"

"I'll decide," he announced. "I'll decide and I'll call you."

Down on the first floor, out of his sight, Saradove stopped and felt the brown walls, the dirt-thick floor, the mist of rain outside, all curl together and slip inside her nostrils. Everything smelled of camellia blooms, of new earth and pads of moss beneath the flowers' dark leaves. Her home's front yard was inside her and growing up into summer. She spoke to the thick peeling paint of a door in front of her.

"Oh my God," she told the shut door, "why doesn't he hurry?"

The smell was so strong that she felt beside her for the sword that might cut a path through it. She could never last through all that sweetness without a shield for her body. She screamed, deep into her dirty palms, "Then what is the use of him anyway, if not for this?"

"Wait!" He was still above her. "Won't you let me kiss you before you go?"

With all her power gone, she left the bag on the bottom step and climbed back to his feet. The kiss was long and stirring, and she felt none of it. When he let her go, she almost fell backward.

Johnson strolled back into his rooms, his face smiling good wishes all over her. If she chose to extract promises from good wishes, it would be her own fault. Bent nearly double, down she went again, retrieved her bag, looked some more at the threat. It hung thick as solid sugar, scented like crepe myrtle, ready to descend and stick her to that floor forever. Her heart thumped. Suddenly everything was gone but fear, which never fails. She could speak for herself.

"Shut up, heart!" she yelled. The paint on the closed door was blistered into thin bubbles. If they split open, she would see the valves of her own heart pumping there against the wood.

"What took *me* to *his* feet? Not him, you! Come out of the wood, heart. If you're his collaborator, get upstairs and live with him! I'll love you and kill you in one lump, all together. Go ahead!"

Slowly, the door opened wide. A fat woman covered by a

small dress and much black skin stood there; eight ragged children hung on her.

"Is you awright, lady? What's that after you?"

"Yes, ma'am. Nothing ma'am." A garden, and the grass around it, sprung up around her. The sugar was the scent of home, getting closer.

"Lady, lady, I ain't ma'am." Saradove began to shake in the hall's heat; the cool rain was all gone.

"Mama said," she whispered, "Mama said, Say yes ma'am, no ma'am, or next time I'll kill you." The fat woman's aching toes splayed from the holes in her torn felt slippers and curved against the stone floor. Saradove had whispered to the pathetic, blistered toes.

"You better go on home to your mama, lady. Run home, girl!" Her children began to chew their cornbread again.

"No I won't."

Saradove turned, called as loud as the heavy flowers in her throat would let her, back up the stairs. "One more thing, Johnson! You just listen to this: art and magic are harder to practice than love. You think it's so easy, you just try it!"

Johnson couldn't hear. He was taking a loud and splashing bath; he was turning the pages of *The Maltese Falcon* with a wet finger tip.

She turned her back on the paper bag crumpling against the step. Saradove ran out into the renewed sun, on all four feet, her hunters fast behind her, their bows drawn.

the wedding present

In a thick row around the neat square of their front yard, things had been set out to grow an imaginary fence. Imaginary, because it kept nothing out. Between the camellia and the pomegranate bushes, there was space large enough for all the neighborhood children to slide through on their bellies. Many dogs had burrowed tunnels between the pine tree and the clump of azaleas; one side of the white azalea seemed dog-shaped. The cornerful of crepe myrtle had gates in their branches for the two sisters from across the street to push open and enter the yard, bearing tin tea sets and enough dolls for a party. After the myrtles, a long line of emptiness greeted the street, a place for cars to stop on a visit, a place where six could alight and pace forward abreast across the grass before they lined up to climb the front steps. At the next corner, the empty line stopped, climbed a young oak that sheltered nothing but summertime anthills, had no shade, and was a torment to the telephone company, which ran its lines through the branches and kept away birds bent on nesting there. Beneath the oak, dusty unflowered bushes began a solid row up and down the yard's other side. Their leaves stank for one short season every year; dogs and children jumped them, and they stood aside for grownups. A splendid Judas tree crouched above the last of the stinking bushes, dropped petals on the bricks of the front porch, and completed the last touch of the house's defense.

Nothing grew but grass between the sides of the fence; it was Duncan's and Olympia's favorite of the things they had planted. Saradove despised it for its mowed, unshadowed vacancy; she knew she could never be tiny enough to climb it or hide behind it.

In the wintertime all three of them ignored the yard. While it was cold, Duncan drove his car in and out of the driveway; and he left and entered his house on a path of cement laid by the front steps. His head was forever bent, his eye forever on the choice of one key or another. His mind would be on getting warm. Bare bushes made him shake all the harder. When Olympia left the house, she faced the door as she closed it; she slammed it in her own face. She would march across the frosted grass, seeing nothing but each step her high heels took, to the waiting taxicab that drove her not very many places. Saradove always, in heat or cold, went out the back door.

It was never very cold, but it was the only cold they knew. In the winter, without the yard, they passed their time before the big brown oil burner in the hall, sat eating in the steamy kitchen; in the bedrooms they lay talking about bills and sickness, doing no-count homework. Except on Sundays, when uncles and aunts came to sit after the big dinner, nobody but Saradove ever went to the living room. The uncles and aunts, while they sat, dozed through talk of heart attacks and those who were not there. Saradove did nothing in the room but look at it.

Saradove loved the living room for the wedding present and loved the wedding present for the women painted on it. Nearly as wide as the mantelpiece, the picture filled a plaster frame rich in golden curls and waves. Inside the picture, bare maidens sat on an enormous rock, more purple than rock-colored; their long arms clasped their long legs, and their narrow shoulders drooped. The sun was setting in front of them, keeping them pink all over.

Nearly every winter afternoon, Saradove found nothing to do but sink on the couch beneath the painting, and clench her fists against the desire to yank the shoulders straight and turn the maidens to face her. But the maidens kept to the painter's intention, with eyes for nothing but the gold and bottomless lake before them and the cloud-blurred, more golden, castle on the shore beyond.

For many winters, Saradove watched and worried over the maidens: Did they ever swim home? Could they slide down that rock without slashing their bodies into purple ribbons? Who kept them out in that cooling, fading light? A girl came home with her one afternoon, ate up all the peanut butter, and told blatant lies about the picture: they were princesses; their father was a wicked king who had thrown them out for refusing to marry other wicked kings. They were going to sit out there and freeze until the prince slew the dragon in the lake and rowed them to shore. One princess would marry the prince; the other, his brother. Perhaps they were Saradove's ancestors.

That night, Saradove threw her supper at Olympia for letting an outsider embarrass her with the truth about the picture; that had been a mother's duty. Olympia picked up the pork chop and ate it herself.

"That girl's a storyteller," she said. "That picture's just what it looks like: a wedding present. Get out of this kitchen and go read another dirty book."

Saradove never brought a clean library book into the house. There was no telling who had handled those books, made those stains and fingerprints. Maybe colored people.

In the summer, while the front yard roasted and melted its sugary smells alone outside, Saradove kept still to the couch, but ignored the cool maidens, lucky to be in frosted winter skins. She lay stripped to her underpants, her eyes on the dirty books, waiting for her own sweat to melt her inside them. Often she looked at her breasts, saw them begin to grow.

But late, when the heat had let up, Olympia went out to water the yard, then to sit, resting in the new scents her water had raised, in the porch swing to wait for Duncan. The swing's chains rattled; Olympia chewed the skin around her fingernails. When the empty street became unbearable, she called into the living room, where she could see the near-naked body of her daughter shining through the dark.

"Come out here and let's dig up that pomegranate bush, Saradove."

The swing's chains rattled; Olympia let herself smile.

"Shut up you crazy old woman."

On the radio, Captain Midnight was creeping through the dark to battle a gang of international murderers.

"I ain't old, Saradove. Don't you talk to your mother that

33

way. Colored boys come trampling on my grass to steal pomegranates. Come let's dig it up."

Saradove rolled over on her belly and felt that something, any minute, was going to bloom big on her chest. She felt the strong fist of Captain Midnight punch a face in. She shut her eyes.

"And chop down that oak tree, too. Telephone company don't like that tree anyhow; and see how no grass can live under it." The swing creaked faster.

"Chop it down?" Saradove screamed. "You won't either!" Saradove was lost. The man on the radio talked about cereal, but she knew all the toasted oats in the world would not turn her into Captain Midnight.

"So we're going to chop it all down, you hear, Saradove?"

The thickening dusk made the chains' clanking louder; still, Duncan had not come home.

"Then I'll paint the stump white and grow some nice ivy over it. How about a big kettle of pink petunias on top? How about that, Saradove—you live here, too."

Saradove pressed closer to the big radio. In a moment, the Lone Ranger would gallop, in a cloud of dust, over her heart. She thought, A faithful Indian companion is what I *want*.

"How come you don't answer me? You don't speak up you'll never get what you want. You know good and well we didn't even plant that tree. It was here when we built. We're going to chop it down, hear?"

Hidden in the sagebrush, Saradove's valiant heart flexed against terror: the outlaws had Tonto.

Without warning, the lamppost at the corner suddenly glowed. The next-door mother began calling her children home, but nothing ran home to her but her big red dog. The driveway was still empty; no car had passed for a long time.

Olympia's voice screeched like the noise of the chains, faster, higher and higher.

"No child ever hated their own home like you do. Anybody, any other youngun could feel just how much I've sacrificed, how your daddy kills himself to provide. And there you sit catching cold, ruining your eyes. Why aren't you out meeting nice people like other girls?"

Higher and higher went the voice; the swing, faster.

"Meaner and sassier all the time, and what about your mother, anyway? Look and see what it's been like for me—nothing but pain from the two of you!"

Next door, the mother hushed, cocked her head to catch Olympia's misery. The afternoon heroes were disappearing into the caves of the radio.

Saradove pressed her brow against her knees. She whispered, "God help me, Tonto, I am sorry. It hurt me as much as it hurt you to see them burn you at the stake."

With a heave, she flung the library book at the screen door, toward Olympia's noise. The book fell short and overturned the bottle of Coca-Cola on the coffee table. Beneath the glass top, the soda began to foam and sizzle. Duncan said the junk ate out your stomach lining; only whisky made it fit to drink. Saradove watched closely for holes to appear in the mahogany.

"Blessed saviour!" Olympia was breathing furiously through the screen's tiny holes. "I never thought I'd see you throw filth at me. You just get up from there, put on clothes before your daddy catches you." Olympia opened the door. "Did I hear Co-Cola spill?"

The screen banged; Olympia came through the dark like a heavy, noisy ghost.

"Look at that," she said. "Look at you."

She swung off to the kitchen; the house vibrated around her.

"It's going to take five dishrags to sop up that mess and you just now ruined my good mahogany—only thing your precious grandma ever gave *me*—just like everything else I ever had." Her voice was wrung out of her like water from the dishrags. "I can't have nothing! I ain't ever had, I never will!"

She came back, turning on lights; she threw the cold rags against Saradove's belly.

"Get up from there, clean it all up. Look, it's going to storm!"

Outside, clouds black enough to show through the dark were coming, brushing the tops of the pine, the oak, the Judas; they started soaking the grass, with thick heavy drops. Saradove mopped the table, the sticky fluid wetting her hands like sweat, or too much mother love. Across the room, Duncan's big wing chair—for his rest only—began to swell through the humid evening storm until it became a giant's chair hugely swimming above the carpet. It waved arms at her, blinked the black grease spot his hair had made, on and off against her face.

"Mama, Mama, I'm tired. When can we have supper?"

Olympia turned from the dark screen. The storm's air had pressed her hair back; her face showed that she had stopped waiting. She leaned against the big chair.

"Don't whine, Saradove." Her fingers picked at the tapestried leaves. "I reckon you might as well eat. Just put on something first, run borrow some milk. Go to the Alleys' house. Tell them I forgot it at the store today."

Saradove pulled on her shorts, her shirt. "But it's raining hard."

"I said stop whining. A child needs milk for supper—go borrow some. I'll pay her back tomorrow. Run between the drops, you're neither sugar nor salt and won't melt."

In the dark, in the middle of the invisible rain, Saradove curled the wet grass through her toes, felt the cotton of her clothes grow soaked and heavy. She began running down the hill to the Alleys'. Her legs poured into the rain: they were neither sugar nor salt and wouldn't melt. Her feet slapped against the hot wet of the street's tar so fast her body tried to roll like a ball to follow them. As she sped, each raindrop that hit her eyelids became bigger than her face. Her secret was beginning to show, but there was no one out in the dark to see it. She had seen it first, clear as day, at school. What a tiny thing she was, she saw! There was the school her daddy paid the Catholics five dollars a month to send her to. It was as big as a horse. There was Saradove, as little as a flea on the horse's tail. In truth, the horse was a house, a gingerbread mansion with its parlors and halls and bedrooms unchanged by the nuns whose presence, whose curly-iron-and-wood desks alone had turned the place from house to school. One day Saradove had lifted her desk top and had seen, for the first time, the message she had made there for herself. Through the tall windows of wavy old glass, over the bunches of fern and begonia that stood in them, a bucket of sun poured and stuck to everything she had there: ten gold stars pasted on a picture of a pink-and-white Our Lady, the reward for reading; a pen-wiper, stitched in blue by the oldest nun and laundered once a week by Olympia; the bottle of black ink, the black staff pen, the Palmer Method penmanship book; the two chocolate suckers the youngest nun had sold her at recess.

All Saradove's things lined up before her and told Saradove, very exactly, this: You are incredibly tiny, the smallest living thing in the whole world. They have scaled everything in your desk down to nearly invisible bits for you; they carved your desk from kindling wood. All you own, and you, would fit into the toe of a slipper. Every morning, Sister must remind the other girls not to stare at you, to treat you as though you were as big and ordinary as themselves. Whenever you feel confused and ridiculous, it is because they have made a mistake, have reminded you of your size. Olympia and Duncan, of course, are used to you and never make a mistake, although they are very sad about it all. Tonight, under the kitchen's yellow light, when Duncan hurls his silver, his coffee cup, his full plate of chicken and dumplings at your mother, you will bless being so small. You will crawl beneath a bubble in the linoleum or curl into the curve of the stove leg. There's no knowing how, but somehow you will also be big enough to go out again into the light, wrap your arms around Olympia and scream, "Don't hurt my mama, don't hurt my mama," at Duncan, who really, you understand, won't be hurting anybody, just making a big mess for your mama to clean up.

When Duncan got mad and threw his supper on the floor, it was always because of Saradove; but it was Olympia who had picked the fight. Just as she turned his meat onto his plate, she would bend her nose to the sizzling juices and say, "You've been down there with those men at the hardware store again, I can smell it. And all my neighbors know it—they see you stagger in just like I do. You think going down there and buying them drink is going to make them give you something, because they're rich and you're not, don't you? Huh? You think so? You don't pay for Saradove's dancing lessons and music lessons and a new dress for me, you spend it all on drink for them and you. I know. That's what you want to do."

And Olympia would set the trembling meat in front of him and go around the kitchen closing all the windows against her neighbors' ears.

And Duncan would clutch his knife and fork as though they anchored him from shooting like a rocket through his roof, would look carefully over the steaming supper, choosing which to throw first. As the salt shaker flew past Olympia's head, he would yell, "Can't a man have any peace around here!" Saradove would stumble in to save her mama and, like mama bird and papa bird, they would both rise up against her and toss her out of the nest of their fight.

Saradove raced down the hill, flapping her arms through the rain. A certain power was returning to her, a power she imagined belonged to her every time Duncan rode her in the car: that her arm was a gleaming, razor-sharp scythe, as wide as the world. As the car rolled along, her arm would go out the window, palm up, fingers flat, and strike down and level off her whole country until all became her own minute size. Her arm sliced heads from bodies, bodies from feet. Men, houses, trees, birdbaths, telephone poles became stumps in the clay.

At the bottom of the hill, the rain stopped and the darkness suddenly dried. They gave her, with kindness and looks, a bottle of milk; and when she got home, his car sat in the driveway, humped and darker than the dark itself. Holding the bottle at arm's length, she jumped the crepe myrtle, carrying away flecks of the crinkled flowers that stuck to her skin like spots of royal blood. Duncan's hands, holding the steering wheel in the loose, exhausted fashion of a racer who has come in last, gleamed out white and bone-tired. Saradove dug her toes into the grass and wished herself as black as the night. She began to plan: first, gobble up supper before he could sit down to his; get all the arithmetic answers, right or wrong, down on the paper; huddle by the radio where Inner Sanctum would creak tonight into her ear, until they ran her to bed. The walls of her plan were thick and safe; his hands could not reach through them and touch her.

But first, the front steps. How could tiny Saradove slither up those tall bricks? The giant girl who had bounced down the hill like a runaway ball was still at the bottom, had stayed behind to look for maypops in the Alleys' little wood, was letting the milk get warm. Little Saradove would have to wait forever in the grass jungle before that big and lazy, willful girl would catch up and get her safely past the white hands in the car, past the kitchen's grits and ham, and fix her against the mesh hole where nothing but the ghosts that strolled out on trembling organ music could get her to turn a hair.

The porch light snapped on. Beneath it, Olympia's head was suddenly there, encircled in a halo of bugs that swarmed a path around the light's heat. Like lightning, Saradove cleared the steps in two giant bounds. Maypop seeds stuck to her fingers; her hair smelled of raindrops.

On her plate, a big yellow eye shook on the hardening white face of the grits. The sharp, red smell of country ham frying in its own gravy cut through the kitchen. On the table, an empty glass waited for the Alleys' milk. Saradove put the milk in the icebox and poured out Coca-Cola. She put the table into action. The egg and butter warmed her fork and tongue; her spoon flashed. Beyond the back door, the sunset happened. She faced it and ate. Duncan's dessert, the sweet he craved every night, waited for him on the sink—a pitcher of molasses, heavy as rock; a mound of country butter stamped with leaf and daisy, slices of store-bought bread. Between drags on a cigarette, he would eat it all up, after she had gone. Saradove ate everything that was hers, dropped her hands into her lap and burped. Out front, someone was falling into the pomegranate bush; two people were wailing and grunting to get from the dark into light.

"Why, you monster, why do you do it?"

"I love you, sugar-pie. Get on down here in the grass with me."

"You fool! One-two-three-*hup!*" Something heavy was getting dragged up the steps. Olympia was panting and laughing as though something like pleasure was happening to her: "This

time I just got to laugh! You don't know just how downright
. . . comical . . . you look . . . all them vines in your hair
. . . grass stuck out of your ears!"

Saradove went to see, rubbing her mouth on her shirt tail.
In a mixture of earth and greenery, bright streamers of blood
flew about Duncan's face. At last, his face was all of a piece:
his nose, crisscrossed with broken veins, matched his blood-
striped cheeks. His hands were that way; they might have
been born in a brier patch. They held a bottle of milk out to
her.

"Duncan, why're you bleeding that way?" Her voice grew
as loud as his breathing. "Why're you bleeding like that?"

Duncan pressed the white bottle to his cheek. The blood
stuck to the glass like a transfer picture of a bunny coming
off, reversed, against an Easter egg.

"Here, S'dove honey, here's your milk." With every word
he spoke, his voice softened. "Some of the blood I got from
climbing over the first bobbed-wire fence, some I got from
the next bobbed-wire fence; the rest I got from both of them
going back over. I just stole from the milk company, S'dove
honey, and got you your sweet bottle of milk. You love me
for that?"

He swayed; Olympia screamed. "All I said was pick up a
quart of milk on your way home . . . all my money went
for those old dancing lessons today . . . you could of paid
for *that*, just the *milk!*"

Duncan shook blood off his face the way a dog shakes off
water, with a shudder. "With what? Pay for it with what?
And any child's got to have milk on top of dancing lessons
then I guess I got to get it for her. . . ." In the mess of mud
stuck against his left ear, a frail blue feather, ragged with
wet, hung out. It seemed, in the blur of Saradove's vision, the
plume on the fancy hat of a cavalier. Out in the night, per-

haps in the camellia bush, a bird with one feather less in its tail warbled itself into sleep.

"Even though," Duncan's whisper went on, "even though you can't get her to drink the milk, you can't get her to play us a tune or do us a dance. Next it'll be art lessons, won't it? *Fart* lessons! That's what I call it, that's what it all is."

From the yard, the drying night crept inside to flap at their faces, first with the smell of grass; then with the roses' breath, sweeter than a smile; then with the turpentined air from the pine tree. The oak tree rustled in its own corner. Duncan fell into his wing chair, his head fitting exactly into its grease stain.

"You, Olympia, you sit down on that couch over there and listen to me. Saradove, get on that piano bench, but don't bother to play us a tune."

Instead of lighting a cigarette, he began to stroke the milk bottle, caressing it with bloody hands until he had convinced them that some cow had given blood, not milk. Saradove's thighs stuck to the piano bench; her elbows bent into the soundless keys behind her. Olympia stayed where she was, only her finger moving, twisting the gray hairs with the brown around it.

"You stop this, you hear, Duncan?" Her voice, glued together by nerves, strained to impress him with the same gentleness as her finger did her hair. "Stop this being so silly and go eat your supper. Fried chicken, sharp cheese. Please. You want her to be like other girls just like I do. Why can't you be like other men? Why do you come home bleeding like that?"

He winked at her. "Stand in the light so I can see through your dress." Rage took him; he clutched the bottle. "I said sit down on that couch!" Olympia sat, her dress rumpling high on her thighs. She curled her hands into their thick, white nest and smiled down at them. Duncan watched her, his eyes reflecting the milky glimmering of her skin, his hands tighter than ever around the bottle.

"That's just what I'm bound to talk about," he said. "Trouble with both of you is you *don't* want her like everybody else . . . especially you don't want her like me! She *ought* to be out on that bread truck with me taking bull from the whole world instead of damn dancing! She *ought* to be having a swallow in the back room with me and learning how to make her way. It's no good being a goddamn girl . . . just look at you, Olympia! Just look at Saradove . . . she believes me! It's wonderful to be me . . . and you, like a fool, want her different!" His head lurched; dried mud crumbled and carried the blue feather down the front of his shirt. The ivy leaves slipped and curled in his slick hair. "How do you think she got here anyway . . . by *magic?* That's it! You think enough dancing lessons, music lessons, enough milk and party dresses, *fart* lessons, and she'll be something magic, something way off and different from me, something I never had nothing to do with!"

Olympia whined, "It's not my fault." Her finger released a corkscrew curl. It bobbed gently against the wrinkles branching from her pale eyes.

"You shut up!" He watched her knees uncross and spread. He twisted the bottle between his legs. "You think you're fixing it now, don't you? Think you can pour enough *fart* and milk in her and she'll forget how she got here in the first place. Look at her humped over there, all skinny from indoors and Co-Cola, her hair all curled like a paper doll's— she ought to be throwing that crate of loaves down to me every morning of her life! We'll just see how magical she is. You think you can rub me out, make *me* never happen! Little girl who got here by magic never had to have a daddy—just a *mama* who finds her in a rosebush or a cabbage patch one

43

fine day and takes the pretty thing on home." He pounded the words through the top of the milk bottle. "But I'm still here. Y'all are just going to have to kill me to get rid of me. You can't forget me with no rosebush or cabbage. Here and now I claim that girl to fit my boots, and she better do it!"

Olympia began twisting her curl again; her bare feet arched against the rug and turned their toes toward Duncan. Saradove drew her legs over the bench, dropped her head down into the cold ivory keys. She watched herself being hauled from the broken rosebushes. She was hurling a plate of supper, across some distant kitchen, at Olympia.

Olympia stood and straightened her dress over her knees. "Go wash the front yard off your face, clean up the blood. You talk like a crazy man." She bent over and held his leg. Her thoughts were somewhere else, so she said, "But I know how you feel, drives me crazy all day long." Duncan leaned against her arm and rolled the bottle of milk across the floor to Saradove's feet. He got up and started for the kitchen.

Olympia called, "But not in the kitchen sink, you hear, Duncan? That's not sanitary."

For a moment, Olympia looked at herself in the mirror above Duncan's chair, then sped through the screen door into her yard. Her voice came from the night, "I'm going to water them azaleas!" In her relief she screamed, "Saradove, you do one more thing like this and I'll kill you!"

The screen slammed. The dark yard grabbed Olympia and held her with a black hand. The water began, and the flowers slapped it back against her legs. In the kitchen, hot water hummed from the faucet and roared into Duncan's hands. Saradove listened to torrents sloshing from his hands to the floor.

It seemed to take a long time, and was painful, to get her skin unstuck from the piano bench. When she was on her feet, Saradove smelled of furniture polish. She stretched her arms as far as possible above her head, believing that if she could dive *up* instead of down, she could go like an arrow above the naked backs of her maidens and crawl, a champion swimmer, through the pink water to safety and her father's palace. Or, just to stand on the mantelpiece and ease herself onto that rock, where the maidens would spend the coming night kissing their love all over her face, would be enough. She imagined, at the end of love, flinging sharp cheese against their heads, destroying their lovely, invisible faces with flying fried drumsticks and thighs.

Duncan said, "You're at it again, ain't you? Am I going to have to talk all night to convince just one of you you're not different, you're ordinary? Just like your daddy, your house, your face! Were you planning right then just to fly off through the ceiling and head toward some of them lovely people you know? Which one?" Duncan's skin was clean now; only his blueberry eyes made color in his pale face. He leaned on the door, weak, waiting for her to take his weakness from him before he fell. "Which one? Huh? Is it the piano player down at First Presbyterian? The girl-scout leader? Is it that loveydovey on the telephone with all the arithmetic answers? Which one are you going to fly off to, love it up with, instead of with your poor old daddy?" Saradove brought her arms down, slashing the air, sending it flying. She saw the smile on Duncan's face.

"I love you, Duncan."

"What did you say?" His shoulder came away from the door.

"I said I love you." Duncan rubbed his hand through his hair. Sprouts of grass came off on his fingers. He yawned.

"When I'm through with it, you can look at the new *Saturday Evening Post*. I'm tired and don't give a damn." He hurried toward his bed lamp and his restful pajamas.

45

sea gulls

The rough black pages of the photograph album made her flesh crawl as she flipped them backward. If Saradove had been a cat, her hair would have stood on end and crackled. When the pages lay still, she saw a shiny Olympia, in black and white, looking up at her with the coy, secret smile of one who had nothing to gain by motherhood. Her hair was marcelled close to her skull. One slender arm, polished as a piano key, crooked around a long-stemmed bunch of gladioli. The other arm linked elbows with a woman wearing the same hair, the same dress, and a superior face, the face of Olympia's eldest sister. Blurred, in the background, was the sister's husband, all in white, a Panama hat shadowing his smile. Beyond him, there were the fences of a rich Virginia farm, and horses.

Saradove shuddered, went on looking for herself. Let her mother go on standing there, having a good time, wasting her smiles on flowers and a sister while she, Saradove, was somewhere that was nowhere, waiting far off to be plucked from the dirt beneath a rosebush or a cabbage plant. But on the next page, Saradove was everywhere; she had made it. A fat baby, the only one in the album, sat outdoors in an enameled tub of water, throwing a duck at the photographer. A little girl, sashed in white, buckled into black patent leather, knelt in a clutch of her grandmother's hollyhocks. No one could ever make her smile for the camera. Near the end of the album, Saradove found the picture she was looking for. Kneeling together at a little table, wearing white pinafores that seemed like starched birds pouncing on their shoulders, she and the two sisters from across the street lifted tin teacups to each other. A big doll sagged against the table, its tea untouched. The crepe myrtles held them all in leafy shadow. The light was all wrong, and the faces lost.

Saradove gulped the whisky as though it were good fresh milk.

"Put more water in that; you'll be sick," said the woman, speaking from the dark across the little table. The jukebox, with its belly full of lament, slipped a bright band of neon around the fingers seeking Saradove's hand.

"Give the water back to the ocean. It's too dark in here for water."

"Perhaps you'd rather get drunk in broad daylight. I'll get spotlights turned on this table."

"Suit yourself. Will you kiss me in the light? Will you put your hand down my dress in the light? Will you hold me?"

47

"Come out of here with me; sleep with me. You haven't seen the light for weeks. Saradove, will you come out of here with me?"

A bar stool scraped, a glass crashed to the floor. The sound from the jukebox crept closer to Saradove—love, lost, stay with me—trying to catch her for the woman across the table.

"Answer my question," said the woman. A green light flickered from the music and washed over the woman's face, for an instant letting Saradove see it, wonder at its color. What a long journey for the moss to make from the Alleys' maypop woods, crawling up the hill, over this city's concrete, just to cling in front of me to that damp skin.

"Please repeat the question." The moss dried, split by a sigh, crumbled to the floor. The music thumped, crossing the sigh with lust.

"God love you, Saradove. I do. Look: here's the difference between love and need." From a long distance, the woman was wading through the stink of cigarettes, and the sweet grasps of female fingers, females' mouths, for each other. Saradove was held, then kissed, then slapped across the face. "There, that's all of it. I won't ask you again, but tell me the answer, the way you would answer if you could."

The snap-to's of the bathroom door came closer. And a hand, the same hand, took her by the head and shook it to hear the dry, sweet rattle inside. It was nearly closing time. The bar held its customers above its head, ready to slam them to the ash-strewn floor, when the long hand finally crept to three, when the music went dead. Crumbled in heaps of skirts and female trousers, the morning light would find them there; and the music would light up again, spit out more of love. Saradove could look and see them all: folded in one secure lump, they would dream of peacefulness while

48

the sun shone through to fade their colors like clothes left too long on the line.

Saradove struck a match. "Here's your answer, approximately; here's the way I would answer just to deceive you," she said. She imagined that her light had set the woman's face on fire. "Before I go on, look and see that you're on fire."

The woman laughed, relieved. "Oh, how good you are to notice, at last! When I said, come home with me, I said I am on fire; when I say, sleep with me, I say I am on fire; when I say, God love you, Saradove, I am on fire; when I say, come and let me have you, I am on fire. I'm on fire . . . answer me!"

Saradove thought, She is trying to give birth to me, have me, catch me; her face blooms on me, it will burn my house, pull me out alive, catch me. She had come too close; but, even drunk, she could run backward, zigzagging, losing herself in disguises until even love's chase tired out.

Saradove answered, "I'll nearly answer you. I'm nearly the girl you met at the party, nearly the one you took home, then back to parties, then back home. I'm nearly the one you sat beside on the rock while the sun picked out our flesh tones before it crawled back across the firm water to Papa's castle. I'll have you if you'll make that picture for me, if you'll keep the wind off the water, if you'll keep the night forever locked behind the sunset, if you'll keep your downy bottom sitting still beside mine on that rock forever. And keep your back to the world, your mysterious bosom from the eyes of little girls. Will you?"

"I said nothing about forever. . . ." The woman's voice was off the scent, tired, running more for home and bed than love. Her cigarette fell into the glass ditch of ashes and butts.

49

"I did." Saradove, winning, rejoiced. With nothing behind her, she ran freely, both fast and slow. "What I am," she said, "is the smaller girl in the picture, the one with the darker hair, the younger spine. You're the one who plans things for me, perhaps a future of swims across the lake for breakfast on the battlements with Papa, a hike through those mountains in the misty distance with a late-afternoon cuddle in the leaves. We'd only have to be back in time for sunset on the rock before we make it to the bars. Look at my happy answer. Do you love me?"

The bar rushed for three o'clock. Little silences began to wedge themselves between voices and the crash of ice into glass. Then the bar opened its hands and let go. The women, with incredible energy, got to their feet, brushed off their evening, and walked out the door.

"Come outside, Saradove, and I'll let you go." In the street, the kiss stopped her breath, but only for the shortest time. As Saradove inhaled again, she found the woman had let go, had gone, had given Saradove her wish. She was alone in the black street, feeling as sharp and distinct as a steel pen point the instant before it begins to scratch the curving words along the line. To no one at all, Saradove said, "I didn't mean it. I meant, I love you. Wait, I'm coming." She began running; it was the wrong direction, there was no one to chase her.

She thought, There is a plague in New York City; everyone's deserted and left me alone without a warning. But the silence was nothing but the city holding its breath, with its eyes closed, in the few hours after night had rushed to a standstill, before morning came to shake it awake again. She turned into a crooked little street that became ever darker in its trail past a failed little theater, past the special grocery stores, past the pretty, brass-plated houses. She ran through the dark. She ran, thinking, When I come to Sixth Avenue,

I will sit down and in a little while will remember how to get to her. Sixth Avenue was ahead of her suddenly, still glittering in the few headlights of cars, in the flare of Howard Johnson's serving nourishing hamburgers. She sat down on a curbstone. It was simply a matter of waiting for the sun to break out, suck up the ink, and write the solution down in front of her.

Far off up the avenue, peacefulness poured over the asphalt and rolled downtown to soften the few people left to feel it. Saradove leaned against a lamppost, dreaming she sat in a fresh meadow or in her grandmother's hollyhocks. Ants began construction between her feet. Grass and ivy crept around her head; trees fresh as dew branched from the parking meters to lean over her. Azaleas, sprouting bushy and brilliant from the ears of Howard Johnson's, multiplied and spread to every roof. But for the bleating of the sheep trotting over the hummock of a sandal shop, all would have been quiet.

She was going to become a shepherdess waiting for morning on a mountain; she was going to be a Judas tree springing ripe and pink beside a winter house, but a horn's toot made her open her eyes.

A young man, his hair greased flat and waved respectably, his transparent shirt all creased and pointed at the elbows, stood beside a little black car and gaped at her. In such a shirt, he would have been ridiculous bowing from the waist. Instead, he put his hands in his pockets.

"Miss, can I help you? You seem to be a nice girl." Perhaps, thought Saradove, if he wore a powdered wig and concealed a lace handkerchief in his sleeve.

"Perhaps," she said, "if you wore a powdered wig."

"Oh no, miss, don't think I'm that way! I am not what you're thinking I am." His face cringed with honesty. "I wouldn't even be in a neighborhood like this if I didn't have to wait for my buddy. I got to drive him home to Jersey."

Saradove eased herself up the lamppost until they were eye to eye. The young man seemed awash in a navy-blue sea threatening to soak her too. She thought of becoming a life raft for him, one of those nice girls she could have been if she had listened to her mother. Instead, she thought, I spend my dawns tossing those girls from the back of my truck; they're store-bought bread, I have them with molasses.

The young man sat down on his car's dusty fender. The ocean pouring out of him was only morning coming. "Oh," he said, "I guess you suspect the worst, me talking to you like this, but I can tell you what my mother's always told me about the New York girls . . . the lipstick and rouge, the hair all tied up in knots. . . ."

"I know," said Saradove.

"But yours isn't—I see it—yours is plain." His nerves got the better of him, and he laughed, shaking all over with it, hoping he'd been plain enough to match her. "I don't mean plain like it sounded, like that. . . ." He waved his hands vaguely toward his shoes, which, astonishingly in the coming light, were turning into wide, neat humps of tangerine suède sewed down to crepe soles. "I mean you're pretty and all—but a nice girl—like my mother used to be. I could tell when I saw you sitting here all sad with your eyes closed. Not the kind of girl who belongs in a place like this. I knew—it was funny—right away, something terrible had come to you to bring you here this time of night, I mean, right where I'd find you."

Saradove imagined watering the African violets with his mother for the rest of her life, and the tears poured easily into her eyes. But after all, he deserved his chance: his mother had told him to go look for a nice girl in a desperate situation; and the nice girl would become his and hers forevermore in New Jersey. He could have approximately what he sought.

She thought, My unpainted smile is worth a Sunday dinner to him; my brimming blue eyes, a modern maple bedroom *suit*. Truly, my tears flowing down unvarnished cheeks can bring all the nourishment of a Thanksgiving turkey on a checkered tablecloth to him.

At that moment, the New Jersey hills sucked all the country air back into their own real meadows. The actual city morning emptied over their heads like a lazy man's garbage from a third-story window. Far away, and coming closer, the sheep's bleating turned to the choking of traffic hastening forward for fresh supplies of sandals and hamburgers.

"I'm a stranger here myself." Saradove blushed, burlesquing the sun before it came out to show her up.

"My name is Arnold; that makes two of us." He dove for her sorrowing profile like a fish for the line. He twisted one orange shoe around the other, hung his head to shake the words out more easily. "I know what must have happened. I know how it is—you know—when I get a couple of beers in me back at Fairleigh Dickinson—that's where I'm a senior going to be a lawyer. I wouldn't *criticize!*" His brown eyes bobbed like corks on a pond. They told her that he yearned to serve up bowls of his mother's tomato soup to her, to frame her poor head in yards of organdy curtains. Instead, using the material at hand, he grabbed the lamppost above her head and leaned, like a tree half cut down, as though he were shielding her from the ax that had already broken him.

Saradove shot him a mother's look and lied. "It's not what you think," she said. She stepped off the curb, leaving him alone with the lamppost, without losing a single tear to the gutter. Her lashes beat the breeze; she remembered her up-bringing. "I suppose you might say that I have been . . . cruelly abandoned. I was going to . . . consult . . . a policeman when you were so kind . . . so kind just to happen along." Arnold went up like a red balloon; she held the string for him.

A strange chin, drifted with doughnut powder, stuck up above the back fender. Wearing the blue twin to Arnold's shirt, the buddy vaulted the car hood and grabbed Arnold around the neck in the crook of his elbow.

"Hey, big man!" he yelled. "So this is how you wait for your old buddy! Takes you to sunup to find one and then—" he examined Saradove's face, tracing it with a breath of beer and sugar doughnut—"and then, you old devil, by God, you make it cry!"

Saradove reached out and claimed Arnold; she mollycoddled him with her voice. But across the street an early-bird supermarket, snuggling next to Howard Johnson's, opened its doors and set off its nighttime burglar alarm, shouting down all her comforting.

"You misunderstand!" she screamed at the buddy. "I have lost something, my . . . my money! And I'm on my way to a friend's house for . . . for aid and comfort . . . and after that to my grandmother's on Park Avenue!"

Arnold grunted like a tuba. "You always misunderstand! One thing on your brain all the time. Only one thing!" But suddenly he sounded like a loose and raving maniac: someone had shut off the alarm; in all the peace and quiet, Arnold was shouting about one thing only. Saradove peered up at him from around a shirt sleeve and laughed at it.

Saradove made herself sound like a buddy. "I won't hold you boys up any longer. You want to get home to New Jersey. I know what you want." She reached up and tickled Arnold, with one finger, inside his shirt sleeve. "Now it's daylight, so long, guys."

It was daylight with a vengeance. Sunlight merged with a

sky shelled in the hard, sticky glaze of blue *petits-fours*. The night had left Saradove's side without a single good-bye, had left her head rocking alone in shreds of fantasy: beds and perversion, liquor without sleep, hundreds and thousands of maidens leaving barstools without first saying that they loved Saradove. A pigeon strutted by her feet, gurgling after its mate. Villagers refreshed with sleep and orange juice banged out of their doors on Waverly Place and crossed efficiently to the subway. They had many selfish reasons for not taking Saradove by the hand and leading her into their shining kitchens.

"She wants to go to her grandmother's," Arnold's buddy shouted. He shook with the strain of facing daylight with nothing to show for it but a doughnut.

Arnold smiled a mother's smile. "You're wrong, old buddy, she wants to go to her friend's house." He beat his fist against the transparent shirt. He had come up from the microscope with the answer—look at her, cured at last!

At once, without another word, they all agreed to drop their night's failures at each other's feet. They nestled together in the front seat of the car, each shoulder weeping against another.

All along Fourth Street, running east, the traffic lights turned green the moment they approached. Reprieved, they all relaxed, gliding through the city's speed limit as one. Their barge was flower-strewn, gilded and spotted with cupids. Forests bowed before them; on either bank, children waved and curtsied. The violins tuned up; the conductor swayed with a favorite tune. They sat at the address, motionless, to hear the waves lap at their feet, to hear the final coda lapse from the bows. The music could have shivered on one note until noon.

Arnold's buddy opened his eyes. "Here we are."

If I were the girl, Saradove thought, he has taken all night to find, he would help me to the shore now, open the basket and bring out the cold chicken and wine. I would let him watch me trail my fingers, like willows, in the water all afternoon. Who is it I've taken all morning to find? Arnold opened the door and led her by the fingers to the sidewalk. Across the street, the tombstones of Marble Cemetery floated up, flashed their shadows and fell down again through the trees, lively with the hearts of the oldest citizens. Arnold stood still in the sun, his eyes closed, his jaws apart. Saradove let his hand drop, and his face came awake with hope.

"Tomorrow," he said, "tonight, I mean, we are all going on a beach party to the beach. Will you come with me? This *is* my car." Saradove patted the shirt sleeve, felt the breeze go through it.

"I'm afraid I've delayed you." She gave him the smile of a princess who needed to sleep for a hundred years. He bowed low from the waist and kissed her hand; he saw that her legs were marked with curbstone dirt, that her white sneakers had come untied.

The boys sat far apart in the front seat, and Arnold promised Saradove to keep his buddy awake at the wheel.

All the way up the stairs, she dragged her fingers along the stuccoed walls; they were brown and smelled of coffee. L.E.'s door was wide open, the rooms beyond it empty. Her lamps still burned, shining on expensive modern clutter, fresh flowers, half-eaten food.

"Where are you?" said Saradove. She went up another flight, to the roof. L.E. lay in the shadow of the chimney, unmussed by the morning. Her face felt, to Saradove's hand, like fresh, newly raked earth; it had grown too young to

56

ments, the night's first star, revealed to them without fanfare for their wishes. Soon they dressed, trembling; and it was wholly dark again on the roof.

The roof's door swung open. Evelyn stood in it, watching them in the blaze of light from the stairs. Her breasts jutted like bombs beneath her sweater. Evelyn lived with L.E., and sometimes kept her sober, sometimes made her eat, sometimes got her to the job of hammering and nailing at a framer's shop. L.E. moved from the square of light back into the dark, grasping Saradove by the hair; it was hard to tell which of these terrors that took her from drink and sleep needed her fidelity more.

"Ah, dear love, it's you!" L.E. rushed to stroke Evelyn's long, amber-colored bristling hair, but warily, as though she feared a carving knife hidden beneath that thick sweater. "I've just been wondering out here, with Saradove's help, how you explained the lack of me at work today."

Evelyn moved out of the hand and blocked Saradove's sight of the star. "I told them your father just died," she said.

"Again? But my darling Evelyn, you told them he died last month, or the month before. . . ." She slid neatly back into the light, taking Evelyn by the hand, making her evening's choice. "But it doesn't matter which month, does it, Saradove? It couldn't interest you—either was such a long time before your time."

"*Our* time," said Saradove. Evelyn stroked her own forehead, aiming an elbow directly at Saradove's heart. Her hips swung back and forth, made a white moon pendulum knocking against L.E. before she settled herself to answer. "No," she said, "dear fool, L.E., last month it was your *uncle* who died and kept you home; the month before it was your mother." Evelyn let go of her forehead and swung her arms out against the sky. Their dead white gleamed in the dark.

All of her that showed was alabaster, amber and pink; and cops that caught her shouting after L.E. in predawn streets loved her for it. All of L.E. began to twiddle inward: the toes of her boots touched, her shoulders tried to meet, her elbows tried to kiss. She bent her back against the chimney and hung her head.

"Mother?" she said, with great charm. "Mother? You really shouldn't wish Mother to die, you know, Evelyn."

Evelyn shook her bombs, stretching, at the stars. "Come and eat your dinner, L.E. Here—take my hand and come with me." She crossed the alabaster of her face with pink lipstick, produced a smile for Saradove, the least she could do. "Why, hello, Saradove! What are you doing on a roof?"

"I just dropped by." From what? thought Saradove, heaven, an airplane?

Evelyn took L.E. by the hands and gently pulled her, like a sleepy, bad child, all the way down the stairs to home.

a Russian Jew
from Sevastopol

The morning, at 2:00 A.M., glistened beyond the street lamp's arc like a painted lake. Outside it, in the dark, there was a Gothic rockpile carved like a church. To the left of the church door, there was a niche large enough for two to crouch. And there were L.E. and Saradove, crouching, escaped from Evelyn, bending, snarling their bodies, kissing. Occasionally, some sound would shake L.E.'s nerve; she would insist that they peek around the stone to spy out the street for danger. Instead, Saradove would look through the curling iron spikes growing from the church's black and silver grass, protecting the graves from live ones like herself. But after the long night they were exhausted from the use of each other; and L.E. could no longer bear Saradove's indifference to the dangers that lurked like sea monsters out in the light, ready to pounce on their rock. She began to talk, noticing the scenery for the first time, noticing how close it came to resembling her life, a romantic revival.

"It reminds me," L.E. said at last, "of what my mother and Elizabeth Barrett Browning could do with it. It would become a major poem. How marvelous if they were here instead of us. Think what art could be made!"

The city washed against their scenery. L.E. shifted, Saradove moved; and their long arms clasped their long legs, and their narrow shoulders drooped. The light that reached them turned their hands and faces frost-colored. Saradove closed her eyes; she thought of the art that they had made. They reminded her, not of poetry, but of painting. They were a picture she could not remember. "You mean," said Saradove, "like the time last winter in the alley when you said that Cocteau could have made white flowers from the snow on the garbage cans . . . if only Cocteau had been there instead of you and me."

L.E. was disgusted. "This is different. But what can I expect? Only Elizabeth would understand, and she would be too sick, there on the couch with Aurora Leigh, to let me in." L.E. unzipped the pocket of her secondhand motorcycle jacket and took out a pink pastel crayon. With long swoops and careful capitals on the gray stone, she wrote: ELIZABETH BARRETT BROWNING LOVES MY MOTHER ARNA HARTSDALE. There was nothing of the Fuckyou Helpme scrawls of the subway station about it. L.E. pressed her cheek against the words and smiled, not at Saradove. "This is my memorial," she said, "to my mother and Elizabeth Barrett Browning in this age that insensitively puts down Elizabeth."

"It doesn't put your mother down, does it?" The pink on

gray reminded Saradove of Olympia's summer Sunday frock. She had worn it with white kid gloves and white high heels. When, one day, she had lost one of the gloves (she said the counter girl had stolen it) in the drugstore, it was the last time she had ever gone to church.

L.E. patted Saradove on the head, in her favorite disguise of dirty rich old man visiting the poor orphan girl. "This age doesn't *know* my mother's poetry," she explained kindly, "because it destroyed her faith in herself before she could come to the full height of her powers. Now . . . now, she does nothing but read Swinburne, live in Los Angeles, and write letters that are masterpieces from a beautiful soul, to me." L.E. kissed Saradove. Beneath the kiss, Saradove wondered sadly about motherhood. It seemed to be pink and gray, seemed to come from a crayon.

Lights from a patrol car caressed their faces, moved back, pointed at a tombstone. A policeman leaned out to look. In an instant, L.E. had unwound herself from the hole and was in the light. She leaned against the fence as though it were a piano, smiling at the policeman's light as though she were preparing to sing to it. She called, "Oh, Officer? Officer?" The policemen put out their cigarettes. "You haven't, have you, seen a Borzoi hound in this vicinity? I've been half the night, with my sister here, looking for him." L.E. moved closer to the car, stroking the iron spikes with her fingers; her smile grew more fantastic. To Saradove, L.E., out by the graves, seemed a dancing skeleton hiding its bones in mean, zippered leather and sneaking close to eat up the innocent. She began to sweat against the church rock. But the policemen were due for coffee and Danish. Their motor idled; it took them only a glance to agree on the incident. One of them leaned out his window to see if L.E. could possibly belong to him.

"You girls get on back home," he said. L.E. let her head

droop in such a charming mime of disappointment that Saradove knew for sure that ill-luck intended to back up on them and take them into custody. But the car sped on; L.E. leapt back into the rock.

"That was my Kit Cornell voice," she said. "I was weaned on that voice. It's for emergencies of a personal nature." Saradove could breathe again; it was L.E. she breathed, freshened with the scent of graveyard grass and free night air.

Somehow they managed to spread themselves out against the rock. Saradove plunged to the bottom of the lake and there seized the sea monster. In her grasp, it turned beautiful. When she surfaced, her first thought was of the graves and of her mother. But it was L.E.'s mother she spoke about.

"You and your mother," she said, "think so much of Mrs. Browning . . . "

"Miss Barrett," L.E. interrupted. "I like to remember her before she married."

"Well, you and your mother think so much of her I guess you must get together sometimes to take flowers to her grave."

L.E. hid her face against the rock and laughed, shaking all her bones hard against Saradove. In spite of everything, Saradove could still amuse. "There's that Southern shit again. I swear, Saradove, sometimes you *are* real, real as fatback, grits and collard greens! Flowers to the grave, indeed!"

Saradove hid her own face in her hands. "Don't tease," she said.

"Don't tease!" L.E. mocked.

Saradove desperately remembered literature. "I mean," she said, "don't you know even Dame Edith Sitwell used to run around Swinburne's grave, and pour milk and honey on it? And dance around?"

L.E. did not know, was enchanted, folded Saradove again

into her arms. "Of course! How wonderful, of course! But that's not . . . you have a lot to learn, Saradove . . . that's not fatback—that's elegance, that's true honor! And if my mother, Arna Hartsdale, had only thought of it, that's what she would have done. For Miss Barrett, though." L.E. withdrew to her own part of the dark. Saradove could not even hear her breathe, but the voice was clear, reaching into her memories and strangling them into new, exotic shapes. L.E. began dreaming of a new past for Saradove.

"I know you, Saradove. I see you now, you and your mama and daddy and uncle and auntie and your idiot family-skeleton cousin—I see you burping your fried-chicken dinners, then driving in your Easter hats out to Grandma's plot to change the water in the vases, put in a new bunch of . . . what? Carnations? That's your style."

"No!" There was still a chance that L.E. might remember the true things. She spoke quickly, harshly, pushing at the glittering, subtle structure of new lies L.E. was trying to build for her. "No! They wouldn't have *bought* flowers . . . carnations are things you buy! They would go in the back yard and pick gladioli for her; or go back to my grandmother's old house by the railroad tracks and take her some of the flowers she grew . . . ragged robins, sweet william plants, hollyhocks. L.E., my grandmother isn't dead yet!" And Saradove conjured up a live grandmother from a dead one, added to L.E.'s shining lies.

"Listen to me, Saradove . . ."

"No! You're just putting my grandmother down because she said one time the same thing you just said about your mother."

L.E. gave up, began stroking her own head, began wondering if anyone famous was planted by this dismal church. "What's that, Saradove . . . I don't understand." But she didn't listen. She was admiring a vision her mind was making of Arna Hartsdale dancing, in shimmering evening dress, around a grave, then dancing up close to the church to watch her daughter make love to Saradove. She thought of breaking into the church and whispering all her sins to Saradove through the confessional grille; and then Saradove could whisper all of them back to her. L.E. didn't know that it was only a Baptist church.

". . . that this insensitive age ruined my father, of course. That's what my grandmother said. The Depression kept him from his rightful place in the world. By rights—and I know it!—he should have had the big white house, the slaves, the cotton, the thoroughbreds held in by white fences; plenty of bourbon, and beaux for me. It was despair at his lot that made him run away and join the circus—this was before my mother and me—where he became a side-show barker and ruined his throat and married a trapeze artist!" L.E.'s clouded castle could never be good enough; Saradove could build something even airier, even more marvelous. She could make a more splendid lie. Who could love the daughter of the bread-truck driver who threw plates at a little woman named Olympia?

"What are you saying?" L.E. came closer, amazed, wondering hard about where Saradove left off and L.E. began, in both fantasy and flesh. The difference had somehow been lost down the throat of a hungry and beautiful story. "You lie, Saradove!" L.E. needed difference; she needed to control the difference. "Go on, light your cigarette. It must be safe enough to smoke here if you're still alive after lying like that in the house of God!" L.E. grinned, waited for fun; but Saradove didn't see it.

"It's perfectly true. He was away from home for over ten . . . no, twenty years . . . married to this trapeze artist,

66

traveling with the show all over the South . . . no, even before the crowned heads of Europe. He told me . . . he used to sit by my bed at night and tell me wonderful stories . . . he told me his best friends were clowns and elephants . . . that the King of England pinned a gold medal on his wife."

Saradove stayed still, waiting for the lightning to come strike her down; but nothing stirred, not even a grave, and the only sound was from a bus belching blocks away. Or was it the motor of the bread truck, revving up, speeding fast as lightning to catch her? She watched L.E. strike a match and hold it high above them, saw L.E. turn into the ghost woman who used to creep from the radio, carrying a candle and her severed head into Saradove's bedroom, scaring her into a nightmare. Smells of sulphur and the rock's damp slid between them; tobacco smoke gathered it all up and spread it outside on the grass. L.E. chose Saradove's truth. She began to paint the castle pink and make the story her own.

"Haven't you ever considered," she said, "that you might have been fooled all these years with an impostor for a mother?" Never, thought Saradove.

"Never!" she gasped. "Nobody but a real mother would have let me love her . . . Olympia isn't . . . ?" Saradove fell deep into the shining trap. Her new past was becoming clear as a picture on the wall, more truthful than the life beneath the picture. Hope juggled her heart from hand to hand; it could have been a china plate twirling in the air. L.E., in a moment, would give Saradove a new name, a new bloodstream. Saradove would be a Catholic from Atlanta, a Russian Jew from Sevastopol, the King of Scotland's bastard daughter. L.E. would give her seven sisters, alive and spinning, in the Black Forest. L.E. would change into her noble father, come to claim his own. She sat very still, though, prepared for trickery.

L.E. turned her back on what she had made; she began outlining ELIZABETH BARRETT BROWNING LOVES MY MOTHER ARNA HARTSDALE with a huge pink heart.

"I didn't say," said L.E., "that Olympia is an impostor. I only meant that it's possible. Listen to this: have you ever thought that your real destiny might be to wear ballet slippers and a spangled suit and ride an elephant? To follow that *real* mother's profession? Listen, Saradove, don't you see? Doesn't it seem real? After your trapeze mother fell tragically to her death in the ring, your father, brokenhearted, gathered you up—an infant sleeping in yards of dirty tulle—and ran back home, defeated in his dream, back to . . . where is it?"

"New Oriental, North Carolina."

"New Oriental, North Carolina," L.E. repeated. She added a bunch of roses, a sheaf of lilies to the pink heart. "And there your father married again: a nice, average girl who was only too happy for a chance to get off the farm, so happy she was even willing to raise you—tainted as you were by show business—in the bargain."

Around the church, the breeze was freshening up for a try at dawn; the silvered trees brushed at each other. Saradove could see it all, could see herself as she should have been, a wet infant head pushing through a silver-spangled crotch a thousand feet high above the sawdust ground. Her mother bent, pumped, swung back and forth on the trapeze bar; and Saradove was born, midair.

But the story, for that moment, was too wonderful to be Saradove's mother. Saradove imagined she heard the bread truck honking its horn behind her.

"Olympia?" she said. "Not *Olympia*, way up there!"

"Of course not Olympia, you idiot Saradove. You're not listening—she's the second one, the nice girl off the farm."

"I don't believe it." She didn't believe it, she was Saradove.

She was still Saradove, stretched out on a couch, worn out from looking at a painting. She was not in a picture frame, lovely and at her ease before her father's castle; she was not fantasy, she was flesh.

L.E. stood and zipped up the leather jacket; she was offended, prepared to go off alone in the dark. "Of course," she said, "if you wish to reject reality—you're *immature*, Saradove—reject reality right off the bat, not even give me a chance, then far be it from me to destroy your little dream of *real* Mama suckling you in the homey rocking chair with Daddy standing by!" L.E. posed in the fashion of tragediennes waiting to exit stage left.

"Wait, please!" said Saradove. If L.E. went away, the story would never end. To keep her, Saradove said, "Yes, you're right. I believe you."

Straight through the sound of leaf rustle, leaving the graves where they lay, Saradove kept with L.E., kept with the story. They were headed across town, for a bar. Evelyn would be already there, arranging free drinks with the bartender who waited every night for the three girls to come in, lean their breasts across his bar, poke him in the belly, taunt him. Happy to walk, to be near familiar ground, Saradove took the hand that touched hers and kissed it, sipping at each finger. She reached for the waist, felt for the face.

L.E. felt horror. Some fairy tale she had made up was coming to life and trying to love her. "Either stop that," she said, "or come and do it forever."

Saradove unzipped L.E.'s pocket and put her hand in it as they walked. "We're taking a dreadful chance," she said happily. "You know, he almost had Evelyn in that back room of his last night before you started rolling beer bottles at him. And he's not so fat in the belly that he can't *rub* when he makes us dance with him."

L.E. wished Saradove would disappear. L.E. wished she were home, with Evelyn, in bed; or out getting in a fight; or even framing pictures; or driving the smiling Arna Hartsdale down the Los Angeles freeway in a speeding Mercedes. She realized that if she didn't stop and pee immediately she would have to grab her crotch and dance around, something that Saradove was sure to misinterpret. "Stop, Saradove," she said, "I've just got to pee." L.E. screwed her mouth into a little rose and rolled her eyes. She hopped back and forth from the curb into a slick of rainbowed grease.

Saradove turned away, regretting every kiss, every passion. The castle was falling; beside her, in the painting, there was a grown-up woman who couldn't wait to go to the bathroom. She hunched her shoulders in the cotton dress she had spent all afternoon with, striving to iron it into regular creases. She looked at the sky, longing for Radclyffe Hall to descend and clutch her to her pin-striped, bow-tied bosom. She began easing L.E.'s head beneath the glittering knife of the guillotine— no, better the noose. She gave the chair a satisfying kick and watched L.E. swing in the breeze. Saradove stamped her foot in frustration. At the last moment, just as L.E.'s tongue had begun to swell and protrude, Saradove had dashed, whimpering, to grab her by the knees and lift her up to safety.

"What's the matter, Saradove? You have to pee, too? We'll never make it to the bar—but look what I see—a fresh green garden, with its pretty gate wide open, just waiting for me to pee on it. Just like Shakespeare, isn't it? Lots of moonlit gardens in Shakespeare . . . what's the matter, Saradove? Where's your sense of humor, Saradove? Between your legs?"

Saradove loved the movies; in New Oriental, they never did Shakespeare. "You go ahead," she said. "I'll watch out for people coming." Forgetting Saradove, L.E. grabbed herself by the crotch and let the hours of drinking that had led her to the church catch up with her. She swayed, came close to Saradove; her eyes grew luminous, like the tip of the god-mother's wand.

I'll give you anything; I'll be your heart's desire, thought Saradove.

"You're going to let me go in there all alone?" said L.E., reaching for her heart's desire. "All alone where there are lions and tigers, tigers and lions? Aren't you afraid of losing me? And I know what you'll do . . . the minute I've been eaten alive, you'll run away. You're going to run away, Saradove."

L.E. was afraid of losing her! Delight made her feet itch to move and run. "Oh, no!" Saradove laughed.

And L.E. answered, "Then go ahead and run!" L.E. stumbled for the garden gate, laughing too.

The gate slammed shut. Saradove, alone, listened to all the varieties of night coming to get her, roaring like a bread truck. She listened to the shrubbery behind the garden wall heave, part, shake still. A sound of rushing water began and, before it stopped, the moon came out over a warehouse to give its final display, shining like a candle. Then where's my birthday cake? thought Saradove, asking the moon a hard question. In answer, it burned through her flesh until it found the thinnest vein; and the sounds Saradove heard was of her own blood rushing home.

Saradove began to run away. Down the street that might have been a forest she went, an urgent hunter whose prey of rabbit, deer or lion might hide behind any door the night held open. Every corner became a thick tree, and something behind each thick trunk reached out to frustrate her kill. And beyond, in the next dark alley, the animal waited again, using its intelligence to stop breathing, to lick its paws and rest until Saradove's feet again pounded close. At the last moment, in a dark motion of fur, the animal sped out of a shadow's triangle, leapt through an oval O of darkened neon, over her head, and on.

"I *am* the hunter!" Saradove cried. "*I* catch things!" But she stopped running. She could not forget how to breathe. Her head hung, her tongue fell loose in her mouth; and she opened her eyes on a shop window and spoke to it. How long can I last, she panted, until we come to the end? There, in the empty places, how quickly will I be caught? She stretched her back upright, feeling the wonderful muscles swim into place. The sound of four paws, or hooves, beat and beat, then stopped. It would wait until she was equal again. She pretended she did not hear the roaring of the motor, the grinding of the gears, the soft bounce of bread among the crates; magically, no matter how near, Duncan's truck was still behind her.

In the shop window was a faded jumble of books, stacked in dust; tacked to the window frame there were valentines, old hearts already written on with thin and curling strokes that did not look like words. It was June, no month for valentines; Saradove leaned her head against the glass to select one. Its edges were tucked into the fur of the shop's fat and tabby cat that slept like the dead. The valentine had the face of a girl staring up into the pallor of the street's light, looking for Saradove. Her lacy bodice supported a gold locket, painted half-open to show the vague, squint-eyed face of her sweetheart, his ginger, handle-bar mustache. Her face was round with chins, rosy cheeks, blue eyes; the pink mouth, like a wax flower, was curled slightly open to reveal her little teeth. Round yellow curls toppled beneath her red hat; her arms, like two little white bananas, curved around her bodice. Her fingers held flowers that had never sprouted on earth's surface.

What a shame, Saradove said to her. You're gone so old-fashioned, your smile's so arch, pouting like the lips of a goldfish. Saradove told her, I've known you, loved you for years. Where is your bathing suit and billboard and giant Coca-Cola? It wasn't that long ago—you promised to wait and stay the same for me. Who's on your billboard at the fairgrounds now? A huger girl, a more delicious girl? Does New Oriental miss you? But what a way to treat me, your first and forever lover! When they pasted you up, other people took one look and bought Royal Crown; not me. I watched you burn in the summer, wrinkle in the rain; I smiled back. When I saw you freezing through the winter in that skimpy latex, I nearly shimmied up the poles to get you, take you home with me and warm you up. The last time I saw you, they had you in that Easter hat, that yellow corsage, vulgar as they come, but I waved good-bye, promised to return. What are you doing here? Did the Coca-Cola rot your stomach lining? Is that what brought you to New York City dust?

Saradove breathed in deeply, shook from so much oxygen all at once. Her forehead quivered against the glass. The cat's eyes opened into quarter moons; he stretched out one foreleg, five nails open, and knocked Saradove's girl over, covered her with his rump. Saradove followed her head to the glass and rested there against it. The hunter walked out of her, left her, the beasts at heel beside him. He left her alone with all her heart's desire beneath the cat's behind: herself, sunny, banal, sweet as Coca-Cola, certain love on the fourteenth of February; no feet for running.

The street, empty now of any sound, began furling forth little gray flags of light. Saradove pushed herself through them, hoping for home before the sun could catch her and make her sick. Definitions of herself occurred to her: I am the two-headed dog the Russians invented. I am the centaur. I am Christine Jorgensen. I am the many joking faces of Jehovah. Halfway home, she took L.E.'s crayon from her pocket and leaned against a new, unrented apartment building that had the façade of a pale-blue public toilet. In careful capitals, she wrote all over it, all her definitions—CENTAUR, JORGENSEN, TWO-HEADED DOG, JEHOVAH, SARADOVE. SARADOVE RACEPATH she scrawled at last. As an afterthought, she added, with vicious intent: WHERE ARE THE GARGOYLES OF YESTERYEAR? She left the crayon where she dropped it.

She climbed the stairs to her fifth floor, yawning, deciding that being God would be best. Centaurs are extinct; Christine Jorgensen a miracle of modern science, *urp;* two heads go with a wagging tail, not for me. Saradove, she told herself, be God. On the last flight of stairs, her legs began to pump; her lungs gasped. I am not God, she thought; in me, dissolving in drink and the nonsense of a silly girl, are the last vestiges of the splendid fencing champion Saradove could have been.

At the top of the stairs, she rested against her door and felt the single, lustful eye peer at her. It belonged to the janitor, who lived next door to her in an apartment lavish with filigreed saints and a glaring Virgin Mary. His brown rayon bathrobe was caught, with the wet eye, in the door; it sweetened him, made him unlike the dirty man who rolled out the morning garbage cans. When she smiled at him, he slammed the door; but for his benefit, she swung her keys twice against the wall, like bells, and called out, "Oh, what a night! Oh, what a night!"

Saradove had left her room smelling of carnations; now it stank. The flowers against her fingers had thinned and wrinkled to the texture of old yellowed newspaper. At each stage of life and decay, her fingers told her, there is a different smell. She sat down in her own dark. Across the street, the windows of a trucking company burned, always, day and night, with enough light to cast the glow of a single candle into her rooms. It was enough. Saradove wrapped herself in her raincoat and lit a cigarette, both to keep off the morning chill. She considered the person nearest her, the janitor, who would probably take his chances as a maniac rapist, given the slightest opportunity. Saradove got up and unlocked her door.

Saradove thought, He throws the garbage cans around and rages at this brutal age that has kept him from his rightful place in the world, has made him a janitor. He can't relax, get drunk with the boys, spend all his pay because that's what janitors are supposed to do. In his rightful place, in a little hot country, he would come charging down from the mountains waving his rifle . . . no, it's a machete clutched between his bright teeth . . . to liberate his mother and sisters from the clutches of the landlord, so that he could be landlord. I know for a fact that when he passes my door on his way down to the garbage, he insanely sticks his nose in my lock hoping to sniff my perfume. And I haven't any. It's no way for my revolution's hero to behave.

Saradove closed her eyes and dropped her cigarette in the carnation water. For her head's sake, she pulled the chair cushion to the floor; she tried to tuck all her body inside the raincoat and when she did, there came a smell to high heaven of carnation's and tobacco's incense. She was very comfortable; the dust curls on the floor came and powdered her face; but when she spoke, out loud, they blew in wild directions on her breath. Get up and go get her, said Saradove. Right now she is bouncing beer bottles off the fat belly of the bartender, needing me. How long will I take to get there? When I come home, I'll bring back her empty bottles and bop the janitor over the head for dishonoring me with his nose.

Saradove clasped her hands together in a prayerful, Rodin

fashion and slipped them beneath her cheek. Marriage to the janitor, she whispered, will make a real life. Within a month, I will have taught my eager, passionate husband all he needs to know of Marx. All day long he will gratefully hear me while I explain to him parliamentary procedure, how to explode the train, sneak attack, strangling with a piano wire, what necktie to wear to the White House. We'll have secret-cell meetings. I might be the hardy Communist wife of a hardy Communist; I might wear safari pants and a bush jacket full of live grenades. I'll be fit for picket lines. No children, of course, to grow up in this corrupt, insensitive age . . . all our youth ahead of us to organize all the janitors, drag them out of their beer and into the fire. In our old age, covered with the honorable scars of prison, we'll retire to an efficiency on Riverside Drive. We'll walk our fox terrier, greet the dawn of a new day.

Bright as a button, the sun climbed over the window sill and rolled over her face. She managed to get to her hands and knees, to crawl over, to knock herself in the head yanking down the blinds. When it was dark again, her knees butted the little phonograph, its turntable still revolving from days ago, hot as an iron in the fire. She groped to pull the plug, but the needle hopped and skipped ahead of her and, after a gnash of sound, flute music by Mozart poured over her like streams of purest drinking water. I know, wept Saradove, that Mozart was not French; but I have always wanted to visit the gardens of Versailles. The phone rang.

The Kit Cornell voice had become the monster-movie voice. "And well you might cry," said L.E. "You're not alone . . . I can hear the music . . . not the kind of music to be alone with. Don't lie to me."

"Wait a minute," said Saradove. "I can't talk in the dark,"

"The dark doesn't shine on you, does it? Crazy Saradove, the sun is out."

"Not here." But her hand couldn't reach the light switch; and she was afraid to leave the voice alone. Some smoke hissed at her from the line's other end.

"I know," said L.E., "your apartment's been magicked off to Australia . . . you got another sun from mine in your back yard someday . . . I didn't, I won't chase you through the dark any more."

"Didn't you? Yes, you did."

"Hush, crybaby. I don't love you any more . . . no more. I'm coming over."

"You're drunk, it's daylight, you have to go to work." She heard something, L.E.'s phone, clang against a metal wall. The sound, like hot oil, cured Saradove's aching ear.

When L.E. spoke again, the monster movie had reached its rousing climax. "No work," she said. "My uncle just died and the funeral's at your house. Daylight? I thought you said it was dark."

Saradove dropped her phone and turned to look at the room. The blinds flapped in and out, the cord twirling in a darkened, then lighted gyration. The candlelight from the trucking company had been snuffed out. In its place the sun sloshed melted butter over her floor . . . in again, sucked out again, as the blind flapped.

Saradove spoke in the phone again. "We're both right. You may or may not come over. As you wish; as I wish." Nothing answered in her ear but the buzzing of a clear line. Saradove thought, It doesn't matter; she will come or not come. Her whole body curled up in just the small and terrible place between her legs. "It doesn't matter," she told her body.

The room reeled in and out of Saradove's head, fixing her

with its dirt, telling her she must not sleep until it was clean. She took off her raincoat and thought she would clean her room in case company came. She threw the coat on the floor, went to yank out the phonograph, gagging Mozart for his impudence, his filthy ease in making telephone bells ring to his music. She wanted to dust her books; they were lined up, wall to wall, beneath the windows, and sported black soot the size of sand grains. There was nothing to dust with; instead, she sang a song, involving Mozart's tune and words Olympia crooned when she bent over white shirts on the ironing board. "Mailman's gone by an-nd left me no letter; melancholy ba-aby, sun's going shine in my back yar-rd someday. . . ."

One carnation was still just soft enough. She brushed the flower over the books, letting soot and petals fly. So much for you, Edgar Allan Poe. . . . So much for you, History of the English Language, Saradove sang. One more remark, I'll give you to the bread truck, Gawain-Poet! Saradove's eyes were closed, but when her head hit the opposite wall, she knew that things were clean and finished. The pink petals garnishing the books improved the looks of them, but still no one had come. But still, thought Saradove, soon she will come and I will sink like a stone beneath the water's pink surface. It will be black and golden and carved with jewels in the treasure-trove at the bottom of the lake. Before that, she would eat and grow strong for sunset swimming, for the twirl from the trapeze, for the sunshine in the great meadow of her heart's desire. In the kitchen, cockroaches scuttled and leapt like frogs from sink to stove and back again. Some, falling to the floor from an enormous height, simply turned back over to run again. You should have seen Olympia, Saradove told them. She ironed those sheets, scrubbed those corners, sterilized things like you with strong ammonia. The whole house, once a week, was hot with the smell of ironed cotton; and Stella Dallas boohooed at Mama; and I saw her one day get seduced by an English Lord off the radio. Look at her daughter . . . infested!

With a great leap, the Russian Ballet in Swan Lake straight behind her, Saradove hit the kitchen floor. When she could get to her feet again, she danced among the roaches, slapping her hands against the walls. One out of ten was her victim. She tried especially hard to murder the pregnant albino, born, raised, knocked up in the bowels of the stove; instead, it lived on, and Saradove overturned the cornflakes, more roaches in the cornflakes.

The front door slammed. Saradove, caught in the sound, was in the green meadow, in L.E.'s loving, in the glazed faces of buttercups, in the noise of bees, in the bursting hearts of maypops; she was outside her own skin again, trying to re-make the child, become, with a new and beautiful past, a new Saradove. But the child was gone, unrescued, down the road, jolting another time, for another day, in the clangorous insides of the bread truck. Saradove woke up. "No," she said, "it is the maniac rapist janitor here to . . . to . . ."

"Fuck you royally," said Evelyn. "No. I think not."

It was Evelyn in her house, not L.E. come to build a more wondrous past for a more wondrous Saradove, not L.E. come to be the new father, the new mother and make lust the new birthplace; not L.E. Nor the janitor with the future. Evelyn stood before her, sweet as candy; the real thing. Her amber hair was coiled on her head in a crown. Her little red shoes were tucked into the fifth position, pristine, something of a Degas drawing safely behind glass. Saradove waited, sweated among the cockroaches.

"Not the janitor. Me. You won't get him any more than you'll get L.E.," Evelyn said harshly, full of purpose. "*That* lover-to-be of yours just came up the stairs jabbering away in Spanish to a pretty little thing just off Pan Am from Puerto Rico. Listen to the bedsprings rattle!" Evelyn jangled her huge pocketbook up and down to imitate bedsprings. The pocketbook was big and bulging; but not, this time, her breasts. She had changed from the big bombs into little round cups.

Evelyn smiled a merry, grown-up smile; the preliminary, thought Saradove, to the ferocious duel with rapiers they would presently fight for the priceless hide of L.E. Keep her body, Saradove wanted to say, just let me have the dreams she means to change my life with.

Evelyn said, "Sit down, Saradove. I haven't come to put a silver bullet through your heart, though that's what you de-serve—*vampire!*"

Vampire, thought Saradove. That would do, would make a changed Saradove. Who can catch a vampire?

"I'll just heat the coffee," said Evelyn. "Oh my!" Evelyn was staring down into the coffeepot. "Give me a spoon, Saradove." Saradove shook open a metal drawer and did. She would do everything Evelyn told her; perhaps Evelyn was the one to point the hose at her roots, so that she might bloom and flower, like bushes planted in a summer yard. Perhaps Evelyn was the other maiden in the picture.

Evelyn drew her dress between her legs to keep it from the greasy stove; she began stirring up the coffee with a big wooden spoon. Saradove watched, fearful, as she had watched the spotless white hands of the nun stir up nouns and num-bers and saints' names on the blackboard before she called on Saradove, the ignorant, graceless Protestant; Saradove, the black influence in a roomful of the saved.

"Don't stare that way, Saradove! Look!" Evelyn held out the spoon. In its bowl floated a drowned and legless cockroach. "The sharks probably got him before I could save him," said Evelyn. "Don't worry, throw it in the sink. Protein is good for the coffee." Evelyn's sweet, melodic mood was covering some growling intention. Saradove knew it. It would be the rapier through her gut, the bullet through her heart, a bash on the head or a kick in the teeth. Evelyn's fun was murdering the little fishes in L.E.'s silken net.

The blind still flapped with sun and shade. Saradove watched it and recognized, in that moment, Evelyn's real identity. Obviously, she was the real, the original Coca-Cola girl, the darling of Saradove's childhood, the love of her life come from paper to flesh, from the New Oriental billboard to the cockroached home of Saradove! Was she? No. She was only Evelyn. Evelyn who, while Saradove courted, kissed, grew fat on L.E., behaved through it all like a hostess entertaining Eisenhower—taking L.E., including Saradove, on excursions to Bear Mountain, Stratford for Shakespeare, Brooklyn Heights, the beach, the opera; Evelyn paying and arranging, acting like a hostess entertaining Eisenhower, a famous hostess.

Again, Saradove's mind unreeled; she was walking back through her nodding head, back into the Village restaurant where Marlene Dietrich growled through all the dinner hour from the jukebox. Saradove was laughing so hard her hair was brushing the plate of veal scallopini. FALL-ING in LOF A-GAIN, NEVAIR . . . and L.E. was laughing, even harder than Saradove; L.E. had Marlene Dietrich's secret telephone number. L.E. could laugh best of all, up and down the scale, both wild and dignified, in the manner of 1902 actresses playing divorcees. While laughing, L.E. was rubbing her fingers inside Evelyn's mohair sweater; laughing, L.E. was pressing her knees, under the table, hard against Saradove's. Why were they laughing so hard? Saradove's memory began to express itself in dream. Oh, yes . . . because Evelyn was telling the

81

story of how she had got rid of L.E.'s last little love . . . doped her hilariously on marijuana one Sunday night and put her on a train to Damariscotta, Maine. Saradove could not remember the story very well. There was a tight-assed waiter in a powder-blue jacket leaning over them, removing the veal scallopini, looking evil because he thought they were laughing at Marlene Dietrich. And then the waiter brought coffee; no, L.E. never sat still for coffee . . . but the smell was there, of coffee like bubbling mud, ancient coffee, warmed again and again and now tipping into her dream.

"Wake up, Saradove! I can't wait while you nap all day!"

Saradove opened her eyes and faced it. What a stern voice, so like that older one in black and white all over (not seersuckered, not red-shod) that had called out, Wake up, Saradove! The other girls can't wait for long division while you learn multiplication!

"*That's* right, Saradove. Sit up and listen. Take your coffee and drink it." Saradove took it, discovered her fingers icy cold against the hot cup. She saw, in great surprise, it was her grandmother's cup, of fluted porcelain, painted with red berries and green leaves. When she drank it all up, there would be a single green leaf to see on the cup's bottom. What was she doing with her grandmother's cup? Evelyn had another one. Saradove shook her head at both of them.

Evelyn, nestling in the only chair, watched her shake her head. "Don't get obstreperous, Saradove. I don't have the rest of my life to waste here. I've come only to be blunt. I've come to kick you out."

"You can't kick me out!" How good it felt to be obstreperous. "I'm in my house, not yours." What raw nerve of the Coca-Cola girl! To climb off that billboard after all those years just to kick the one who loved her best!

82

"Not from your house; from L.E.'s life. You're an atrocious influence, and she wants you. But it's the end of that."

"I am not an influence!" The Coca-Cola girl had come only to end something. She had to be placated, if not with yellow corsages or latex bathing suits, then with the burnt offering, the holocaust of Saradove. "Evelyn, I am truly nothing at all. Nothing but innocence my mama left me when she fell; nothing but speeches my daddy taught me with his whistling bamboo cane; pointed the way to the freak show out to me. Look at L.E.! How wonderful the opportunities of growing up in Hollywood with Arna Hartsdale, the mother with four divorces, the mother with the Mercedes-Benz, the mother who loves Elizabeth Barrett. And not a father. The best influence of all—no father." Saradove imagined Arna Hartsdale kneeling before rosebushes sprouting up and down Hollywood and Vine, finally, triumphantly, lifting up the baby daughter L.E. "I am nothing to her, Evelyn. How could I be?"

"Goddamn you, Saradove!"

"God love me!"

Evelyn spooned a small hill of sugar into her coffee. "Nothing or not nothing—be that as it may—still, you are the atrocious influence. I will tell you why." As stern as numbers, Evelyn told. "At dawn today, L.E. invited the fat bartender across the street into a playground opposite a police station so that she could beat him up." She rapped pearly nails against the porcelain cup, beating in every word: "To beat him up! To start a fight in broad daylight in front of a police station. And because of you."

Saradove had to believe it. Numbers never lied. "Why beat up the fat bartender? Why? Because of *me?*"

Evelyn sloshed coffee on her seersucker skirt, but nothing in the world could burn her. "The answer is obvious to any-

83

one, anyone with a shred of character! Because you—oh, my God, not *me*—ran away from her, left her, never showed up at the bar where she was wanting you. She got angry, frustrated; because of you, drunk. And when she started throwing beer bottles—bottles *full* of beer—at us when we were dancing—I was trying to distract him—he told her to get the hell out. And then she started yelling that she'd break the place to pieces and then go outside and scream rape until the cops came for him if he didn't come out and fight her like a man."

"And then what happened?" Something had happened because of Saradove, a story more wonderful than any gilded mother on a trapeze bar. She crawled closer to Evelyn, to light a cigarette from Evelyn's pack.

"Use your imagination, if not your sense. The police, of course, came bopping out of that station like mad dogs and arrested them both. Just as L.E. was jumping up and down on the bartender's belly. And she'd already used karate on his sex organs. Why, I don't know. It took ten mean cops to break it all up; and now, L.E., with nothing but a black eye, is cooling her heels in the Women's House of Detention—that dyke-infested hole—a reality far too cruel for one of her sensitivity! Why don't you say something? Don't you love her more than I do? It was because of you!"

"Because of me. God love her," said Saradove.

Evelyn tilted her cup for the last swallow of coffee. She shrieked, "There is a cockroach leg in the bottom of my cup!"

"That's just a painted leaf. And that's the problem, I think. Why do I have those cups?"

"Grandmothers die and leave them to granddaughters." Evelyn's pale eyes popped from their pale lids. She screamed, "And it is definitely a cockroach leg—not a painted leaf— that offends me!" She lifted the cup above her head and hurled it neatly against the wall. There was the impact of porcelain on plaster, the smash of smithereens against the floor; and it became the loudest noise Saradove could remember.

"My grandmother dead?" asked Saradove. And it became true. "Yes, she did die. It seems out of the question. But there are the cups—cup—and here am I the grandchild."

Evelyn sniffed and spat, kept on spitting, thinking there was a cockroach leg on the tip of her tongue. A smell of hair being curled into stinking little wires came to her. Saradove's cigarette was burning into Saradove's hair.

"Wake up, Saradove!" Evelyn snatched the cigarette and yanked Saradove's chin up from her chest. "You're on fire, Saradove!"

Saradove rolled her head, shook off the stones on her eyelids. "Oh, I know I am. I am on fire to . . . and am on fire to . . . " She fixed her elbows against the coffee table to prop up her chin. "What are you going to do about my grandmother's cup, Evelyn?"

"Since it was yours, nothing." Evelyn stood and began kicking each of Saradove's books separately, accurately with her little red toe. "I've always hated Edgar Allan Poe. And you." She kicked the phonograph too. The flute continued; the water returned.

At some invisible time, Saradove thought, the janitor sneaked in and plugged Mozart back in. The janitor must like Mozart, so that's the end of me and the janitor. I'll tell him tomorrow. Saradove kicked the phonograph and ended the flute, the water, Mozart; the gardens of Versailles. She extended her foot, craftily, to trip Evelyn; but the little red shoes, the seersucker, flew up out of reach, revealed a lacey white slip a bride should have been wearing. Evelyn's eyelids flew up, revealed forgiveness, self-pity, envy of Saradove.

"You have a problem, Saradove. It was because of you."

"Because of me. All the Saradoves have problems—Saradove, the Siamese-headed dog, the extinct centaur, C. Jorgensen, God—all of us. We all do."

Evelyn went to her, her mind on rape, ravishment, having Saradove—divide and conquer. Instead, her foot kicked over Saradove's coffee. It flowed, in a thin brown stream, down the tilted parquet. It needed only sand and pebble beneath it, some toads and willows and cattails beside it, a fishing pole dropping in it, to make a new world. But it was nothing but coffee; it wended down the dirty floor to join, not the ocean, but a pool of old water and carnation juice that had spilled beside Saradove's raincoat. Saradove wished for her raincoat. Evelyn took it, folded it, sat down cross-legged on it.

Saradove yawned at her. "What will you do for L.E.? How will you bring her back?"

There was a terrible itch inside Evelyn's garter belt. It brought back all her fury against Saradove. "It's about time," she said, "that you got down to fundamentals. You better bet I can bring her back. But by now she's already had the public enema, and I can't cure that."

Saradove grabbed for the cigarettes. "The *what?* The . . . public enema? Tell me!"

"Give me those!" Evelyn snatched the cigarettes back. She would not answer until she had examined all the cigarettes and selected the best one.

"I want to know!" Saradove shouted.

Evelyn started to tell, but instead she gagged. She had touched the flame to the wrong end of the cigarette; she had lighted the filter. Happy for an excuse, she threw it hard, without looking, over her shoulder. It landed on the Gawain-Poet and turned the book black. Evelyn settled for the second-best cigarette.

"If you knew a single soul, anyone who really lives to the hilt in this town, you wouldn't have to ask."

"I don't know a single soul who lives, only you."

"That's exactly what I mean about you." Evelyn puffed calmly for a minute and then blew the smoke into Saradove's face; but Saradove's own smoke guarded her. "A public enema," she said, "for your information, is what they do to all bad girls when they get put in the Women's House of Detention. They line them up with nothing on but these little beach jackets—hospital jackets . . . whatever—and then they go around sticking them while everybody watches. And then, of course, you absolutely die because there's only one toilet, and that's in the middle of the room where everybody can see. I wonder if you can imagine what happens to you—the agony—until it's your turn to get to that one and only toilet. I know for a fact that I wouldn't care who saw me—I wouldn't care if General, President, I mean, ex-President Eisenhower saw me on it if I could just get to that toilet. Would you, Saradove?"

Saradove shivered, wanted her raincoat to warm her.

"And it's all because of you, Saradove!"

"Yes, because of me. *That* is?" No old world could be as terrible as the new one she was making. L.E.'s bad time had something to do with a golden maiden looking out over pink water. It had something to do with longing for a mother on a trapeze bar, with wanting an end to all bread trucks. "How will you bring her back, Evelyn?" she asked hopelessly. How could a public enema be mended?

"Well might you ask. Just as I'm going you finally get around to it. There's nothing for me to do but wire Arna Hartsdale again."

"I'm glad to hear it! Thank God for Arna Hartsdale."

"You may thank Arna Hartsdale *only*. She's as sweet as

Santa Claus. She's the one who wiggled her eyelashes at strange men to make them go in gay bars and pull out the fifteen-year-old L.E., back in the primal Los Angeles days. She's the one who divorced the TV star and married the school president just to keep L.E. from being thrown out again. She's the one who put L.E.'s hand in mine the day we left for New York and said, 'Take care of my little girl.' She's a *femme fatale* in rouge and chiffon and fancy cars and diamond necklaces that man after man has laid on her. She's still a blast in a bikini on ill-gotten beaches of the Caribbean. It's all for L.E.! She's a wonderful mother—she'll bail us out!"

Saradove let the drowsiness fall down. There was a wonderful mother, there was an Arna Hartsdale sliding down every chimney in the world.

Evelyn was at the door, singing, "Yes, I'm off to wire Arna Hartsdale. She will have L.E. soon by my side." Evelyn's tune swayed to a stop, to a command. "But you understand that in or out of jail, L.E. will make sure henceforth she sees no more of Saradove. You understand it's all your fault— it happened because of you."

"Oh yes, because of me," yawned Saradove, damned tired of all hunts, captures, battles, rescues; all of a sudden sick of fatal women. Despite her Arna Hartsdale, Evelyn could not stop any of it. Next week, tomorrow, if only Saradove could want it enough, L.E.'s aunt or mother or uncle or an unknown daddy would die and will Saradove many days' worth of L.E., wrapped in ribbons; if only Saradove could want it enough.

Evelyn went away; Saradove went to sleep.

"Wake up, Saradove!" Evelyn was back, trying to give her something. "I forgot to give you your going-away present." She dropped some bright thing into Saradove's lap and went away again.

It was the valentine, the old-fashioned Coca-Cola girl, there in her hands at last. And Saradove was out in the hall leaning far over the railing before Evelyn was halfway down the stairs. In her chest, where her heart had been, there was a trapped rabbit kicking in its panic, not blood, but pain and hate down her veins.

"You saw me and you didn't help me! You saw everything that happened to me. Don't tell, don't tell!" Saradove screamed, but the words floated down the stairwell like the bouquet from a bride's hands; or as though they were the bright streamers thrown from a departing, ocean-going ship, useless.

Cooler than breezes, Evelyn's voice went up and caught her words, as though her voice were a brass bowl, as though the words were apples and plums. "Don't worry," she said. "I did help. I gave you what you wanted. I think you were being chased to death."

"Not at all!" Saradove cried back; and the fruit was crushed to pulp and the bouquet thrown to the fire; and the streamers, uncaught, sank to the harbor's bottom. "It is not what I want; and I *was* the hunter. I *am* the hunter. I chase!" Nothing but the sound of Evelyn's huge pocketbook bumping its way down came back to her. "What in God's name, Evelyn, is *in* that pocketbook? Answer me!" There was nothing else to think about.

"Just homemade bombs," came the soft answer. "In case of revolution."

So that is where she hides them, Saradove thought. The building's door crashed shut.

She hung motionless, for a moment, over the railing, feeling her arms dangle, her fingers brush up air and dust. Above her shoulders there was a head like a heavy apple jammed on a toothpick. She closed her eyes. Rest filled the head, sweetening its pulp; contentment, her neck and shoulders. Hair, her own, whispered against her ears, like black birds deciding to nest

there. Looking, she saw far below, beneath the tower of descending banister, the tiny patch of first floor, not big enough to grow a single bean, much less to catch the whole large self of Saradove.

And what a comedown, she believed, to go diving like an elephant for a pail of water when Mama plummeted like a bluebird. Mama plummeted like a bluebird. After she thudded to the sawdust, how long did the trapeze keep swinging before it stopped? Saradove heaved herself straight up, imagining she could dive upward, imagining she had accomplished that thing sometime long before. It was her sport, her exercise, like basketball. Give it a chance, said the gym teacher, flexing her leg, you'll learn basketball yet; come and practice, privately with me, after school. With pleasure, said Saradove. "It feels wonderful," said Saradove. She threw herself against the railing to try again; again, her arms reached for the roof, and it did not feel wonderful a second time. She slouched and could hear the bedsprings rattle in that lavish apartment behind the walls. Yes, they were, they were still at it. She crept to the door, to hear details. She said, There goes another lost to my cause, no dawn of a new day, no marvelous un-American activities. He'll be in the drink, beautiful in brown rayon, with all the rest tonight. She raised her fist and pounded three loud times on the door. The bedsprings crunched to a stop.

"Charge! Charge!" bellowed Saradove. "The British are coming! Puerto Rico, *Sí*, Yankee, *No! La jour de gloire est arrivée!*"

Quickly, she was back in her own house, beginning to tear the buttons from her dress. The blasted dress—she tore and tore at it—caught, stuck in her armpits, crawled like a snake around her thighs, squeezed. Her legs sliced at it; it fell, dead at last, around her feet. But the sneakers were glued everlastingly to her bare feet. Swearing (bastard son of a bitch up yours with a meat cleaver!), she pulled them nearly inside out until they took wings and leapt, like albino roaches, from her hands into the pieces of the shattered cup.

Her bath water poured out hot as a revolutionary's blood, and she was satisfied. In it, she could look up through the bathroom's window and over the roofs of Seventh Avenue. There was a boy on a roof who was letting the clouds criss-cross his butterfly kite, letting his kite dillydally with clouds. Wait a minute, wait a minute! thought Saradove, and threw herself out of the water. For an instant she hovered, parallel with the floor, then landed on two elbows, two knees. "It doesn't hurt, not at all," she whispered, pushing forward her crippled self, pretending that she was the face towel that Veronica had held out. Behind her row of books, there was a wide plank that was to have been a bookshelf. It had done nothing the whole year she had had it but damage the corners of the English language's History. By the time she had it fitted across the bathtub, her scars were dry, blackened, and no different from the rest of her body. Beneath her avocado plant, so dead now it lacked even the life to shed its few leaves, there was her notebook, the ballpoint still clipped to its rings. She eased it from beneath the plant's clay pot, marveling at her own calm and organization. "Get clean," she announced, "and pay attention to my dear grandmother all at the same time. I am a good daughter. I am a beloved grandchild." She brushed away the dirt on the notebook; she saw and ad-mired the perfect white circle the plant's pot had printed on it.

"A certain artist," she told the plant, "won the contest to paint the Pope's ceiling just because he could draw such a circle, freehanded." She bore down on the flowerpot with her foot and yanked, with her hands, the plant free; even its big bulb came free, round and thick and big as her own head. Grasping the avocado's upper branches, she twirled it high through the air like a lariat, let it gather speed until it described the perfect circle high around and above her, as high and round as her arm could reach. The dirt flew; she imagined, as it spattered like hail against her skin, that it could bury her the way hail iced and made glittery the ugly winter earth. The exact moment came, and she let go. The plant sped through her bathroom's open window like a determined suicide; and, naked, earth-flecked, she leaned out after it in time to see it end its spinning and land with superb violence upon a yellow taxi's top. Saradove smiled, waved at it, good-bye, as it sped on down the avenue.

"Hey crazy woman! Hey somebody, there's a nekkid crazy woman over there!" His butterfly kite jerked in and out of the clouds as he danced, and he nearly lost it. Saradove blushed and pulled herself back inside so abruptly that she landed sitting upright in the empty flowerpot, the dead green plant's white spirit come back to haunt and to ornament. For a while, she could not bear to stop hiding herself, wrapping herself in her arms; but when she could, she crawled again to the window and let anyone who wished see her eyes and nose. No squads of police cars, no orderlies in white jackets down there. The traffic passed without a break. Across the street, the bar was opening and the neighborhood men, including her janitor, were shuffling happily inside for the day's first refreshment. Who could be surprised when things fell on New York City? No one was surprised. Only the boy across the roof insisted there was something strange; but no one could hear him, and he had lost his kite.

"Fuck you, little boy," said Saradove. "Serves you right."

Behind her, the water was turning itself into a waterfall going over the tub's side. The plank floated. She held the notebook over her head and waded in; crossed the Congo to get the typhoid vaccine through the savage bush: "Boom-boom-boom, white man, Sahib, ain't gwine shoot no tiger today. Raining, white man! Back to limousine, white man!"

She settled herself, cross-legged in the water, forcing more of it to spill from her side until the plank rested again on the tub.

"Dear Grandmother," she said, opening the notebook, poising the pen. But the first page was not blank and clean. The Greek alphabet, with the English letters beside it, had been copied there as clumsily as a little child wrote CAT. What's CAT in Greek? Saradove turned the page. More rows of handwriting, two to each ruled line: "Johnson, at times, reaches great heights—terrible at others because of erratic habits (Procrastination)." Samuel Johnson had erotic habits, Saradove told the book; she said, "Dear Grandmother, I think often of you sitting down there in the old ladies' rest home." She turned the page, prepared to write that down, but there was more to read of the familiar handwriting, of the very lovely and endearing handwriting. It belongs to me, Saradove decided; it was the handwriting that belonged to me in college. There is my name, Saradove Racepath, in that glorious script. Amazingly, the paper was not old, crinkled and yellowed, in the manner of old and glorious manuscripts; it was still very young, very white paper. "Amazingly," said Saradove. "Dear Grandmother," she said, "on my graduation day, it rained very hard, so hard that we couldn't line up outside, as they wanted us to, and march in to 'Pomp and Circumstance,' with all of us smelling of the white and flesh-colored (the color of Woolworth's rayon nightgowns) gladioli that were banked on the stage; instead we had to rush inside in gangs and stink like wet dogs in our unclean black gowns. All of their permanent waves fell out, thank God, and Olympia and all the mothers wanted their money back because they had waited four years to see their daughters march. That's why I didn't get time to visit you that day—all day was devoted to Olympia screaming about getting her money back, and she didn't hush until the Dean of Women said, to please her, that the mother was quite as delectable as the daughter. Imagine."

A bottle of lavender bubble bath floated up to the tub and knocked. Saradove poured half of it into the water and kicked, becoming a long-distance swimmer, to make froth. The bubbles slithered over the plank; she had to blow at them to make them keep their distance. She became that fantastic old drawing of the North Wind from a children's book, full-cheeked and balloon-headed, flooding the winter with a breathful of bubbles. She blew, the countryside cringed beneath her blast; and she turned the page.

The script was careless, knowing; it belonged to someone (Saradove Racepath!) who must have known Latin from infancy. She spouted out the translations with bubbles; she drew in more bubbles with more air. She coughed Latin.

" 'Girls' " said Saradove, " 'As a flower springs up secretly behind the garden wall, unknown to cattle, by no plow torn up, which the winds caress, the sun strengthens, the shower draws forth . . . many a boy, many a girl desire it: yet when the same flower fades, nipped by some sharp nail, never a boy, never a girl desire it . . . so it is the maiden, while chaste, while she is dear to her own; when she has lost her chaste flower, her body stained, she is sweet neither to boys, nor dear to girls. *Hymen, Hymenaeus,* et cetera.' "

Saradove closed the book, threw it over her shoulder out into the hall. "What a terrific translation, Saradove," she told herself, "and also the God's honest truth!" She pushed the plank overboard. Saradove slept, slipped down in the water until only her head was dry. Saradove woke; her breasts floated like little white balloons, but when she closed her hands on them, they burst and disappeared. Her hands were still dirty, had to soak.

"Dear Grandmother," she said, "you may remember me as somebody who translates Latin terrifically. In case you do, please write and tell me so. Hearing it from you, straight out of the horse's mouth—though Olympia always said anything from you would be more out of the horse's ass—would, I think, make it true. Make me something real . . . make me true." Saradove sank again into the bubbles. The sun streamed in and made her radiant with the soapy rainbows. The sun left; the light left and turned her gray.

Behind her eyes, Saradove was seeing, in the big farmhouse off the highway, her grandmother in the rest home, resting from home, from life. From a distance, immediately before the car began its long downhill swoop to it, the house seemed to spring up from uninterrupted tobacco fields; it seemed a clutter of tall, stacked boards, dauby with peeling paint and green leaves, cluttered with dark and blinded windows. Up close, the fields receded, and around the house, now solid and sure in its hundred years of dead or gone-away farmers, there was plenty of room for much tamped-down earth, stringy sweet peas that bloomed without help, and a wisteria vine that had multiplied its vines until every tree had been done to death. But Saradove was seeing nothing of trees or blooms. The days of her visits were forever clamped in damp November days with skies like wet, dirty sponges that rubbed constantly at the gray sight below.

Do you remember, Saradove was dreaming, how Duncan, your baby son, used to get me out there every Sunday, in Sunday-school clothes? I hated going; he forced me, with stories, to see you there. He would start at dinnertime, over the rice and gravy, the butter beans, talking about a monkey—

95

an ape, I think—that lived in a chinaberry tree outside some tenant farmer's crackerbox on the road to your rest home. I know you. If you ever heard about that ape, you must have laughed in your water glass, rocked hard against your wound-up hospital bed, said, "Heavenly Jesus, what foolery! Of course he sees an ape swinging in a tree," said it to me, the unbeliever in all your good things, and said, "and one time he traded his bicycle for a billy goat. Brought it home, expected me to keep it tethered to my rosebushes. Wound up with no bicycle, no billy goat neither." I was going to be lured out there to your big room, lured to give you a kiss smelling of camphor and damp, to sit, be quiet, beneath your gooseneck lamp, to take in, count, all those medicine bottles, by an ape! By an ape up a chinaberry tree? Heavenly Jesus, Grandmother, what did all of you think of me? If there was an ape up there it was only because he wanted one to be there, wanted me to love him for making the ape be there. The same way he wanted me to love driving off in the sunrise with him once every year to watch the circus unload all their dirty, flashy elephants at the fairgrounds. What his daughter could love, and what she couldn't love, used to bother your baby son. I couldn't learn even one vaudeville step from those liquored pals of his he used to sneak in the house past Olympia. He used to hit back at me with that every time I talked about leaving home and going away to school.

"Some more of that *fart* stuff, I reckon," he'd say. "Why, I remember the time when you were already nine years old and couldn't even pick up a little soft-shoe shuffle from the best in the business. He was black as spades and I brought him in my own house because I don't have nothing against that if they got talent." I suppose it bothered you too, Grandmother. What a concern all of you had about love! But you talked like poets about it, called it by other names. It was an ape up a chinaberry tree, a soft-shoe routine; one time it was a bottle of milk. I wish just once he could have let me go without a story, without dancing, without food and said only, Girl, I love you. But he made love a story I couldn't believe in, turned it to a rhythm I couldn't move to, bloodied it with his hands and asked me to drink it. And listen to yourself! One summer day, the only one I remember happening out there past the ape, you sat there on the screened porch (while the other old ladies lay and napped or looked out at you, blank and jealous), and you licked at the amber-colored water in your glass and said, "Heavenly Jesus, Saradove, you didn't even have the gumption to get in the high-school band so you could march on Confederacy Day and at the football games beating the big drum! I always knew the big drum would suit you best. I *knew* you were suited for the big drum. And you didn't even go do that for us! And now you want to leave home, you want *school!* What kind of girl wants school? Now you want my baby boy to go pay out all kinds of money so you can go off and learn Latin and Greek and godlessness that I *know* you're not suited for when you wouldn't even learn to play the big drum for us. You're just like me, after all," you chuckled, "just like me, always wanting something you can't have!"

"Just like you, Mama!" Duncan laughed. And he would cross his legs and squeeze his knees together. It was always too cold for him in your rest home. He'd say, "Olympia, I literally *froze!*" every time on the way back. "And like me too, like both of us. Slammed the door in my face the other night because she contradicted her mama and I corrected her. Saradove's *always* right, just like you and me, ain't she, Mama?" He laughed, loving you. For slamming the door in his face, he slammed me against the wall, twice, and slapped me in the face, twice. I came home from school next day and

97

found a princess doll and a box of chocolate-covered cherries on my bed. Olympia said then, "Now you're sorry you aggravate him so much, aren't you?"

It went on, you rocking and laughing in your glass. You said, "*Most* like me, like me, like me! That child's just like the time I put the padlock on the icebox door to keep you and Olympia out of the Christmas turkey on Christmas night. I was right, but I was mad as a wet hen! I *did* get to make hash and soup out of them leftovers, and both of you wouldn't take a taste of either. You were mad, but you were *wrong*."

You were in the rest home for a sickness, I believe, of the heart that made you incapable. But I know, if he'd asked you to, you could have got up, wobbled out of that rocking chair, and danced in the tobacco fields with him, your baby son. In and out of the green leaves you'd go, if he'd have you, something like a young girl in spite of your flannel gown, making him an old man, older than you. That other person in the room every Sunday, fat and little, unlike us, biting the skin around her fingers, kept silent, would not have challenged you. Or me; and you were all exactly like me, Saradove.

It was always too dark on the way home to look again up the chinaberry for the ape, but I believe for the first time, this very minute, that the ape was truly there. Don't you? How are they treating you? Is the food good enough? Give me a kiss, Mama, then one to save for later, he always said, before we walked away from you through the home's parlor, where the Baptist preacher, famous for never getting the nerve to ask where the bathroom was, sat twisting in his seat, visiting until the supper trays came rattling down the halls. When I think, Grandmother, of those heavy generous gestures you made toward my infancy, rocking me off the perch of my mama's hand the years we lived in your house with you, I still tremble and go radiant, shaking with delight. But here there's no question of love or delight—it is: can I decide which is which, love and delight? Can I command every single evening love to knock on my door, like three sons coming home, and open the door, once, twice, three times until all three are inside with me; and give, to each of them, my same face.

Saradove slept in the cooling water, shrank. The bubbles exploded, leaving the dirty water around her eventually flat and motionless.

the big doll

Saradove's grandmother, still healthy enough in the heart to be still in her own home, got up from the porch swing and stood staring through the leaves. The leaves sprouted from vines. The vines twirled around crisscrossing bars of string. The spring before that, the colored man had tacked the ends of string from the porch's overhanging roof while she had labored on the ground beneath him, setting out the plants, training the shoots to the string. Now she brushed the thick leaves with her hand, almost leaned to put her weight against them, so much like a support they seemed. The leaves were growing too thick; as usual, she had overdone success. She could remember when she had wished for just one son; and hadn't she had three of them? She had planned, had made with her own fingers this wall when it had come to her, one glaring morning, that one more summer of porch-sitting beneath the fleet eyes of people passing on the trains would drive her to follow them and shoot them in their tracks, and not care who in the world they were. Her sons, and that wife of one son, had complained a little. They ate her food and complained to her: Mama! The parlor's going to be dark as night all summer long with those vines there. But they knew when to hush; it didn't take padlocks to compel them all the time. Anyway, none of them sat on the porch and got caught by the staring eyes of the train passengers. But the leaves were getting too thick now. No point in smelling like mold. Permit a little bit of sun, she told herself, and she ripped off a big handful of green. She progressed, making holes in the green wall, from one end of the porch to the other. Bursts of sun socked her in the eye. She stacked the leaves in her hand, then put them in her apron pocket, where they seemed heavy. Olympia was going to think she'd won when she saw this. Olympia was so slow it'd take her time to see that the holes weren't meant for brightening the parlor but were for her, Doveen, to see through. But give them an inch and they'll take a mile. She sat down to swing again, look through a hole, make a poem in her head to her Saviour.

Give them an inch, Saviour, and they'll take a mile,
Saviour, precious, bleeding Saviour. Love them, Saviour,
and they'll spit in your eye, Saviour, precious, bleeding
  Saviour.
Love me, love me, love me, Saviour! As I do you, Amen,
  precious bleeding Saviour!

That very day Toby was nailing up the string she had gone inside for a minute and heard there Olympia whispering to her

101

husband, inside their bedroom where the daughter-in-law always took him to speak secrets against his own mama. "But it looks so niggery, Duncan!" she'd said. "Like something they do out in the country with sweet-potato vines. What's going to happen when my Virginia sister comes to see me, what's she going to think?"

She hadn't cared at all what her baby son was going to answer. She had left them to their weak old secrets and had gone back outside to plant more vines, more than intended. It was all the same to her, anyway. She took the leaves now from her pocket, began ripping them in half. What's the point, she thought, of troubling to raise three sons all alone, then see the favorite one of them go chase off after elephants and come on back home only when he needed house and food for a common-looking country wife and a baby girl? Her slippers hit the floor, grinding the leaves to pulp, sticking their juices to her soles. How long did it take them to put clothes on a child? She opened the door and called up through the dark.

"Saradove! Saradove! Come on to Grandmother, precious! You want that Co-Cola or not?"

No answer; just Olympia standing like a Catholic statue at the top of the stairs holding the girl against her. Four years old and *holding* her! And Saradove began pushing in her mother's face with the heel of her hand and kicking at her with white Mary Jane slippers.

She writhed in her mother's arms, she screamed, "Put me down, put me down! I want my drugstore. I want my Co-Cola! Grandmother, get me!"

Doveen took hold of the newel post as though she would lift it for a club. Aggravation shook her, then her voice: "Put that child down! This minute—before you fall downstairs!

Listen to me! Speak up. What's going on up there? I won't wait all day."

Saradove slid down her mother's body and hopped downstairs like a bunny rabbit. She called, "Look at me, Mama, look at me! I'm a bunny, I'm the Easter bunny! Say bye-bye to the Easter bunny, Mama!" She took Doveen's hand and pulled for the front door.

"We'll go in a minute, precious. I'm still waiting for the answer up there."

Olympia cleared her throat up in the dark, but if she smiled, it did not show through. "I just thought—I just thought maybe today just you go, and she stays with me. And I take her out in the kitchen and make dough. Dough into beaten biscuits for supper, for Duncan's molasses. She wants it, she wants to learn from me." Olympia's smile showed at last.

Doveen, to her shame, nearly stamped her foot. "How many times, Olympia, do I have to say no fooling back in the kitchen when Libba and me have enough work there already? When we get back it's going to be time to fix supper and I don't want to see dough strung out from one end to the other. Duncan takes his molasses on my biscuits and can't abide the taste of any other. And Saradove goes downstreet with me every afternoon just as regular as First Presbyterian on Sunday, don't you, Saradove? Don't you, precious?" Doveen took hold of the little hands and let the child hop up and down between her slippers.

Olympia let go of her smile, leaving nothing but dark at the head of the stairs. "Libba's going to be helping Toby in the back yard polish the brass. She wouldn't mind. I just thought."

"Good-bye, Olympia. You heard me. Hear the three o'clock train coming!"

The train took Saradove and shook her, like a great iron hand. The dangerous metal, the giant wheels were coming too close; and when the next car sped near it grabbed her beneath it, sliced her again and again all over the polished tracks. She screamed.

"Who's been telling you bogeyman stories, Saradove? Tell me who. Well, then just who do you think you are, screaming out loud in broad daylight? Tell me, who do you think you are?" Doveen loved the power of the three o'clock. She loved to hear it in peace.

"I'm her! I'm her!" Saradove shouted. She was pointing to a gray-gloved hand, a painted face, a pink hat that was waving and nodding and speeding away from them in the dining-car window.

"Stop that, Saradove! I don't want to see you wave at train people no more! Who knows where in the world any of them come from? Who knows but they might come in the night and take you away to be somebody else's little girl? Not mine nor Duncan's any more!" Doveen bent and trapped Saradove tight in a hug around the shoulders. "Now come on, train's all gone until the evening. Let's get the Co-Cola."

They walked the old pitted sidewalks past smells of sweets from the old roots of old bushes, past the damp gardens of their neighbors. They crossed the railroad tracks, still hot from the presence of the train.

"What did you learn in Sunday school, Saradove precious?"

"Jesus is my friend." Saradove was skipping past the stores.

"Come here, hold my hand! Who made you?"

"Underneath the cabbage! Underneath the rosebush!"

Doveen yanked at the hand. "Who made you?"

"You! Grandmother!"

"Hold my hand. Who made you?"

"God. God is love, God is love," Saradove sang.

"Go ahead, sing the rest of it."

They passed the hardware store, its window full with the bodies of stuffed pheasants and one big turtle with a gold-painted back. Its door was open, letting out the thick, harsh smell of burlaped seeds, of nails. They passed the picture show theater, and the popcorn machine beat out at them like a rainstorm, and they smelled the fresh rolls of cardboard tickets.

"God is love, God is love!" sang Saradove. "Love him, love him, all ye little children, God is love!"

"Are you supposed to dance around when you sing that God is love? You don't dance around at our First Presbyterian, do you?"

They went in the drugstore, a damp and hot little cave of sweetness where the marble-topped tables, the dainty ice-cream chairs reared up all alone and empty.

Doveen said, "I see you've kept the place clean and empty for us, Mr. George Winslow!"

"Yes, yes, yes!" The answer came from behind the carved old prescription counter, so heavy and big they must have put it first on the empty space and built the store around it. It was black from years of sickness and gleamed with rows of brown liquid and white powder cures. Mr. George Winslow leapt from behind the soda-fountain spigots, a twitching white mouse dressed up like a druggist.

"Miss Doveen! Miss Doveen!" The black marble fountain counter seemed to cut him in half as he leaned over to them, but he was made no less eager. "How good I feel to see you well and active one more day! I declare it's everybody who counts a thing coming down with something or other bad—they buried Miss Jane, you know that? But Miss Doveen, I tell everybody, she runs that big house, that big family, that little granddaughter like she was still a girl. And you still are just

105

like the prettiest thing in town, you always were, Miss Doveen! I'll say it to you and anybody else, just like I say you don't ever have to spend a dime in my store on anything but a good Co-Cola with plenty of ice!"

Doveen pulled off her net gloves and appeared to count the pink roses lined up across their knuckles. She pointed to a chair for Saradove. She said, "Don't start whining for that big doll, you hear, Saradove? I see you got your eye on that big doll on the counter! Well, you just can't have it!"

Saradove looked away from the slow-moving blades of the big fan that hung from the stamped tin ceiling. She had been seeing herself hanging there, turning in big, easy circles above her grandmother's head. Where was the doll? What doll?

"I heard that!" George Winslow was setting glasses of trembling ice and Coca-Cola before them. His face twisted in delight, his hands and eyes fought for their attention. "I heard that, Miss Doveen! If your grandchild must have that big old doll, then she must have it!" He jittered away through the big shadows the fan was casting, and he nearly tore the big doll from its box.

Saradove sucked through her straw and clenched her glass. A piece of ice got itself stuck in the straw; when she blew gently, it was dislodged. And there was Mr. George Winslow before them, holding the doll by its enormous mitts, dancing it like a savage to a tom-tom above their little table. His voice went high, cracked; he whispered, "Hello, Saradove. Hey there! I bet you don't know my name, my name's Sweet Little Janice, and I got a sweetheart. I bet we got the same sweetheart, and what's his name? Why, his name's Mr. George Winslow! Why don't you give him a kiss?"

It was a big fat face, round and white as a snow-covered globe—not a mouse face—that swooped from behind the doll's bonnet and smacked Saradove full on the lips. She spat, frantically, ice, Coca-Cola, that terrible kiss all over the marble; but Doveen didn't see her. Doveen was busy slapping George Winslow on the wrist with her net gloves.

"George Winslow! The way you go on with little Saradove and big Doveen is enough to make us think you love us enough to leave this whole business of yours to one or the both of us. I can't pay for this doll!"

He lifted his head, ending his grin. Organ music hummed in the narrow mouse throat. "Who said a word about pay? Remember I'm a Christian as good as you, and there're the things I believe in like a good Christian like the spirit of giving. Jesus said, Let the little children come unto me, and I know and you know that Jesus loved more than anything to see a little girl smile. He himself would've give her this doll if he could . . . he would've pinched that fat little cheek just like *this!* Would Jesus Christ have said a word about pay?"

Saradove, pinched, shrieked; the doll's face beamed at her beneath its sunbonnet. The Coca-Cola crashed, splashed in a crunch of ice slivers to the floor's black-and-white diamond tiles.

"Saradove Racepath!" Doveen was on her feet, shaking her dress all around her, though it was still dry as bone, unsullied by an accident. "Look at your dotted swiss! That poor mama of yours spent the morning ironing that tuck by tuck. Now look!"

Saradove was wailing. Her poor mama, all her hot, bending morning gone now for nothing! "It's sticking! It's all wet and sticking!"

"Tut-ti-tut-tut!" went George Winslow, descending on Saradove, counter rag in his hand. "It ain't a thing to cry over! Saradove's sweetheart's going to fix everything, ain't he, Saradove, ain't he, Sweet Janice?" Saradove was screaming; he was pinching her thigh as he mopped at her dress. "Oh-hhh," he breathed, "a big baby!" His hand patted at the place it had pinched. "Look at that Sweet Janice watch you cry. You going to let Sweet Janice watch you cry?"

He stood up again, his ears hurting from the screams. Doveen was drawing on her gloves, their little roses syrup-stained, blight-browned.

"Miss Doveen! Miss Doveen!" he called. "No need to go, no need to go!" He took her gloved, sticky fingers tightly. "How about a little more of the same in a new Co-Cola?" he whispered.

Doveen, grim, took her fingers back. "Can't, George Winslow; don't think I don't appreciate it, but I've got to get the child home before my nerves give out. They spoil the life out of her, spoiled to death—look at it!—then say, You take her, Mama!"

"Isn't that the way! Isn't that the way!"

"Stand up; pick up that doll, Saradove," Doveen commanded. "I oughtn't even let you have it after the way you behave."

Saradove grasped the big doll by its waist and stood it against her, plastering it against her wet skirt. The doll's bonnet came to her shoulders. She looked into its impenetrable black-button eyes. "Do its clothes come off?" she asked.

Unexpectedly, Doveen and George Winslow suddenly, eagerly laughed. "Time enough for that! Time enough for that!" they called into each other's open face. Saradove grabbed the doll's thick cotton hand and bit, fiercely, into it.

"Stop that," said Doveen, "and say 'Thank you, Mr. Winslow' to him." Saradove bit harder, feeling the stuffing grind beneath her teeth.

"I hate you," whispered Saradove into the doll's curly, unforgettable smile. Her grandmother snared her by the wrist, yanked her to the door, her feet and the doll's painted shoes sliding grittily over the tiles.

"Enough, enough!" said Doveen. "I'll be the one to say thank you, George. We've had all we can stand for one day. I guarantee you my baby son will hear about this."

George Winslow shook and shook his head. He rubbed his hands together. When the three were outside his door, he watched the big stuffed one fall nearly flat on the sidewalk. The two human ones, tense, sweating, almost weeping, fell into each other's arms. He locked his door and drew the shade. Smiling deeply, he began to finger his trousers.

a letter to Vienna

In the bathtub, Saradove shook, awoke. The room was dim with the coming twilight. It was horrible to touch the cold sides of the tub. Methodically, sucking all her breath in to compress her body away from the cold water, she stood, then bent and pulled the plug. The drain gurgled beneath her hand. She was sick at the thought of the long metal throat swallowing all her sewage.

Now where had the world gone? She felt wild. Somewhere, there must be a story of how once upon a time a beautiful princess, enchanted by a jealous fairy, fell asleep in her bath and stayed asleep for years, hundreds of years, while the world passed and changed around her. When someone kissed her, she awoke. Saradove looked from her window, and it was a window no longer. It had become the crumbling wall of her castle. Beyond, there was a dry ditch where once a moat had kept out the unwelcome. Beyond that, a stinking highway where once a forest had stood and nourished her, where once she had hunted the unicorn with her father, the king. So she went back to sleep, cursing the handsome prince who had awakened her.

Saradove smiled down at the water curling around her toes like feathers from some arctic bird; she nearly tripped on the writing plank. She was very hungry. She imagined the cold water golden leaves from a northern winter, so she kicked through it. While she slept, wars had been won, streets renamed; everybody (those who could appreciate the sensation) was rich, nobody was dying any more. At this very moment they were tearing down her modest home (hers and the janitor's) to erect a skyscraper to be entirely devoted to the filming of television shows for adolescents. But in Saradove's bathroom the water that sloshed over the floor, and time, were enchanted. Blissfully, Saradove became old hat; but her stomach contracted and squeezed like a fist.

The glass knob of the closet door shone through her fingers, but she did not turn it. She remembered: she had stupidly forgotten to check up on the age of her face. With so much time gone by, who knew what it might be? Her feet were ankle-deep in water, her fingers were pressing the light switch: she was going to be electrocuted. No—the light burned, and she was still alive. In the mirror there was not a change in sight. The pieces of her face could have belonged to anyone but Saradove, to Saradove as she imagined herself. The nose was long and set slightly askew, in memory of a tricycle accident. The eyes slanted down beneath heavy lids, seeming

111

mournful even when she felt jubilant. The mouth was a wide streak of sensuality that needed a French starlet to go around it. There was little else to bother about—just pale skin, black and wide-scattered brows, long, uneven hair that dangled on the brows.

"Not a change in sight," she told the mirror, "and nothing of me is mine." To see what it would do for her, she made her face up with self-pity. The result was a pair of eyes that belonged to Duncan. The nose bent in faint memory of Olympia's, but was mostly the fault of careless Libba, Doveen's maid, who had put her on the tricycle. The mouth was a mystery just as the long-dead, conveniently dead, grandfather Ananais was a mystery. "He was a wretched lecher," Doveen, satisfactorily alive, had once said; had said once only about her husband. "My mouth is like a clown's," said Saradove. She was mistaken.

Towels blooming blue roses began soaking in the floor's water; and one of the same she tied about herself just below her breasts. Her doorbell rang and she ran, heels up, to press her ear against the door. Definitely, there was breathing on the other side. "Here comes the kiss," said Saradove.

"Sarado-oove! Oh, Sarado-oove! Open up your door!" The baritone voice, in operatic majesty, raised her name in song.

"Is that you, Clive? Is that my old friend Clive out there?" she sang back. Saradove believed in the existence of impostors.

"Of course it is! The same *young* friend Clive. Open up, Saradear."

"I'm naked," she answered.

"Well, hurry."

In a moment, Saradove had slithered into the gorgeous green silk dressing gown that the former, more elegant, tenant had left behind in the apartment; and she was back at the door, shaking the towel from her waist. Belted, the gown covered more than enough of her skin, covered much of the floor around her. It had belonged to a very tall man, and it made her feel wonderful.

Clive came inside, coming perhaps on stage, looking directly, as he rarely did, into her eyes. "I understand," he said. He pressed her shoulders between his hands. "I understand so well," he said, like the doctor announcing the number of days before death.

"What do you understand?" she asked, really wondering, and looking, as she rarely did, directly into his eyes. She wondered too, as always, at the awesome unity of glamour that Clive was. His hair was white-gold, valuable-looking, straight and full, and never once fell over the black-lashed black eyes. And the eyes never once detracted from the finest of Roman noses or from the mouth which was, naturally, chiseled. His body was decently shapely but more than anything else was a pedestal for the beautiful head. He was wearing shorts to show his very straight tensed legs which, with muscles, could conceivably have danced "The Dying Swan." His bare legs, his bare arms, sprouted as much silky hair as his head, but black hair. What a rare and most delicate ape he would be, swinging from the chinaberry's branch.

Clive coughed and let his fingers wander through his clothes, hunting down the mildest of cigarettes. The room was too dirty for him to breathe anything but his own clean smoke.

"About L.E.," he said, and squeezed a shoulder. "All I must do to see grief embodied is to look into your face."

"I don't feel bad," said Saradove. And she did not. What was he talking about? Who was L.E.? L.E. was sex, and sex was outlandish and belonged in jail.

Clive had pianist's fingers, and he ran them along his hair. He smoked his cigarette as though he were tossing roses.

113

"Don't tell me that, Saralove." He stalked the room, ignoring the chair she pointed to. "I've known you too long to be unaware of the ultrafineness, the ultra*sensitivity* of your spirit—you *must* suffer, especially when love is lost!" He looked hard at her, glaring out over the footlights. "Mrs. Patrick Campbell once said . . ." But Clive did not say; his voice sank to very familiar monster-movie tones. He groaned, "L.E.! L.E. herself has much sensitivity of spirit. It is a terrible thing to be this way—it drives her to *drink*, to *violence*, to *unhealthy* sexual liaisons!"

"Onward!" Saradove shouted. "And upward!"

"Excluding you, my dear, of course!" Clive added quickly. "I came to help ease things for you." His eyes began glazing with boredom; he was wondering if his trip was going to be wasted. "But she was all wrong for you, Saraswoop, all wrong. And she's gone to L.A."

"Los Angeles!" Saradove shouted. She loved impostors; she hated abbreviations.

"If you insist," said Clive. What a filthy place she lives in, he decided. In spite of misery, one should be clean. By God, there's a roach! Clive sat down and put his feet up.

"I'm terribly hungry. How do you know what happened? How do you know she's going to L.A.?"

"Evelyn called me an hour ago. *Los Angeles!* Before I was supposed to wake. *Long* before. Gruesome girl. She told me it was all my fault, all because of me." Clive looked intently about the room, then ground out his cigarette beneath his heel. "The bitch said that if I hadn't frustrated L.E.'s natural outlets of aggression by instilling in her the methods of our Gandhi, the methods of passive resistance, to cope with all that *hate* out there—" he waved his hand toward the trucking company—"she would never have been pent-up enough to engage in a fight with that barkeep." Clive giggled. "A barkeep? Did she really? Is it true?"

Saradove rubbed her silken belly: clean, warm, empty. "I suppose so. But you're mistaken, Clive dear. Nothing's your fault. L.E. certainly didn't go *limp* when they arrested her."

Clive's hands drooped, the essence of dejection, between his knees. "Ahhh!" he sang, "I imagined not. Clive's lessons never take entirely. But *mea culpa* anyway. It's always *mea culpa* after I spend all my influence, all my strength for others, and then they go wrong in spite of me. But, although disgusting, Evelyn's right. She is. My fault."

"She told me first."

"Told you what?" How childish, how mulish, how *unrealistic* Saradove could be!

"That it's *my* fault L.E. got arrested. She got angry, frustrated, because I, dear, didn't show up in that bar last night. She felt like fighting—the hell of losing me, you know. There you have it. I am to blame." Saradove stroked her hair, began twisting a piece of it around her finger. She felt her mother pressing close through the band of hair. She felt Olympia's dark summer yard of flowers blooming around her finger's skin.

Clive laughed, forgivingly. He got up, to stride—was it a dagger that he saw before him? "It's all right, Saralove, I understand—I always understand! We both know how much Evelyn loves to shift blame around, to give every one of her dear ones the once-over with guilt feelings—something I, personally, however, have never experienced! But she was right this one time about me, although rather stinky about it all. Think, Saradarling! Think how long I've known L.E.! Since we were literally goo-gooing together in that school for the children of artistic parents! *I*—dying of love for Miss LeBon-

115

temps and her sweet repertory! *L.E.*—stunning in the royal-blue shirt and whipcord jodhpurs I'd dressed her in; and coming to me, beating her breast, confessing her passion (*realized* passion—you know our L.E.!) for the wife of the headmaster, knowing so well I'd understand. I understood, of course. It's ghastly how I always understand. I touch—" Clive slapped his own cheek gently—"therefore I corrupt!" Clive washed his hands, stage center. He was, pathetically, Lady Macbeth. "If L.E.'s in jail," he sighed, "that fastidious aristocrat—one of *us*, in jail!—it's because of me. Whenever I lend my little helping hand, I end by ruining the character!" He leaned, comfortably, against the wall. He smiled at his cleaned, wonderfully shaped fingers as though they were a mirror for his wonderful face. "I do have a kind of Mephistophelean air about me, don't I? Where's your mirror, Sarasweets? In the bath?"

He rolled out of the room. He was looking in the bathroom mirror; he was bursting into song over what he saw. "D-rrrink to me only wi-ith thine eyes, and I willl pledge with mine!" He trilled most notes, lifted one arm, held one hand against his chest. Despite his lifelong acquaintance with such a beautiful image, what a shock each time he passed a mirror! He closed his eyes, ended the song softly. He unselfishly returned his gaze to Saradove.

"Look, Sarapigeon, I won't keep you. Arrange some clothing. Let us dine together. Funeral meats. I myself crave Ovaltine. My stomach must have Ovaltine every hour on the hour or things begin to happen."

He was about to drown Saradove; all at once, she began to swim. "Goddamn it! Clive!" She turned her hair loose. She stamped her foot, and the green silk shook all over her. "Aren't you my friend? Love is what this is about! This is the power of love! Don't you believe in the power of love?

You don't know how to love her, and I did! I created her going to jail because she loved me so much! By withholding the presence of my love, I created her despair. Look at me, Clive: I've created love!"

Clive ran from the bathroom, began stroking her back, barely touching the silk.

"Precious child! I didn't intend such an upset! I didn't intend stealing your creative *thunder!*" He began to rub, less tentatively. "I don't know what you're talking about. What's so noble, my Saraloopy, about putting someone in jail? Especially L.E.?" He struck himself on the chest. "I know I'm not noble!"

Saradove hung her head, sulking, twisting her hair again, remembering Olympia again. "Yes," she said, "there was the public enema." She turned her face up to his impatient, amused beauty. She fought to control him—after all, he was her friend. "But think, please, of what control I have! What control my loving has! Then one day I get tired, I turn my back to rest for a while—and look what happens! *Down* they go! The blame—because of me! But, then again, no one has ever killed himself—herself—oh hell, *itself*—for me."

Clive dropped his arms and let his smile rain down. He knew people—my God, just one look at him and they'd do anything for him. "Saramyown," he said, "don't arouse yourself—I see it all, if that's what you mean. Just look at me. Do you think I've had an easy time of it being tactful and kind when they're always raving on about my looks?" He turned back to the bathroom. "Must take a leak. Get dressed, be of good cheer. Tonight I'm having a party and you must be brave and delightful for it." He stopped in his tracks. Laughter was welling up in him, and it spurted out like a mouthful of water that couldn't be swallowed. "Public enema!" he screamed. "Public enema!" He doubled over, in a graceful, helpless dance. "Saradarling! If that's what they do in that jail, then you better believe it—our L.E. will be Public Enema Number One!" The bathroom door slammed and shut him and his laughing tight inside.

Saradove went to her bedroom, regretfully letting the silk gown fall off behind her. She dressed in a blouse and skirt dizzy with scrolls of flowers. Both were stiff from the laundry; both were full of a thrilling school memory of holding someone's hands in the skirt folds, in the evening, in the soggiest, softest, most hidden shadow of the golf course. Where was her sweater? Outside the window the month of June was growing chilled. It was beneath the bed in all the dust.

Clive confronted her, his face gone insane. It glared at her in black and white. Through a thick coat of white, he had drawn every wrinkle, every delineation of skin, every feature out in stark black pencil. Clive stood and glared, was decorated. The gold hair had been flattened out of sight beneath a slick of grease. The fumes of hell blew from his eyes and mouth, and he was forcing Saradove to inhale them. She was suffocating in her pleasant clothes. Clive was waiting for her to praise; his fingers gouged into a jar of cold cream.

She screamed, "Get out of my bathroom! What have you stolen from me!" Clive fell back from her slap, but all hell had come off on the palm of her hand. He had made his mark.

"Come off it! You definitely never use this lush make-up, my naturally lovely, Saraswum! Come off it! I thought to surprise you with the Mephistopheles make-up that Miss LeBontemps taught me. Can't a soul surprise you any more?" He pouted, the devil given the hook. He returned to the bathroom, slapping his face with the cold cream. "Come off it," he called again. "There's no hope at all if possessions are glorified! You're not glorifying, are you, Saraloop? You wouldn't!"

Saradove hugged herself, trembling on the edifice of rage that Olympia had built years ago when her clumsy ungrown hands had dropped and smashed Olympia's prize cut-glass wedding bowl.

"It's no use," she moaned in that mother's voice, "I can't have anything—no, nothing."

"I said, where's your tissue, Saradrum?"

Soothed by the idea of having nothing, Saradove answered, "There's none. Use what we have, toilet paper." Halfway out her front door, she remembered Clive, that she was leaving him dangerously alone to mop up that mask. "Clive!" she called. "I can't stand this place a minute longer. Be careful, while I wait downstairs."

"I can't stand it either. I'll be a second."

Saradove running down the stairs felt something, running far faster than herself, speeding in her chest. Why won't it hurry and catch me, capture me, lock me up in a neat procession of days, sleeping nights, a shining kitchen, hot ironed sheets, simmering stews, two-week vacations, spoons to polish, a little girl to beat and rock . . . ? By the time she reached the street, the downward rhythm had caught her. She hopped on the sidewalk, wishing for a jump rope, chanting spells, red linoleum, plastic fruit, Sèvres teacups, Oriental carpets, piano lessons, lace tablecloth, clean hairbrush, family reunion, Sunday school, heaven when I die, a happy home life!

Across the street, a boy was writing on the shuttered entrance of the trucking company. Delinquent! thought Saradove. Is nothing sacred? The boy ran away, and Saradove could read his white-chalk message: EARTHMEN, WE ARE WATCHING YOU. "I knew it all the time," said Saradove.

119

The voice of Clive, preceding Clive, descended the stairs behind her. "Falling in love again! Nev-air vanted tooo!" And Clive appeared, radiant in his own face, to cross the roaring street with her and go east to the genteel dining rooms of his delight. He dance-stepped in his walking, tossed the gold about his skull, but never over his face. Two little Puerto Rican girls, their own hair in enormous, quivering beehives to crown their tiny bodies, went "Ah!" as Clive strolled past, and clutched at each other. Clive gave them a look to build their hopes upon. They giggled; they whispered, "*Maricón!*"

Clive bowed from the waist, earnestly, to a red-haired patrolman out ticketing cars. "Did I ever," he asked, "tell you about the time I got L.E. to put on my Saville Row suit and my pearl stickpin and my brocade vest? I got her to do it, then I put on my Mephistopheles face (Miss LeBontemps had just *taken me in*) and my red silk Dior shirt and my white ducks and my blue suède shoes, then we went out on Hollywood and Vine to startle people. I *guess* to startle people . . . to do something. Darling, at sixteen, our beauty—look at me! This is a pallid ghost of what I was! I tell you, I was nearly raped—men, women and children! I was like a lifeboat for those poor ugly souls. We wound up diving for the nearest taxi and rushed home to Arna, who gave us lemonade, laughed most merrily, and told us we were awful naughties! And that night, full of *my* mummy's brandy, L.E. went out simply glorious in rented white tie and tails, bearing six gardenias—no less!—in a florist's box to induce the headmaster's wife to go with her to the Spring Promenade." Clive hung on Saradove's arm, nearly blind with laughing, and ran head on into a businessman, who started walking backward, quickly, the other way. "The poor love was back in fifteen minutes at my door, doubled over and white at the gills. Cramps. It was her period! God help her—us all. And it was sad—I defend its sadness—so don't mention irony to me, Saradove."

Saradove didn't mean to. All that beauty gone wrong. It made her sick. She moved around to the street side of Clive and took his arm to comfort him with that pleasure.

"No, you never told me about that time, Clive. Tell me more. Beguile me, Clive, beguile me." The houses of people richer than Clive passed him by on either side as they walked, and made him sigh.

During the meal, Clive talked about virtue, old-fashioned virtue, and how much he believed in it. Around them, the little old ladies sipped and tucked in, smothered in service and white napery. Saradove thought the little old ladies admirable, lovely; she wanted them. Clive baffled her.

"People like you," he said, "see nothing but my grand design." He smoothed an eyelid, stroked his throat. "You don't see how deeply I feel about all this—" he waved at a particularly lovely old thing burping behind her napkin—"and motherhood, and keeping families together, and submissive wives and domineering husbands and peace among men. Because I'm so beautiful—I admit it, I am—you expect me to be some prancing flibbertigibbet whoring Lincoln Continentals off dirty old men, sitting up all night in those bars. When you're younger it's a different matter."

"Not me," said Saradove, considering Clive's grand design, wishing she had one too. She burped, lifting her napkin just in time.

"I didn't mean 'you' like that. Normally I say 'one'—when *one's* younger, it's a different matter—and people think me snotty for it. American is loathsome. Do you speak French, Sarajujube?"

"No. Why should I?"

121

"Because one's never thought snotty for speaking French; only original. And then one's gasped at, and one can have rich, varied communication with one's French lover."

"I don't know any of those," said Saradove.

"You're not supposed to know them, you're supposed to have them."

"I don't have them either." Saradove rolled a bread pellet and shot it from her fingernails at the sweetest of the old ladies. She must be approaching eighty, Saradove decided.

"*One* doesn't know them, one *has* them. But *you* should."

"And I don't. Perhaps you'll have a surprise for me at your party. Do you speak French, Clive?"

"No," he said, and paid their bill.

Outside the restaurant, Clive went running for a taxi, his jacket billowing behind him like a heavy, sumptuous parasol caught in the wind. Every single one of the yellow bugs swerved, snarled; resisted Clive. How could they? thought Saradove. But they did and, instead of Clive, fought to take silken women away from hotel entrances. I can't blame them for that, thought Saradove. But she looked for a place to hide so that Clive would not remember her as a witness to his failure in the important things of life. There was nothing wide enough or thick enough to conceal her. Only childish trees ringed with tiny iron fences like bracelets; only the slender, narrow doorways of town houses. Pretending would hide her better than anything. She turned her back on the street with an exaggerated expression of disgust: Oh hell, her attitude told the world, I've come out again without matches; and she inserted her fingers between the two full books of matches in her sweater's breast pocket. Beneath the wool, her breast heaved into the palm of her hand. People passed her, not thinking her strange, smelling of cocktails and air-conditioned Italian food. The chill wind, except in the sleeves of her sweater, was dying. One hand, against her own breast, was warm and beating. The other played the air like a piano or hung still and was cold. With her eyes closed, she could see what the passers-by saw of her: a girl perhaps gone crazy, wrapped in old-hat clothes, without high heels and (on a June evening!) without a generous boy friend. And she imagined the passers-by clothed in the tinted draperies of lush religious paintings, angels of authority, hovering around the Mother of God, their wide-open lips prepared to sing some anthem, their wide-open eyes staring coldly down at the damned.

If I open my eyes, thought Saradove, I hope he won't be there. So she kept her eyes closed. Clive my good friend; Clive my perfect little dressmaker pinning the pattern for an establishment of perfect happiness to me—nothing necessary to wear Clive's dress but the energy to breathe in and out, to care and clean for that splendid order; to learn French and then teach it to Clive.

She opened one eye. It saw a black bowler hat twirling by on an ivory ladle. Then both eyes saw the man wearing the bowler look hastily the other way, toward Clive. Clive was still there, and it was getting darker. Curtain rings were clacking together behind the open windows. Street lamps were coming on, showing Clive to the world; and around the lamppost, Clive was swinging round and round with a stiffened arm. Around and around, his right arm dangling, his fingernails clicking in and out of the fluted column, his face beaming forgiveness on all cabdrivers. He swung; the gold hair bounced like a butterfly. Saradove's heart jumped up like a frump at the sight of a new frock: look at Clive, trampling all over her mean gifts of shame and failure! The lamppost

123

was there: he swung on it. The taxis filled up with women and parcels; and he was more beautiful and expensive than any of them.

Clive waved at her as he circled once more around and flicked his wrist at the street as if he were dusting it off. A cab stopped beside him. He got in it—no, he was exiting through French windows onto a green lawn. He called back to Saradove, one hand by his mouth, shading his words with a secret.

"Sarastar, remember! Black and pearls only! Be there at ten."

Left in the dark, she was too poor to do anything but wait. Ten o'clock was a long wait. Down at the end of Fifth Avenue was Washington Square. She could sit and watch pigeons swoop shamelessly for the popcorn that fools threw them. She was going to sit and glance impatiently to the right and to the left, in case there were mothers and aluminum strollers left in the park, in case the students trotting around NYU suspected that she was waiting for no one, that she was waiting only for time to pass. The mothers, of course, were gone. Only a few students were left, and they strolled in gangs to the pizza parlors at the west of the park, feeling and patting each other, laughing in each other's faces.

Beneath the neon glow of the newfangled street lamps, she discovered purple grass; and she sat on it and felt it like purple beneath her. When she had watched it nearly too long, she began to look at the blackening sky for stars. She turned her head from shoulder to shoulder, but there was none. They will think I am watching for flying saucers. Earth-Saradove, we are watching you. She studied the buttons of her sweater. She took out a cigarette and began to hunt for matches among all the matches of her pocket, but she needed to smoke too much to pursue the game any longer, not even if Radclyffe Hall and Humphrey Bogart and Miss America all together were watching her sit alone.

"I am a dragon," she told her knees, and blew the smoke strenuously from the corners of her folded lips. "Snort, snort!" When that was done, she looked at a tree that was budding into green later than the others, and she imagined it to be a mirror. "You are my glass," she told it. "You are seven feet tall, curved at the top, and square, flush to the ground, at the bottom. Your frame is gilt and has been expressed by a tiny knife into hundreds of flowers and leaves, delicate as feathers. An enormous rosette, with fifty petals and a thousand points of pollen in its center, adorns the top of your curve. When I stand before you, your rosette is my crown, waiting to settle, at the moment of my success, on my head." Saradove stared into the tree. "I do not look like anything on earth," she told it furiously.

She covered herself with promises, to hide from the dark and from the people who saw her sit alone. "In my closet at home," she promised herself, "there is a stiff black dress that goes only to my knees. Its sleeves billow a little at my elbows. Its neck is square, severe, seductive. In the dresser, there are stockings of the serenest nylon, nearly as pale as my own skin. There are pins to make my straight hair curl— or perhaps it should stay straight and make shadows and lessen the health of my cheeks. Beneath my bed, there are black satin shoes. When I lie down on the floor to look for them, their old silver buckles will wink out at me. Here I am ringing Clive's bell, and there I go under Clive's arm to be introduced. The guests are stock-still, seeing my eyes beg for protection from the hordes of men, women and children who have chased me through the streets, a rare, passionate animal they wish to chain to their beds. Slowly the guests are setting their drinks aside, drawing heavily on their cigarettes to cover gasps of delight: they are watching me try to smile bravely at each of them. Scattered about the room, artistic young men, their throats strapped in neckties that look like Persian dreams, their fingers drooping with heavy rings, will uncross their legs. They will murmur, Now she is one of us, quite as beautiful. On the silk sofa—and this is the most important part—three women sit, as motionless as their lungs will allow, waiting to see if I will go to them.

And here they all are, the whole heartbeat of Clive's party. The fabulous women, as real as unicorns. The first will be black-haired, like me. Her brown eyes, like mine, are all afire with the protection and love she's offering me. She'll wear a dark silk suit; her perfect legs will end in high-heeled sandals. She'll wear a huge ruby ring (her one true love gave it to her before she died; a dig drop of blood, the last the one love coughed up, set in gold). As she beckons to me, she will slowly draw the ring from her finger and toss it to the floor, like the cellophane from the lollipop. No—instead, she will place the ring in the exact center of her palm and offer it to *me*. The second will be an actress so famous I can't even imagine her name. She will wear a heavy jade necklace for the sake of her brilliant red hair. Her eyes will dart nervously, two little green birds, not daring to land on me, the great tree she can nest in forever, the great and green tree no one's ax can split. The third is pale all over. Her hair is the color of country butter; her embroidered dress matches it; her nearly yellow shoes are brighter than her hair. She's a famous writer, and all her future books are now dedicated to: Saradove Racepath!

All the women are approaching fifty, my favorite age. Which will I choose?

From the corner of her eye, Saradove believed she could

at last detect a star's twinkle. But when she looked, it was only a tear in her eye. She touched it with the tip of her finger; it was barely large enough to wet the skin, and it dried instantly. The sky was all black now; the world had become a decent hiding place. But her bare toe, pushing out of the hole in her blue sneaker, the blue sneaker itself, had become purple, like the grass. Modern science, thank you! said Saradove. She moved out of the miracle bath and went into the decent hiding place.

A young boy, a younger girl flew out at her like prized game from a covert. They ran, hand in hand, into her dark. They were urgent and hot. Saradove stopped breathing. If they saw her, she would be lost. What they saw was the thickest shadow beneath the greatest tree. They pushed each other, they fell to the ground; and their fall sent a puff of green smell into Saradove's nose. A green smell growing damper, fresher: its name was grass, grass growing wetter, its essence pressing into the dark of her brain. Whispering, their heavy breaths became a snarling of love. Saradove, on her feet, bent from the waist, crept away like a cripple. On coolie feet, elbows stuck to her sides, she drew the heavy carriage of herself away, away from the smell of grass, from the grim sounds of love.

She passed three more trees and dared to straighten herself. The jumping Village night was ahead of her, and she went to it, one foot, then another appearing from beneath her skirt. Disappearing into shadows, emerging into lights, she went like a little fish feeling its way through a cage of water, bumping into the narrow tubes that fed it fresh water and extended life. The water did it all for the fish. Saradove went, like the fish, doing it all for herself.

Inside an apartment above her head, a little clock chimed seven times. She waited for it to say more, but it did not.

She stuck her elbows through the arrowhead points of a fence railing to think dutifully, without love, of L.E. Without love, L.E. lay bound and gagged on Saradove's long plank table, her face contorted with spasms of fear. Saradove, unafraid, swung above her, a thin and brilliant blade tied to a pendulum. Without love, Saradove was sharp and dangerous and perfectly happy, swinging, in a black rat-ridden cellar, closer and closer in gentle, predestined movement, to make mincemeat of L.E. L.E. spat her gag out. "Stop, stop!" she screamed; but when Saradove swung away (only to gather speed and come back), L.E. called, joyously, "Oh please come back! Don't go away—come back, come back and hold me!"

Saradove started home. She had become impossibly strong and the lover of a world's worth of women because Olympia had been impossibly weak, weak as water, and had loved no one but a man weaker than water. Saradove swam through the pair of them: some day, if she could keep afloat long enough, it would be her daughter's impossibly strong arm that Olympia would cling to and save herself from drowning in the rushing weakness of the water. And then she would love her rescuer best; she would love no one but Saradove. She swung her arms through the thick summer air, stroking it past her, making an ocean of it. Before long—it had to be—she would lift her mother's face from the water's deep death. On the baked, sandy shore, the mother would have no one to love but her daughter. Until then, any woman would do.

She pushed her way into Eighth Street's Saturday-night gangs. The biggest gang, clumps of the middle-aged, happy to be out of the suburbs, made the biggest noise. The mouths of the women might have been Waring Blenders, terribly merry to be running at top speed, chopping, chopping. Their curls were tied up tenderly into rhinestoned nets; their husbands, in plump little naked arms. They let Saradove through, winking at each other, thinking of their own daughters settled safely in long convertibles parked in drive-ins, allowing their soft sweaters to be lifted, to let a hand inside. They were going to dine; and later, much later, they were going to descend to a basement and watch the new faggot show. The husbands thought: The men, the men will wear high heels far higher than our wives'. The men will wear tight sheaths of gold lamé and show round, gloriously soft asses, to show bosoms as young, as peach-soft as our daughters'. The men will dance and sidle around the floor, their golden bodies bathed in green light. They'll swivel their hips and waggle their long nails at *me*, thought the husbands. One man will stand in the center, throw back his teased, platinum hair, raise up his sinuous arms and mouth the words to "Somewhere Over the Rainbow"; we will pretend that Judy Garland's voice is coming from the young man's slender throat. It touches the heart, doesn't it? thought the husbands. It will be better than watching Judy Garland sing the song, won't it? It will be better. In the end, the men will take it off, reveal themselves as impostors, oddly the most wonderful thing of all.

The men unhooked their wives' sleeveless arms and began to walk in step with each other. We will dine, they were thinking, and then we will go and see the new faggot show. In her heart, Saradove wished them well and passed on.

Across the street, she stopped to smell the bookstore. Its swinging door fanned the scents of fresh-printed paper and slick jackets over her. Close your eyes, she thought, and you will think that they cook books here, cook them up in saucepans that clang together with the sound of cash registers. She shuffled in slow, small circles before the store window, like a dog hunting for the right space for sleeping; she was trying to put herself in that same place where she had first caught sight of L.E. In the empty spaces above the new poetry, Saradove could see her again. The smile that had lighted on her that first night had come back—the gamin smile, the drowning smile, the sadistic smile inside the charming nursery rhyme.

Beneath the smile, Saradove began to melt, again. She melted and watched, again, the smile creep up through the thin lips and into the thick cheeks. She held the smile in her hands. Quickly, Saradove began to hunt for matches in her pocketful of matches. She had done that for the first time in the face of L.E.'s smile. In a smell of books, L.E. had come out of the door and for the first time touched Saradove. She had bent the knees of her flannel trousers into a debutante curtsy, a forefinger to her chin, her hand plucking at the corner of her coat. She had laughed like the shyest of schoolgirls.

L.E. had laughed the laugh and said, "Madam, pardon me. Madam, can you spare a match?" Promptly, Saradove had gathered all those books of matches from her pocket and dropped them, from shaking fingers, into the street. She had ended in giving L.E. her empty hands. Saradove had answered yes to a simple question and had given L.E. her empty hands. L.E. had laughed again, the laugh of the boldest of schoolgirls. L.E. had taken the hands ("Madam, shall we walk?") and had pulled Saradove into the emptying Eighth Street of her first freezing northern winter; and before they had reached the corner, L.E. had made Saradove run. When Evelyn had come up from the bookshop's basement, five mystery novels tucked up the sweater with her great bombs, an anthropology paperback in her hand, only Saradove's matchbooks were waiting for her. L.E. and her smile were gone, with Saradove, into Saradove's first bar, her first alleyway, her first housetop, her first New York bed.

L.E. and her smile were gone. From the shop window, the nighttime image of Saradove looked out on the other Saradove and told her what it wanted, what it insisted it must have: a cold roof, a hot and rainy roof, a snow-filled alleyway with garbage cans to hide behind; a morning bed. The image floating transparent and free over the new poetry sneered at the flesh-and-blood self and its need for black and pearls, its need for a life pinned to it like a tissue dress pattern. Saradove moved her hand through the matches again, hunting for the thick letter that had been in her pocket that night and after that night, never mailed. Saradove opened her mouth and moaned for the letter. The bookseller, lean and suave in the legs, bumptious in the shoulders, grinned through his window and waved at her. Come on in, he was saying, stop showing that face of yours through our window.

Saradove turned and ran, beating her way down the street to the tune of unsent letters. She dove, like a footballer, between the chests of the A-trainers, the big boys from Harlem down for the night to wrestle with the Village. She fell into a circle of barely teen-aged girls with hair like lacquered blond dust mops: a pink circle of female bubblegum. "Not an apology," they yowled. "It's the Village for you! But she can't be an artist!" Saradove twisted through the parking meters, building a maypole with the ribbons of her self, and shot through the traffic like a lost dog courting death without its leash.

She landed on the sidewalk, safe and dwarfed to the size of an ant by the mass of soot and brown that was the House of Detention for Women. The prison windows were lighted. Opposite them, a small tangle of people, their ears pricked to hear the slightest sounds from the prison, stood, tough and still, against fire hydrants, against shop doors. In the shadow of the prison door, Saradove watched them; and she listened too.

The sounds from the prison began: sirens of screams, catcalls, I love yous, get me outa heres! The sounds gushed over the heads of the listeners and made them flinch and draw together; but this was what they had been waiting for. The listeners moved closer to the curbstone to select the messages meant for them. A big colored dyke, big and hard as rock but with hair waved and brushed into peaks and valleys of grease, pushed aside a little pimp and his packages and took over his fire hydrant. She balanced herself on top of it, cupped her hands and bellowed at the lighted prison. Silence collapsed around her.

"Lissen heah, Angela, you heah? I'm goin' on home now, home do you heah me? And I don' wanna heah tell of you messing round with none of them girls up there! You heah me? *You heah?*"

From high in the prison, the answer came, faint as a violin mew: "I hear! I-hhhh hear!" The big dyke bowed to the little pimp and marched into the crowds.

Saradove waltzed, past Patchin Place, past antiques and jewelry and wallpaper. I am outside, she told the things. I don't belong in jail. There is just enough time—she leapt through the leaping streets—to get home and find the letter I never mailed, to exorcise the poor first love inside it, the first and poorest love that L.E. stole me from. I will set her free, just as jail freed me from L.E. Then comes the black dress, the white pearls, the satin shoes and the wonderful party where my life will begin again.

She looked inside her apartment and told it what a junk heap it was. After the party had set her on the new and shining course, she would not need this terrible mess any longer. She tossed her door key into the wet heap of raincoat. Tomorrow, she promised her home, I will rise up early, I will scrub your floors, disinfect your bathroom, paint your walls, dust your furniture, shine your windows. I will poison the cockroaches and put a big pot of vegetable soup to simmer on your stove. My dishes will sparkle through bubbles of detergent. I will go downstairs and come home with a white bag of crisp rolls that will snap to it in the aroma of fresh coffee. I will open the fat Sunday *Times* and read every word about foreign war. In a big jar by my open window, thick bunches of rhododendron leaves will take on a glaze of sun. I will invite a mere acquaintance to dinner and make spaghetti and green salad; then I will have a new friend. The time has come for health, sanitation and learning! The rooms, not understanding, did not answer. The apartment gloomed around her. Promises, promises, it seemed to say.

"Where is the letter?" Saradove asked the room. "Where have you hidden the letter?" Her sweater sailed off to join the raincoat; she rolled up the sleeves of the blouse and became frantic. If she had stayed off the street, the memory would not have returned. Her betrayal, for the sake of a smile, of that poor first love, came back on her, alive and with a feverish, open wound. She must find the letter before it died, feed it bowls of chicken broth, give it a warm bed, dress it in clean, secondhand clothes and send it miserable but healthy from her door.

The letter was not beneath the couch, not in the underwear drawer, not stuffed between the cornflakes and the apple juice. Saradove sat down, rubbed her perspiring hands through her hair, and looked for herself all over the room, looked for the Saradove of one winter ago sitting quietly down to write a letter.

And there she was. There I am, thought Saradove, in a corner of my room, pulling the last sheet of paper from the typewriter. And there she was. There I am, thought Saradove, uncapping the pen and writing at the bottom of the page, "I will love you truly forever." Saradove ran her tongue across her lips and tasted the glue of the envelope.

Had she been naked? No, of course not: the girl in the corner naturally wore something no one else on earth would be caught dead in. It all appeared, solid before her eyes: a dark green corduroy jumper, long black stockings, sneakers jammed into rubber galoshes, a gray sweater that Olympia had once worn long ago to hang out the wash in, to keep the breeze away when she was transplanting bushes. A red plastic barrette had held back the hair.

Saradove rubbed her shortened hair to make that girl go away. But before she did, she still must walk across the room pressing several bright stamps against the envelope. The unbuckled galoshes squeaked and clumped against the floor. The wintertime Saradove was putting herself inside a loden coat from the closet and the letter inside the pocket, along with a checkbook. She was going out to cash in more of the money Miss Doveen had left her, was going to walk through the streets' black slushy snow and sing a song that went, "Poor Ellen Smith, lying cold on the ground, with her hands 'cross her breast, it was there she was found. . . ." And she would make a hum in her throat to sound like a cello; and the real cello would stop humming and rest when that poor first love, that musician, received the letter. That letter should have gone in the box at the corner, and that Saradove should have gone back through the winter and into her home again. Instead, in front of all those books, someone had caught her with a smile.

At home, Saradove dropped her hair and flew to the closet. The coat lay in piles of dirty laundry and broken shoes and made everything smell like a rummage sale on a hot Saturday noon. Back in her hands, the letter felt new and fresh, cold as a flake of snow. She ripped the thin air-mail envelope apart and began to read the old story by the light of the bare closet bulb. She read, and she became a cadaver warming itself on the memory of its living flesh.

The letter said: Why did you leave me before you taught me everything you know? Why did you leave me? Just once, once long ago, I roasted in the little oven of thighs and arms. Stop telling me about Vienna and those other, awful music students. Stop telling me that you turned on your radio and out came *Tristan and Isolde* and that you felt, all over the city, gloom, gloom, gloom without me. Why did you leave me? Do you remember that I dived through the ditches of the college woods to go to you? It was as light as day because it was spring. I went through the drafty halls of your dormitory, tiptoeing to keep you safe. You did not even get up and open the door for me to come in. You lay in bed and said, Come in. Come here. You told me you were playing stringed instruments, you were strumming the cello without a bow. Did you know that I once sat up a persimmon tree and watched the little boys and girls play with each other's genitals behind our garage? Their little cotton pants choked their ankles. Their little bare feet were gray with dust. They kept calling for me to come down. I stayed up the tree. Don't tell me you are writing music for Greek plays while I have nothing to do, nothing to make but letters to you. Do you know how my skull felt when you took your hand from it and held my scalp aloft above the bed? My eyes were wide, staring open; and yours were sleepy. The moon was on your ceiling. You left me on your ceiling, took your award and went off without me. Here's how it went: study hard, Saradove. A kiss. I love you, Saradove. A kiss. I can't live without you, Saradove. A kiss. And then you went and lived without me. You left me naked on your ceiling. When I came down, you were gone, and my body was covered with sweets where

135

your sticky fingers had touched me. Did you think that after you were gone the sun wouldn't shine on me, that the summer flies would not come, smelling my body sweet for the first time? They came in a swarm and stuck to me. I will betray you. Why did you leave me? But the sun is gone, nothing flies here through the air but snow. I am going to take all my grandmother's money and take a ship and go to you. You will cover me with new honey. I will snap your cello bow in two. No, I do not look for a job; yes, I sleep alone. Yes, I cannot sleep. I walk down the street and sing Poor Ellen Smith. You always want metaphors from me. I am your metaphor for love. Standing, once, on a mountain, you pointed to a mountain. What is this? you said. I said, I am tired, it is a big ship to carry you away. What is this, you said, pointing to a little waterfall. I said, I am tired, it is a crowned king kneeling to give you a tray of diamonds. You hauled the cello to the top of the mountain on your back. You sat on a stone and held it between your knees, strumming it. What am I? you slyly asked. I said, I am tired, my mouth is dyed blue from the berries you picked and put on my tongue; I taste nothing but the calluses on your fingers. You are an ambush. From Vienna, I read that you want me in your bed. I am staying; no, I am coming. The ice on my window sills is dreadful. Some day soon I will be in your room when you come home. I will be in your bed when your key fits into the lock. I will not get up and open the door. I will stay in bed and say, Come here.

Saradove tore the letter in half. Through the tearing of paper, the clock ticked loud. It was time to forget everything but the party and what Clive would have prepared for her there. She ran to the bathroom, to wash her face and make it new for her new beginning. She stripped, watching every move the mirrored Saradove made in the long glass on the wall. The closet was empty of the black dress; there had never been such a dress. The satin shoes were not beneath the bed, their buckles did not glitter through the dust. The beautiful shoes had not been lost there, or anywhere; they did not exist. Saradove went back to her bathroom and watched, warily, the girl in the mirror come toward her. She laced her fingers across her belly to protect it from the girl's fist that would soon smash the glass and punish Saradove for the pestilential poverty of her life and her wardrobe. Through the silent caution between the two girls, the clock ticked on; and Saradove, to waylay the mirrored girl's anger, went to the glass and kissed the girl inside it, pressing her own breasts against the girl's cold ones. Saradove reached out to wrap her arms around the girl, to tighten her hands against her back; and Saradove did nothing with her movement but stun her own elbows. Her curling patch of black hair met only the cool reflection of sex.

"Get out of here," said the girl in the mirror.

The costume, intact, was rolled tight inside a grocery bag and jammed into the back of the closet. Saradove sat on the floor and spread it around her. The corduroy jumper still had the smell of schoolbooks in it. She pulled it over her bare body, and the skirt circled her. The jumper held on to her body like a loving, familiar hand. She pushed the sweater back into the bag and dragged out the long black stockings, sweet still with the darling smells of her own feet and crotch. They held her legs and welcomed her home. She found low, run-down shoes that melted into the fabric of the stockings and seemed to disappear there. Saradove spun around her room, the warm air flapping like a celebratory flag against her chilled buttocks. "Hello! Good-bye! Hello! Good-bye!" she shouted. "On this finger, her ruby ring will catch the sun. Her jade necklace will knock soon against my own corduroy! Which of them will love me best of all? Which will have the look of Olympia?" Saradove spun like a top, whirled like a child on wet grass, in and out of some lawn sprinkler, opening her mouth to catch the water on her tongue.

Saradove soaped her face, she wet her hair and brushed it hard into straight lines around her face. She went out the door, one subway token tight in her hand.

reunion

At the beginning of every cold school morning, Olympia stood in the little hall outside Saradove's room and called, "Saradove, Saradove, wake up, time to get up now, you hear, Saradove?" She stood there, a fat little monument of patience, impatient for her daughter to slip from beneath all those blankets and see the marvelous new rips the night had left in her nightgown. It was nearly impossible, Olympia could see, for Saradove to get out of bed: she had been buried, like a child in a cave-in, within a tunnel of heat that she, Olympia, had been at work making all night long. At twelve o'clock, at two o'clock, at four thirty, Olympia had slipped from her own hot

139

bed and had piled blankets, one by one, on Saradove's to make it hotter. Each time, Saradove had called out from sleep, "No, I'm too hot, I'm too hot, not another." But Olympia knew best about the goodness of heat, had done it anyway; had wedged the blankets tightly between mattress and springs, so good and hot and tight that she could at last get some sleep herself.

She watched Saradove pull the pillow over her head and play dead. That's all very well, Olympia thought, but she will have to sit up and see me very naked in my rayon tatters very soon. Olympia's voice shot like a needle, full of the dope of her daughter's name, into her daughter's brain: "Saradove, Saradove, Saradove . . ." The dazed, dozing head shifted to the edge of the mattress. Olympia moved closer to the oil burner and began toasting in its warm breath. The heat traveled up her legs, puffing at the secret hair in the secret place. It made the corners of rayon, torn from the seams, flap out like maypole streamers. She waited for Saradove to open her eyes, come up stupefied from sleep and wake on the vision of her mother's breast exposed, of an inner thigh white and thick as Georgia marble. And Olympia would have no part in the vision—it would seem an accident of the tropical weather; she would be as aloof from her own nudity as the figurehead of a wrecked ship from its exposed and salt-rotted beams.

But Duncan's cup was clinking with an empty sound against the saucer. She must rush and fill it, get eggs started; morning wouldn't last forever. Morning was closing up in the thick coughs in Duncan's throat, in the heavy shiftings of his weight against the kitchen chair. Olympia, in the kitchen, poured coffee without a word, with no one but him to look at her. Duncan reached over and stuck his finger through a hole in the taut rayon around her leg. It was hateful, like the nervous, humming legs of a horsefly against her skin on the hottest days. She slapped his hand away, almost with the burning base of the percolator.

"Stop that!" she said. "Don't act like that in the morning!"

"Didn't act like you minded last . . ."

"Saradove is coming! Shut your filthy mouth." She held the pot tighter than ever; she needed, terribly, to fill him to the brim with coffee through the little holes deep inside his ears. Duncan's eyes widened; his hands clenched the table's edge.

"Your eggs are coming too," Olympia said hastily.

Saradove shuffled in among them, her drooping pajama legs hiding every step she took. The steam from the pot of popping grits, the sizzling butter in the frying pan started the sweat down her body. She held her cheek hard against the pane of icy glass on the kitchen door. Outside the yard was bare and cold, friendly through its calm and peaceable freeze. Someone was early burning trash in the vacant lot; even the smoke seemed frosted. Someone was warming up his car with loud rhythmical roars. Saradove lifted her cheek and drew a circle on the steamed glass. A touch of her finger made two eyes, a nose; a swoop of her finger made a broad, smiling mouth in the circle. Quickly her finger added a stick body, arms and legs. The little man was dancing from the breathless jungle and all its noise into a lovely arctic waste where he would be alone. A hand took her, sat her at the table; and Olympia, even then, did not let go: she was going to keep Saradove's face between her breasts until at last she *saw*. Saradove saw; she saw the hair, too, sticking through the silky hole like some false clue planted to fool the detective. Saradove was fooled; she turned to her empty plate.

"I want some coffee," she said, "like Duncan's."

Olympia spoke to the ceiling: "What did she say? Ten years old and wants coffee to drink!" She was exalted; she let go of her daughter's arm. Saradove had seen her, someone had looked at her. She wore the bathing-beauty crown; it was like a miracle.

"Grits are ready!" Duncan barked. "Bring her some coffee with lots of milk like Mama used to for me. She's going to be just like me: can't stand it without her coffee."

Olympia began scraping the eggs up. The grits grew silent. Saradove and Duncan looked at each other across the table.

"Can't say good morning, can you, to your old daddy, can you, Saradove?" His face was like the ashes of burned paper rising through the air in the coffee's steam.

"Hey, Duncan."

"Now say hey to your poor old mama over there. Look at her over there. Hardly no sleep last night and there she is working like a nigger for us." Olympia pressed herself hard against the warm stove. They could see her buttocks grow still and tight beneath her torn gown. Duncan leaned back, rubbed his shirt to push his cigarettes up from his pocket.

Olympia stood between them, balancing her torso between the heavy skillet of eggs in her left hand, the pot of grits in her right. She pushed the food on their plates.

"Now eat," she said, "or else everybody in here's going to be late. Butter those grits!" Duncan rested his cigarette on the lid of the jelly jar and obeyed her. She began washing the skillet, picking the thick slabs of yellow from the pan's bottom with her fingernails; she turned it round and round in the stream of steaming water. She looked out the window over the sink and sang to the view: "Je-sus loves me, this I know! For the Bible tells me so!"

From the throats of Olympia's female kin, the hymn wavered forth and hung in the air, solid as music could ever be, solid as fallen apples waiting for a hand to find them on an autumn ground. And the male kin boomed the music back against their wives and cousins and sisters. The little country church was a furnace; but it had to be summer for the family reunion, and people had to sing before they ate the dinner waiting in the yard. The women, perched and proud in their pews, held the hymnals against their bosoms and sang from the heart. Not one was sorrier-dressed than Olympia; but Olympia could hunch her shoulders in the cheap Rayless dress, and smile around at everybody during the singing; let them know that she meant to look this way, this bad, forever, so that they could forever recognize her. The distinguished cousin, the president of a Baptist college in the Piedmont, said from the pulpit that he felt joyous at the sight of their wonderful multiplication, all to the glory of God and the family. The sum of Olympia's multiplication was Saradove. Saradove sat and longed to divide, to triple and quadruple herself until she had made of herself a family of daughters, curly-haired and darling, that would amaze Olympia's kin. On the seat between her and her mother was a shiny white box filled with the almost-new, clean and ironed castoff dresses of Saradove's first cousin. Saradove crouched stiff in her corner to keep away from the touch of the box; she looked steadily through the floor-length open window beside her, to keep away from the sight of the box. Out there were empty spaces of white sand, a few runty pine trees, and escape from the bulging-topped box. It was only a few feet to the ground. Saradove jumped out the window.

Without missing a beat of the hymn, faces from all sides and corners turned on Olympia and sang, "Saviour, like a shepherd lead us!" straight at her. Saradove alone did not turn and look back at her. The streaming gashes of turpentine coming from the slits her cousins had made in the pines were enough to see. The flies hovering above the cellophane-

143

wrapped cakes, waiting in the sun for the singers, were enough to make her sick. The white sand that poured hot inside her shoes was enough to feel.

Olympia, finally, was going to feel humiliation. She was going to stop sighing with relief over secondhand clothes. She was going to stop hugging herself with pleasure every time her sisters patted and pecked at her; she was going to stop grasping for their powdered, ringed fingers. Olympia was going to be saved; her daughter had jumped out the window and had become a hero, rescuing, with her one action, her mother from her long history as the poor little orphan child, the woeful, used object at the tail end of a long family. Saradove had jumped from the window; and, at any instant, Olympia could tear off the ragtag and bobtail of the orphan baby and, burning with shame, drive home and be the beautiful enraged mother again with a switch in her hand. No more talk, thank God, of good sister Lady who had got married first and had taken Olympia out of the County Home to help swab out her new toilets and brush up the wall-to-wall. No more cheating herself, thank God, of new winter shoes to buy a Christmas present for brother Hanson, who'd contributed the big twenty dollars a year to help keep Olympia fed and dressed at Lady's. Duncan had tried to save her by marrying her and see how he had failed! Saradove, ramming her footsteps deep into the white sand, shivered with the loveliness of success. In a moment, Olympia was going to come running out of the church and the singing, snatch her by the hair, drag her to the car and home. At the end of the ride, Saradove would collect all her mother's shame and, forever after, all her mother's gratitude.

Another hymn sweated over the air. Some prayer was said. The little cousins bounded through the door screaming for chicken and four-layer cake. When they saw Saradove, they made a clump of full skirts and short trousers, danced all together and covered their mouthfuls of giggles. Saradove pretended to spit on them; she went and sat on a stump. Her dress stuck to the balls of turpentine; splinters long as hands dug into her back and made a hard thing of her happiness: beyond caring, she was also beyond her kin and the churchyard, far off already down the dusty road, going home with her mother.

Under Lady's twinkling fingers, half-sheltered under Lady's big hat of flowers, Olympia came outside last, talking fast to Lady.

"Is that what you think it is, Sister Lady?" she was saying. "Lord knows I feel like killing her, but if that's what you think it is, I'm sure grateful for you pointing it out. I didn't have the advantages the rest of you all had; sometimes I'm just dumb. I worry so." Olympia sagged against Lady's beautifully built seams.

"I keep telling you, Olympia, and I'll tell you again. It's just that age, twelve years old, that's the age girls start acting up."

Olympia leaned, the sun grazing at her, nibbling at her hair dingy with either gray or sweat, butting into her uncorseted hips, rubbing against her bare legs. Lady stood in the shadow of her baby sister, cooled, waiting for her own daughters.

"But Mela Lee and Jeannette—look at them, Lady!" Olympia kept on, never knowing when to stop. "Pretty, perfect daughters, they always have been. You never have a bit of trouble—look at them!"

Lady looked at them, standing above their heads at the church door, spotlighted by the same sun that tore into Olympia; nodding, smiling to their relatives, their clear skin polished by the hard light, their blue eyes crinkling against it, their ringleted hair bobbing. Lady thought, Oh how well they stand up to the heat! She laughed happily and patted the bunching shoulders of Olympia's dress.

"Stop *blaming* yourself, honey! I told you it's just a stage. Some of them get it, some of them don't . . . depends on a lot of things." Lady thought of some things: her bank account, her own pretty purse-size checkbook; her junior college certificate, her garden club, the nice boys trying to get Mela Lee. She poked Olympia in the ribs to make her join in the laughing, to make her squirm and cover her wet cheeks with her plain, unsparkling fingers.

"Listen, listen, Olympia!" Lady whispered. "This is funny —a girl jumps out the window just about the time she's ready to *fall off the roof!*"

Lady and Olympia arched their backs, arched them so much their buckled stomachs bumped; and they went off together into roars of merriment. Laughing and entwined, they bore down on the other women, who were passing out paper plates bending with fried chicken topped with chocolate cake. Olympia hugged her sister tight. "Oh, Lady, it's just like the old days at home—your home—when you're like this!" Lady's girls were running to her; Lady's loose smile tightened into a mother's.

Saradove imagined that by the magic of her mother's careless laughter she had somehow been grafted to the tree stump; that she would be left there, forgotten, to grow in her own time her own sticky pine needles until a flash fire took her down one day. Her mother had dissolved her future into one liquid dirty joke that she didn't understand but which held, she knew for sure, a whole sorry time she'd never escape. She looked at Olympia and blushed: with incredible familiarity, Jeannette was hugging and kissing Olympia; Mela Lee was pulling at her arm to show off the big birthstone she'd got for her birthday. Olympia was swimming in it.

146

"Umm-humm, um-humm!" Olympia was singing, "And who gave you that? Daddy or a boy friend? Mela Lee, come on and tell me the truth!"

"Oh, Aunt Olympia, you know!" Mela Lee crowed. "Daddy!"

"You're awful, Olympia," said Lady. "Girls, you go get something to eat and be nice to Cousin Bee. She doesn't hear good, that's all, nothing mental involved. Olympia's going to come with me to the outhouse for a minute. And Jeannette, stay away from anything chocolate!"

The girls scampered; Olympia called after them, "Saradove's still taking dancing lessons!" But the girls only scampered and didn't listen.

Olympia had to skip to stay up close with her sister. As they passed Saradove, with nothing but a look, Lady whispered something to Olympia. Olympia laughed behind her hand and whispered back. Lady stiffened, hard, but Olympia was too happy to notice, too happy to contain herself. She said, out loud, "And what's round and juicy and pink and has a lot of fuzz on it? You hear, Lady, what is it?"

"Little Sister!" Lady gasped; and she broke away to walk on alone to the outhouse. Olympia's giggles stopped too fast, as if someone had rammed a wad of cotton down her throat. She folded herself up into a little trot and went after Lady, calling, "Lady, Sister, wait! It's just a *peach!* That's all—just a riddle about a peach!"

Lady shut the outhouse door behind her. Olympia leaned against it like an advertisement for Apple Blossom Snuff, glued tight enough to the wood, but weathered, torn, the message barely legible.

From her mind, Saradove urged her mother to turn and face her. Olympia turned to her daughter and tried to call out. She tried again, with more voice. "Saradove! Saradove," she whimpered, "go get something to eat before you faint in the sun. Get out of the sun, Saradove!"

Saradove stood up, her dress ripping, her legs burning with turpentine, to go away.

And her mother called again, "And Saradove, stay away from anything chocolate!"

"Eat, Saradove," said Olympia. "Put some butter on those grits and eat before they get stone cold." Saradove, eating, watched her mother's face. It was lively and refreshed from soaking in the water's hot steam. She had wrapped herself in her flowered housecoat to show that the morning was over.

"See, Duncan, see!" she said. "Not only have I got to do everything else around here, but I practically have to put the food inside her mouth after I've gone and cooked it." Saradove made her fork move faster.

Duncan's lips wobbled from the effort of trying to chew, to speak, to smoke his cigarette all at once. Saradove remembered an old tin toy, made in Japan, she'd once had. Wound up, it performed an elaborate hodgepodge of tricks for nearly ten seconds: it beat a drum, danced, opened and closed its mouth, raised and lowered its hat, then fell sideways. Nearly, that was Duncan at a meal. His cigarette dribbled ashes on his toast. He dropped the toast and held the cigarette over the floor.

"Lincoln," he said.

"What?" asked Saradove.

"Lincoln," said Duncan. "If it hadn't been for Lincoln and other common Yankees, poor Olympia wouldn't have to work so hard. We'd have a houseful of colored people waiting on her and we'd treat them right. But Lincoln had to go and get the slaves in a lot worse trouble and now poor white women who ought to be resting on their beds in the evening when their husbands get home have to get down on their hands and knees and mop the floor instead."

Duncan reached for another cigarette, and more toast. Saradove imagined their eight little rooms filled with the dark people who lived in shanties across the river, floating through Olympia's work while Olympia lay on the bed and waited for Duncan.

Olympia looked up from the sink. "All I want," she said, "is one colored girl to come in here once a week and iron them white shirts of yours. No bed for me. One more summer—and it's coming soon—of standing over that ironing board and the both of you are going to have to find a new one."

"A new what?" Duncan laughed at her.

"A new wife! A new mother!" She wrung out the dishrag, treating it like a neck. "You hear? You both hear? Now get out of here. You all are going to be late. Saradove's going to fail arithmetic anyway, but I don't want her failing at anything else. Girls don't do that kind of thing."

"My coffee," said Saradove.

Olympia flung the dishrag back in the water. She shook her wet, red hands at them. "Forget that coffee!" she screamed. "I'm not no precious Grandmama!"

A flash of silver flew from Duncan's hand. His chair fell against the floor as he leapt up. His plate twirled through the air and landed in a smash of hardening egg yolk. "Not Mama!" he shouted. "Not Mama, Olympia! I've heard all I can of complaining. You made me leave the poor old lady all by herself in that big house—my childhood home!—made me saddle myself with debt, work like a nigger, just so you can build this house here—this *home of your own!* What do I hear then? Bad words about Mama! Stop it—from now on, stop it!" His mouth still chewed fast on pieces of toast. He raised his fist. Olympia covered her face, her fingers dripping into the sink.

"Don't hit my mama!"

Duncan's arm dropped; his whole body dropped. Olympia began to cry into the dirty water. Duncan straightened up his chair, sank into it, held his head in his hands.

Olympia raised her head from the water, her eyes streaming, her nose running. "Only a minute. I have . . . to warm your petticoat, undershirt . . . your socks . . . sit still." She ran away to the hot oil burner.

Saradove sat still, her back turned against Duncan. She pulled her pajama shirt away from her body and stared down at her chest, watching the skin press and flatten against her ribs as she inhaled. She held her breath to make of her body a slimmer and slimmer little purse of organs. She breathed again, drinking in the warm air of her own flesh. In arithmetic class, she thought, I'll pull my sweater over my nose, I'll breathe only my own air. When the priest comes to give out report cards, he'll see just my eyes. He'll have to hold my card up high to make me see I failed arithmetic again. I'll be breathing my own safe air when he gives it to me, my tiny report card, no bigger than his thumb, for the teeny, tiny person at her teeny, tiny desk. They have to make allowances for me. Saradove bobbed her chin against her chest, three times. "All for thee, Jesus, Mary, Joseph," she chanted.

Duncan came alive, furious. "Olympia! Olympia! Come in here now!"

"I'm only warming . . ." said Olympia from the doorway. She was trembling, as though she could be cold, in the heat, holding the petticoat against her cheek. Duncan's finger shook at Saradove.

"You didn't hear," he shouted. "You didn't hear her! She's saying more of that Catholic manure again! Make her stop it!

Be a mother! What if they heard her down at First Presbyterian—they laugh now at her going to the Catholics all week. How does my mama feel with them talking about this only child, huh? Answer me that!"

Olympia bit down on the petticoat. "Let you know," she spat. "You're not the one's got to get up and take her to Sunday school. And the Baptists were good enough for my people!"

Duncan slammed his fist against the icebox. "Goddamnit! I don't have to! I'm the one makes the living around here, remember?" He stared at the petticoat. "But I'll never make it if you don't stop treating her like a baby, warming up little things all morning like she was something special. You hear? Make that youngun dress herself, I mean it. Always. Dress herself, undress herself. Not you." He held on to the icebox to keep from falling.

"Your blood pressure, your blood pressure," Olympia sang. "What do you do that for? Your blood pressure's going to kill us all." She huddled into the petticoat that had grown cold in her hands. Duncan sat and looked at his knees again.

"Come on, come on, Saradove, quick out to the heat," Olympia called. Olympia's fingers were damp and cool as they drew the clothes down her body; but the clothes were so warm that dressing was like falling asleep in bed again. Olympia knelt at her daughter's feet and tied the shoelaces, double knots.

"Don't act like a baby all the time, Saradove," she whispered, holding her close. "Makes him so mad. You're my baby, just my baby, aren't you? And you're going to be just like all the other girls and make us proud." Saradove pushed her mother away. Duncan stood watching them from the doorway. Saradove asked him, from her mind: What is going to happen to me?

151

He answered, "Don't worry. We'll stop in at the Silver Moon for our coffee."

Together, they moved through the dark living room, stale with last night's cigarettes. From the kitchen, the little radio began whining high, then low, and the Arthur Godfrey show started with a burst of applause. "What is a boy?" moaned Arthur Godfrey. "A boy is . . ."

Duncan held the door open for Saradove. They walked across the dead winter yard to begin their day.

the element of poetry

Up the steps, out of the subway, Saradove climbed, her heart jumping in her chest as high as her feet. It had rained while she was riding underground. She looked at the city through the street's mirrors; and they reflected her too. Rollicking, drunk with rain, the neon circling the discount drugstores, the all-night supermarkets of Clive's neighborhood slipped their tubes and poured down on everyone. A taxi splashed a lady's satin pumps; in return she showered her escort with complaint: she wanted him to go presto! chango! and make them clean again.

"I am a girl going to a party," said Saradove to herself, to the city.

"So what?" answered the escort, tubby, stony-faced, his evening ruined by a pair of shoes.

The light changed. Saradove ran across Broadway, splashing puddles. Her shoes and stockings were black as night and would show nothing, not even dirt. In the dark calm of Clive's block, Saradove did not show. Her skirt rolled with shadows; her face went by like the headless horseman's. Here, the buildings had been made by someone with a short memory of a Gothic castle seen once in a stained, cross-hatched drawing. The gray New York stone had made the memory come true and new.

A Negro, dirty, and loose in his joints, sat on the top step of a building, high above the street. A glow from the forty-watt bulb above him made his pint bottle of Thunderbird twinkle in her eyes as he sucked on it. Saradove passed him by, and smiled, going to her party. The man wiped his mouth with his hand before he spoke, slow as molasses.

"How . . . much . . . you . . . wa—nnnt for it, Ba-aaby?" The way he said it, it sounded like a song. Saradove ran on; and the Negro tipped his soft gray mess of a hat.

The light burning outside Clive's building was powerful and many-watted. Saradove, watching it burn from the dark across the street, considered how it would be standing in the light until the answering bell opened the door of the party to her. When she went from the dark into the light, would she still be a girl going to a party? She thought on the question; it remained nothing but a question. In the light above Clive's door, the women the news of the party had created for her—the women with the ruby ring, the jade necklace, the pale hair—would, might be, insubstantial, as odd in the real light as Saradove's white face seemed in the dark. Per-

154

haps, Saradove decided, I am too early; perhaps, without the black dress and the beautiful face, it is crazy to face those three women. Saradove slid her hand down her smooth hair. It was cool from rainy June air. It felt ready to blossom with grass. She walked back down the street, away from the lighted doorway. Let those sweet women smell their own rainy hair; who needs mine?

The Negro decided to go and meet her. He lurched into her path. "I sa-aaid, how much, how much you wa-aant for it, Baby?" For an instant, Saradove truly faced him; in that instant, he forgot her. She pointed to the Thunderbird still waiting on the steps above him. His eyes followed her finger as if—presto! chango!—she had just then made it appear. But he would have to climb that tower of steps to reach it; and he had just come down them for Saradove. "Oh fuck it," he whispered, and wobbled off to Broadway.

It was extra quiet when he had gone; she could hear Clive's buzzer, faintly, ring; she could see a faintly glimmering party guest vanish through his door. Someone has come, she said; she ran to let the door's light let her inside too, but Clive took a long time to open up to just anybody. For company, she lighted a cigarette. There will be a big clump of people in the center of the room, and damn their lurid neckties! In twos and threes they will dash to the punch bowl, away from me. But what I plan to do is lean against the wall and smoke my cigarette, so who cares? Hurry, Clive! Ring the bell and let me in—this cigarette won't last forever.

The bell rang, and Saradove was running to the second floor where Clive waited, his arms and fingers stretched out to the sight of her, his eyes rolling to spread the news of the wicked thing that was happening behind him at the party.

"Darling! Don't be alarmed, but L.E.'s here and drunk and Evelyn's here and drunk, and L.E. is going to forgive you

155

for getting her in jail—but I promise you she'll never forgive me for doing to her what I did in the first place—but Evelyn is going around punching people in the spine and hoping it'll be you when they turn around—she says she's going to smash you to smithereens. . . ." Clive's breathlessness smelled of ginger ale.

"That's all right." Saradove hugged him around his cough-syrup-colored smoking jacket she'd helped him buy at the thrift shop. "One time I beat an enemy to pulp in the girl's room of the junior high basement. I bet I crippled her for life."

Clive hugged her back, clutching at straws in a high wind. "God! How did this happen to me, and Lettice is here and watching all proceedings with a very very jaundiced eye and not weighing a drop over eighty-five pounds any more and I happen to know that this dreadful enactment is going to prejudice her against me and she'll never invite me to Park Avenue again in my life for New Year's Eve, though she never served a thing but half a glass of New York State, oh, darling, what have you done to me!" He hid his face in her hands and Saradove could feel the sweat of his excitement on her palms. She could see beneath the collar of his smoking jacket: he hasn't washed the Byron shirt since he last let me wear it, I wish I were inside the shirt again, with Clive, treading across a lifetime of parties inside Clive's speedy shoes, my feet on top of his; me too a beautiful young man loving beautiful young boys.

"Let's go in," she said.

"*One* second!" He took out a comb and began pushing her hair into new, electric directions. "No black dress, no pretty black dress, Saraloon?"

"No black dress, Clive. No lovely women, no ruby ring, no green necklace, no red hair?"

"What? You must write me a poem about it, whatever it is. *Try* to." He pretended to tear his hair. "Listen! Gary Spoon is coming! Isn't it wonderful, Gary Spoon! I wish I were you, meeting him for the first time! A famous poet in my house for the first time, and look what's going on!"

He lifted his arm, suddenly, like a curtain revealing the lighted stage; and Saradove could see the party and could see, in bits and pieces, L.E. She was crouched beneath a big round table, half invisible behind the lace tablecloth and the legs of people dipping punch from the bowl, which floated like a great inverted glass crown on the oak above her head. Saradove, at the sight of her, was safe from the eighty-five-pound Park Avenue, from the famous poet, from the smash to smithereens, from the dream of beautiful women about fifty years old. L.E.'s eyes and smile swam through the table-cloth's flower-shaped holes, like little fish slipping through the net.

Evelyn leaned against the wall behind the table, casting the net. Her legs in their tight pants were spread and poised like a prizefighter's. The bombs beneath her thick white sweater were no longer mere bombs—they were missiles, going to go off. She was aiming them at a man as crisp and round as a fresh head of lettuce; but he was wilting from bewilderment.

"More to drink, umm?" he asked Evelyn, and rustled his hands, drying them, down his shirt front. Evelyn grabbed him by his lapels.

"No. Stand still. You're not leaving until you admit I'm stupid. Go on, admit it or I'll have to smash you to smithereens. Say I'm stupid and that all the people who tell me how beauti-ful and brilliant I am are dead wrong and stupid. Are you crazy? Say it!" The little man held tight to his punch cup and stared hopelessly into the missiles pointed at his chest.

"Yes, I'm crazy!" he howled through his perspiring lips.

"Crazy! Crazy! Is it possible . . . you could be . . . average?" The missiles rammed into his shirt front.

"You bastard, you liar!" Her hand swerved out in a perfect arc and got him hard in the face.

Saradove slipped and landed on the couch between two startled pairs of knees. Clive's favorite party music, Schubert's *Die Winterreise*, began ringing through the party; above it, in tempo, Clive's voice wailed through Evelyn's screams: with the strength of three ballet dancers, he was tossing her gracefully through the kitchen door and making her understand that she had just slapped the best second-rate accompanist in town. Immediately, a boy jumped out of his corner and smiled a smile as tight and white as his Levis. He shouted nervously, intimately after Clive: "Clive Baby! Let's have some pachanga, let's have some Stones, let's have some rock *and* roll!" A clump of people swiveled all together around to face him, seriously; and then they turned back to each other's faces, wondering. One man among them raised a hairy finger to his lips and smiled, a very little bit, in secret, to the others. No one else noticed the boy, who unclipped a comb from his shirt pocket and began making his pale hair glisten.

Saradove thought it would be nice to find out what was under the table. There were two silky legs pressing against the table and there was space enough between them for Saradove to crawl through, and beneath, and find out what was there in the lacy dark. She started for the legs, loving the feeling of going home.

Clive's hand touched her. A cold glass touched her cheek.

"Here," he said, "drink this. The punch is just for the waxworks and the mere acquaintances." It was dark brown whisky, floating a slim ice cube. Clive was stretching his mouth in and out of his cheeks, relaxing, preparing to soothe the accompanist. He settled it into a line of earnest distress.

He said, "There. Now I'm going over and kiss those talented fingers so he'll love me again. Good-bye. Enjoy yourself like a darling."

"Clive?"

"Saralove?"

"Who is that yelling boy?"

Clive swallowed. "Just a boy. Uh . . . archaeology student, out of Central Park. Early Indians. You know my interest in digging, why ask? Good-bye." He went off humming Schubert, into the hum and the clink of talk, to make the pianist happy, to get him to love him. Instead, the waxworks, full of mere punch, got Clive. All together they raised their naked arms, thin and looped with papery wrinkles, to flag him down. All together, they sat in an oval arrangement of kitchen chairs near the door and landed Clive with their blessings. "Come here, dear boy!" they called all together. They had modern, even teased, hair sets which perched, lavender and insane, above their little 1912 faces—their perfectly preserved (in tissue paper) little faces, all ready (like a state) to wither away at the first touch of a smile on their lips; but they smiled, and everything stayed the same. Old ladies, Clive knew, nearly in their arms, but definitely not *little* old ladies: the one with the teardrop earrings had the most wonderful money, a Park Avenue penthouse, a dead husband who had been something famous in the twenties. Who would call that little? The one in the spider-web stole that she used to cover a bosom no longer there, but still bare, was regrettably poor in the world's goods but so very rich in style—she had three divorced husbands whose sexual prowess she would murmur about to Clive during their afternoon window-shopping strolls ("He could stay inside one *so* hard *so* long, Clive dear, look at that sweet boa!"); and without effort she illegally collected a small but neat-figured unemployment insurance check every week.

159

Nothing at all little about any of that. Clive pressed her thin fingers to his mouth. The third lady had no claim to distinction but her friendship with the other two; but, as Clive often pointed out to his younger friends, her face was truly the most beautiful in the world—her face reminded him of that time when he was eighteen, in front of the Plaza fountain, when Garbo herself had seized him by the shoulders and whispered: "Young man, so beautiful! So beautiful!"

Clive bowed low to all of them, patted the most beautiful's knee and did what they wanted him to do: he ridded the room of the young man in the tight Levis with such subtlety, such discretion, that hardly anyone heard the noises of hurt feelings coming from the hallway.

Saradove swallowed her ice cube and felt herself go drunk: she would have to be drunk to think of pouring her second drink into Clive's Georgian cream pitcher and sipping whisky from its shining spout for all to see. She shuddered at the thought; she knew perfectly well that only the most beautiful ever got the use of the Georgian silver tea set; it was once a month, the third Wednesday. Evelyn was still in the kitchen where Clive had put her, her back blocking the path to the cupboard and the silver tea set.

"Would you mind moving, please?"

More than anything, Saradove reminded Evelyn of the illustrations in an issue of the *National Geographic* she had once stolen that was entirely devoted to the North American reptiles.

"You are truly an unfeeling monster," said Evelyn.

Anything but that, thought Saradove. "A Gila monster?" she asked. "Why? Who called me that?" She put her hand to her face: no hard shell, no bright prickly scales had grown there yet.

"L.E. did. I didn't agree at first. I said you were just vastly neurotic, probably you had a secret, hopeless kind of thing for Elizabeth Barrett Browning."

"Why did L.E. say that? A Gila monster?"

"Yes. Like Elizabeth Barrett Browning. Coughing on a couch. A secret, hopeless kind of thing for George Sand. An unfeeling monster."

"I'd rather be George Sand," said Saradove, but gave up. To be a Gila monster was not that bad; not anywhere near as bad as How Do I Love Thee? Evelyn had folded up on the floor; the way to the silver was open, but Saradove stopped. In the light from the party—or, perhaps, she had just now opened her eyes—she could see that Evelyn had been, still was, slicing at her wrists with a dull butter knife from Horn and Hardart's.

"Are you trying to commit suicide?" Saradove held tight to the cream pitcher. If Evelyn had more blood in her than the pitcher would hold, it would be up to her to get sober and hunt for empty milk bottles, firemen's buckets, bathtubs. She felt suddenly full of accidental importance, as though she were witnessing a murder at a bus stop or just happening, from luck, to see Maria Tallchief carrying her toe shoes on the subway.

Evelyn held the knife still and looked up, amazed, disgusted. "My God! You make it sound like I'm washing my feet or eating Jell-O! You *reptile!* If you were really Elizabeth Barrett Browning you'd be binding my wrist and taking me to Italy!" Saradove looked away. It was like stepping on Maria Tallchief's big toe and crippling her for life.

"All you can think of is more booze, right?" Evelyn shouted.

"Shh! My fault. I'm sorry, it's just that I always thought that kind of thing happened in clean bathtubs, you know, with a lot of hot water to wash it clean away, you know?"

She put her hand back in the cupboard, snatching the whisky, hearing the silver teapot clink.

"Goddamn anal compulsive! If I jumped out the window you'd just feel sorry for the Sanitation Department, right?"

Saradove put the pitcher back on the shelf, poured, with firm self-discipline, into a glass. She drank, filling herself with charity. "Listen to me, Evelyn. Truly you're just as pretty as Elizabeth Barrett Browning, don't get upset about her all the time, I mean, what has she got that you don't have?" Nothing occurred to either of them. "You'll be a *star* someday, if you just keep it up at Stella Adler's, and what will Mrs. Browning be?" Evelyn's eyes glinted through Saradove's glass. The butter knife plunged, toward Saradove's heart.

"Don't you talk about Elizabeth that way! I have a perfect sado-masochistic relationship going with *Casa Guidi Windows* and you're trying to screw it all up!"

Saradove got to safety behind Clive's ironing board. George Sand, she realized, would have offered Evelyn a cigar and then taken the first cab back home to Chopin.

"Get the hell out of this kitchen!" Evelyn went to work at her wrists again, both still white and unbroken by blood. Back inside the party, Clive's favorite gaity record was playing: *The Toy Symphony;* it jingled over the heads of everybody and roosted in the ears of a social worker sweating through his blue suit and laboring to tell the punch sippers about the problem of dope addiction among the children of subway transit workers. As though she were part of the pretty noise, L.E., still behind the lace tablecloth, was waving and blowing kisses at the people she knew. L.E. could be hungry, L.E. could be cold, could be lonely: Saradove delicately eased all the little cream-cheese-and-olive sandwiches into her pockets and crawled beneath the tablecloth, to whatever was there, to L.E.

162

"How was jail?" L.E.'s eyes were distant and sober; the light shining through the holey tablecloth made pale flowers all over her face.

"You get one hundred per cent for nerve. Besides, who asked you into my little house?"

"You did," Saradove answered, reaching. "Is this your house? *Some* house!"

"A better house than you've ever known; and yes, indeed, mine alone, as the poetess would say. I am playing house in here. I suspect that you don't know how to play house. I suspect that you never played house in your entire life." And L.E. reached back.

"One summer day, I sat in the porch swing at our new house and lied to some children about my mother."

"You're always lying about your mother, Saradove. Come here. It seems only yesterday that I was listening to a lie from you, about your mother being some glamorous trapeze artiste. Why does everyone insist on telling lies about their unhappy childhoods?"

"My childhood was very happy." L.E. let her go and crawled back outside into the party, bumping the table, sloshing the punch overhead. Saradove still talked, softly. "One summer it seemed to rain very hard every afternoon. The rain hid me and made me cozy with myself. I took all my dolls and stuffed animals out and arranged them in the swing. Then I went back inside and got my bedspread and pulled it over all our heads. It made a quiet, warm tent for us. We rocked there as long as the rain lasted, all summer."

Saradove focused her eyes to see through one of the lace flowers: just outside, lying alone on the floor, was a single, many-petaled rose, made of wool. She flattened the lace against her nose and looked harder—it was nothing but a picture in Clive's carpet. The table shook; the punch made a sound like a little lake's waves beneath a wind. It was L.E. coming back, carrying Clive's whisky bottle, making herself comfortable.

"I've decided to drink a farewell toast with you." She unbuttoned her shirt and let the silver cream pitcher and sugar bowl fall to the floor between them. "How your eyes pop, Saradove. Doesn't Clive think you're old and rich and beautiful enough to have tea with him from these? I thought not." She poured the whisky and gave the sugar bowl to Saradove. They drank. L.E. let her eyes glaze, her smile appear. Not charity, but faith; then hopelessness filled Saradove.

"Let us hear, Saradove, how you play house." Saradove spoke of the porch swing and the rain. She saw that L.E.'s face had become a motion-picture projector pointed into the dark rooms of her brain. The shadows of lace flowers that floated on L.E.'s face were crossing Saradove's mouth and sticking there. Fear began to turn her story into a fairy tale, making it cross the forbidden forest. L.E. was projecting images of snow and freezing alleys; L.E. was pushing flocks of pigeons into flight through her mind; L.E. was making over her brain into a morning housetop burning with summer.

"One day, I told the children who came to sit with me in the swing . . ."

"What did you look like?"

"I was bare all over except for little flowered rompers; my toenails had my mother's red polish on them."

"You were bare all over."

"Bare and stuck all over with sweat; sweat made my hair stick to my skull, but my daddy wouldn't have it cut. Rubbing my feet against the bricks of the porch set my teeth on edge. With every swing forward, my foot would rub against the bricks. We wore those rompers because they seemed like jungle clothes to us; we'd been playing Tarzan in the trees

on the vacant lot. It was the first time we'd ever put on anything special to play a game. We didn't put the curtains on
and steal flowers to play bride with until the next spring."

"What did the others look like? How many children were
with you?"

"How many?"

"Yes. To play house there have to be others."

Saradove closed her eyes, to count them. "There were three
others in the swing, three of us crowded and sticking together. It was noon and hot. Every time a car went by, we
could smell rubber tires burn. We had been playing Tarzan
all morning, and nobody's mother would let us turn on a
water sprinkler and play beach because of the water bill. They
all looked like me." Saradove opened her eyes: it was true,
they were all the picture of Saradove. "I had to whisper the
lie about my mother because I was afraid she would hear me
from the house. She had just got a colored maid to come
and iron Duncan's shirts, and I was going to stop taking dancing lessons. After the colored maid started coming, I could
never be sure where my mother might be hiding in the house.
Before that, she was always in the kitchen at noon."

"What was the lie?"

A pair of brown Oxfords, a pair of black suède pumps
nudged at their legs beneath the tablecloth. The punch ladle
was clanking and pouring. The second-rate accompanist, who
had been asked to the party to meet Clive's singer friend, had
finally met her. The singer was trilling her laugh on B-flat.
The singer was making her seduction of the accompanist part
of a song.

Saradove whispered, "I told them that my mother had a
beautiful long black dress with big pink roses pinned to the
shoulder and waist, that she had a long pearl necklace and
diamond earrings to wear with it. I think I'd seen Linda

Darnell wear all that at the picture show. Then, I said that long ago in the olden days, before she'd got married, my mother had been a Southern belle and the daughter of a king in a freezing Yankee country and that she'd worn big hoops under her lace skirts. That she'd been very rich and well loved."

L.E. refilled the cream pitcher and the sugar bowl. "That's not much of a lie. Crazy geography! Lace skirts in freezing weather!" She laughed. "I find it too odd that people have to lie about their mothers."

"All of them are not so wonderful, like yours. I just wanted, terribly, the best for her. I thought you had to be rich to have snow and ice. It was always hot."

"A poet for a mother," L.E. sighed. "It's incredible, my luck." L.E. lighted two cigarettes, generous in her good fortune, and took off her loafer to use as an ash tray. "Then what happened?"

Saradove smoked and whispered, "Then we went back of the house. The others wanted to go in a garage that belonged to the house next door. The garage had a dirt floor, very soft cool dirt that the sun never struck. I've never felt dirt so fine and soft, with black grease mixed through it. The grease made the dirt stick to our feet in little clots. I wouldn't stay in the garage. I climbed a tree in our yard and watched the others go inside. You wouldn't believe how it was: flies buzzed all over through the summer. They clamped on to your skin and you took them inside with you. And you had to watch out where you walked because ground wasps circled over the grass. We always took off our shoes the day school was out. I caught a wasp one time in a Mason jar and kept him there to be cruel. He beat himself to death against the glass."

166

"What about the garage?"

The Toy Symphony ended. They could see Clive pushing the social worker away from the phonograph, with smiles and no explanation; the social worker wanted to play the Modern Jazz Quartet record he'd brought along. Clive slipped something else on the turntable. Noel Coward and Gertrude Lawrence started to sing "Bittersweet." They could see Clive comforting the social worker, taking him off to see the blown-up life-sized photograph of Miss LeBontemps in her L'Aiglon costume that hung beside the door. The Modern Jazz Quartet slipped to the floor and someone stepped on it; later, someone else threw it against the wall and broke it.

"I told you," said Saradove. "The others went into the garage and I climbed a tree to watch them go. That's all." L.E. put the cream pitcher on the floor between them and took Saradove's face in her hands. Smoke slid from her mouth and into Saradove's eyes as she spoke.

"This is a story about playing house," said L.E. "Tell me about the garage." Saradove talked between the hands, into L.E.'s face.

"They kept calling and calling me to come with them. But I didn't, I stayed up the tree."

The heat of the day when she was ten years old and up a persimmon tree began to melt the snow in the alleys. The sun came off the sky and felt L.E. and Saradove wrapped in coats and galoshes behind the garbage cans. The sun pierced and dried the snow between them. The coats became suffocating.

"They called and called," said Saradove, "and I came down from the persimmon tree. There was a row of ugly green bushes that separated the two yards. When I went through them, a branch scratched my belly, a thin red scratch. It

167

seemed cooler, more like snow, in the garage because it was dark there, but even so we sweated more. Our hands and feet got all gray with the soft dirt."

"And what?" L.E. asked. "This is a farewell drink, remember? You must tell me." She did not let Saradove's face go; all of L.E. was projected onto it.

"We took down our pants and looked at each other. We sat down against the wall of the garage beneath the shovels and rakes hanging there, and we spread our legs, all our spindly little legs. We had pretended it would be winter in the garage, but when we touched each other, it felt like heat and summer still. That's all." There was a driveway, white with fine sand, stretching out of the garage and into the brilliant outside. A car bumped from the street and turned into it, and all the children ran.

Someone outside the tablecloth screamed, and it was Clive. "Gary! Gary Spoon is here at last!" Someone, Clive, lifted the tail of the tablecloth and said, "Stop that! Stop that kissing! You've got to come out of there now because Mr. Spoon is here and everything must become more . . . something . . . more *banal!* Quickly, respectable!"

Someone heavy, making the whole room shake, at the sight of Gary Spoon was jumping up and down and clapping his hands. The phonograph needle leapt, and the voices of Gertrude Lawrence and Noel Coward gurgled as one. Saradove opened her eyes and saw it was true, she had been kissing L.E. They stood up in front of Clive and tried to focus on the party. L.E. had no trouble.

"Lettice *saw* you!" said Clive, infuriated because Lettice had grabbed Gary Spoon at the door and seemed to want to keep having him. Clive's first real poet stood kissing the brow of Clive's only rich old lady and drinking from his own silver

filigree flask, ignoring the handfuls of punch cups being offered him. Clive went for them, money and fame waiting
for the grasp of his guiding hand. L.E. went for the singer;
the accompanist had gone forever, and the singer needed
music. Away went L.E.

"All I wanted to say in the first place," said Saradove to
L.E.'s back, "was that Evelyn's in the kitchen committing
suicide."

L.E. looked back over her shoulder. "She usually reserves
that for Monday nights. I expect she's asleep on the floor by
now. See, won't you, darling?" The singer turned to her,
clearing her throat.

Saradove did not see. She looked at Gary Spoon, whose little
tongue ran on with wit and the liquid from his flask. Gary
Spoon looked almost like the cracked Humpty Dumpty,
equally hairless, but without Humpty Dumpty's hauteur. The
guests around him each held two punch cups and waited for
the great fall. The rest of the party—those who had not read
far enough into the Twentieth Century to get to Gary Spoon
—clustered again around the drink. Two women, one fat in
the rear, the other plump in the front, fought over the phonograph, over which came next, Irish Rebel Songs or Enrico
Caruso. Clive interfered and settled it with "Bittersweet"
again. Gary Spoon was smacking his lips and looking at Saradove and Saradove was drawing her skirt aside to let his gaze
pass on.

On the couch, which was not silken, which supported no
lovely women, the social worker, finally drunk and wearied
with drug addiction, was trying to push a woman's thin knees
apart so that his hand could go up her skirt. His glasses had
slipped so far down his nose that his nostrils were rapidly
steaming, then unsteaming, his vision. Lightheaded with the

169

possibility of a husband, the woman was trying, and failing, to do two things at once: keep the social worker's hand up her dress but off her (as she thought of them) privates.

"Stop it, Barney!" she gasped. "Honest to God, our relationship hasn't, I mean, our relationship isn't . . ." Biting his lip, concentrating hard, Barney made a last desperate plunge and got his hand stuck home free against the nylon crotch. The woman's punch cup, which she had been balancing perfectly over her head, simultaneously plunged its rum and orange juice over Barney's face. His glasses fell neatly into the empty cup. She put her hands over her eyes, facing the empty years of spinsterhood ahead of her, moaning about them. She had finally done the wrong thing.

"Blast it, Iris!" Barney yelled. "I mean, blast it, look what you've done! Bring me here with a blasted pack of inhibited fairies and look at me, my eight-dollar shirt . . ."

Clive said, "Quiet this very instant!" He was wearing his terrifying Grand Inquisitor's face, copied exactly from one of Miss LeBontemp's more commonplace expressions. Clive did not believe in social work; nor, for that matter, did he believe in the subway transit system. He lifted Saradove to her feet.

"Miss Racepath here," Clive said, "will show you to the door. When you can conduct yourselves, when you can conduct yourselves . . ." He began moving backward, again toward Gary Spoon, who, with swift explosions from his dirty mind, was drawing even the nonpoetry readers to his side.

The nice, quiet place left at the party, Saradove saw, was behind Clive's thick, long blue curtains. Beneath them, the singer's suède pumps and L.E.'s dusty loafers were rubbing odd but interesting patterns against the floor. Saradove crooked her finger at Barney and Iris, and they followed her,

170

wringing out their clothes in little fistfuls, snarling and weeping and waving good-bye. The social worker bounded down the stairs, alone. As Iris took her first step down, Saradove said, mimicking Evelyn's way, "None of us is getting any younger, right?" After Iris slapped her, leaving two long red streaks, and ran away, Saradove pinched and pulled at her cheek until she was satisfied with the hurt.

On the floor, sitting next to Gary Spoon's feet, she decided his socks must be perfumed, that his pointed boots, also, must be polished with perfume.

Gary Spoon said, above her head, "The element of poetry in all of us—especially you, my dears—" he patted each of the little ladies on her knee—"lies right between our legs!" He drank from his flask and looked through his eyelashes down into the faces of the two boys who had trailed him to the party. One was blond, one was dark; they looked at each other and giggled, although the blond tried not to—tomorrow Gary Spoon was buying him the Lincoln Continental.

Lettice, who could vaguely recall the twenties and the things her famous husband had said, tried to laugh; she touched Gary Spoon on the shoulder. "Tell me," she said, "dear Gary, what do you think of contemporary poetry? It gives one a terrible time sometimes. Sometimes I think one was meant only for Mrs. Browning."

Gary Spoon held his flask like a spyglass before his eye; he shook it, but heard nothing. "Dear lady!" he roared. "I am not interested in contemporary poetry. I am interested only in contemporary *cock!*" He had forgotten the check, "In support of the Arts," that Lettice had promised him.

Lettice waved her fingers in the air, flashing signals to the waxworks with the emerald and the diamond. They draped their thin shawls over their shoulders and, all together, rose from the kitchen chairs.

171

"A taxi, Clive dear?" Lettice called. Clive ran before them, and they were gone.

Gary Spoon passed the empty flask to the dark boy, who held it before him like a chalice. Gary Spoon stood, stumbled, remembering too late the check from Lettice that could have meant the Lincoln Continental, that could have meant . . . He stumbled through the floor sitters and collapsed on the couch, in the social worker's sticky punch stain. Saradove and the boys followed him, perching before him on the coffee table like sparrows on a telephone wire, hoping to feel the messages and transmissions even if they did not understand them. But the blond boy, suddenly sick at the sight of his rival bearing the flask, jumped up before he had barely sat and rushed to a vase of pink roses that stood on the bookcase. Gary Spoon watched him, measuring the care the boy took to select the best flower. Convinced that he was going to get second best, he ignored the boy and pointed a fat finger at Saradove.

"You, sad ducks, sitting there before me. What is your name?"

Saradove pressed her reddened cheek to make it gleam out at him. "Saradove Racepath," she said.

"Whoops!" Gary Spoon batted his lashes at the blond. "It is a name that sounds like an *act!* You know, an *act!*" The blond bowed before Gary Spoon and held out the flower. Gary Spoon lifted his head, but not his hand. He opened his mouth and bared his teeth.

"Don't you understand, sweets?" he whispered. "The mouth, the mouth, put it in my mouth." The boy's fingers, tightening, shaking, broke the stem; but he managed to lay the rose across Gary Spoon's bottom teeth. Gary Spoon snapped his teeth together; and the end of the boy's little finger was bitten through. He sat down at his place on the coffee table again, sucking his finger, trying to smile. Gary Spoon took the flower from his mouth and put it behind his ear.

"That's right, sweets, suck it. Best old-granny treatment in all the world. Suck it, sweets, make it all better. You're a good boy and deserve everything you're going to get." The boy's smile grew wide. Gary Spoon brandished the flower at Saradove.

"I tell you," he said, "teaching them the value of symbols both in love and art is the hardest part of all." Saradove inched her finger along her cheek until it pointed, very casually, to the largest scratch. Gary Spoon closed his eyes and stroked his forehead with the rose.

"Sara—dove—Race—path," he murmured. "Now what does that make me think of?"

The apartment door slammed, Clive returning to his party. Saradove felt things behind her back grow lively again. The floor sitters drew Clive down among them; nearly all of them wore peace buttons. Those with bare lapels were listening earnestly to those with buttons, listening with shock in their faces, to tales of jail. A very tall young man, with a crew cut, a Hawaiian shirt and two peace buttons, was pointing his eyes through the ceiling toward heaven, was telling them how he had received the scar across his chin. Clive sat down next to him, slowly shaking his head, letting his fronds of yellow hair brush back and forth over his brow.

"Joseph," he said sadly, "you are the very essence of California. Take your eyes off my ceiling. I just had it replastered." Discreetly, Clive brushed Joseph's hand from his knee.

Joseph clenched his lips together and covered his scar with the hand Clive had given back to him. "You should talk," he answered. "When have you ever been to jail for the movement?" Clive stood up and went to play Noel Coward again.

Joseph followed him. "When?" he nagged. "When did you last lie down in front of the U.N. and protest?" Noel Coward sang, "Some day I'll find you!" Clive said, and sang, nothing.

Joseph tugged at the hem of his Hawaiian shirt. "I asked you, Clive, when did you ever go to jail for the movement?" Clive turned from the phonograph, love in his face.

"Look, Joseph," he said. He put his hands on Joseph's shoulders. Their foreheads touched. "Don't I go to Europe nearly every year and don't I spend absolute hours at a time sitting still in some scorching or freezing little pension writing letters about the international situation back to the movement which the movement has never seen fit to publish? And didn't I try with every last ounce of personal charm to gain a personal interview with Bertrand Russell last time, for all our sakes? And last, but by no means least, can you actually see somebody like *me* in jail? I mean really and truly see me there?" Joseph stared straight ahead, into Clive's eyes. "And how many times," Clive continued, "have I tried and tried again to read my little piece on Sacco and Vanzetti at the League of Liberators meetings and you, our president, have always chosen some cute little nothing from the *Catholic Worker* to give a . . . what do you call it? . . . a *personal testimony* instead!"

Joseph shook his head, saying no to everything, feeling the silk of Clive's hair against his face.

"Saradove Racepath," Gary Spoon repeated. "What *does* that remind me of?" Gertrude Lawrence, through the crack in the record, sang back at Noel Coward.

"Oh, that!" Saradove held the rose tight to her scratched cheek. "That woman, did you see her? She was behaving so badly on the couch, did you see that? She did it. When I showed her to the door, she just turned around and for no reason whatsoever clawed my face like this. I can't understand it. Look at me!"

Gary Spoon sat up. The boys shifted, ready to follow, but Gary Spoon was just tucking his heels up, more comfortably, beneath him. He pulled his blossom back from Saradove and held it beneath his chin.

"I understand it." His eyes narrowed. "It's always the beautiful and the sensitive who are treated in that manner. No other reason. The world does not require another reason. The world simply slaps you down for being beautiful and sensitive. Look at Frédéric Chopin!" He rubbed his lips with the flower. Saradove turned around. The dusty loafers and the high heels were still beneath the hem of the curtain; but one high heel and one loafer were hanging midway, now, at each leg. Both pairs of legs were crossed and facing forward. Saradove looked back at Gary Spoon.

"Am I beautiful?" she asked.

"Now I know!" Gary Spoon cried. "Saradove Racepath! It reminds me of a balmy summer, of gnarled, half-dead trees bending beneath Spanish moss. Luxury! Licentiousness in the air! Of long drives ending at the great, many-columned porch where gay young blades rock of an evening and sip mint juleps. They talk of good horseflesh! Tell me the truth now, Saradove Racepath, isn't that what you come from? Every gesture, every word, tells me so!" Gary Spoon giggled into the petals of the rose. Saradove smiled down at the rubbed, worn place in the lap of her corduroy and imagined that it could be true.

Gary Spoon leaned back, settling himself for a story. The two boys had relaxed; their backbones bent a little. The blond was biting his fingernail at the thought of the Lincoln Continental that he would drive tomorrow, if only . . . Joseph stood at the door, tucking in his Hawaiian shirt, his backbone rigid as cinder block.

"O.K., Peace Marchers!" Joseph shouted. "Are you coming with me or not?" No one moved to join him. The floor sitters sat on, held still by Clive's perfect face, by the story his hands were acting out in front of them. Clive sat before them, their Indian chief, and told them of the international situation. Joseph waited a moment too long; his face reddened and moistened. He ripped his peace buttons from his shirt and threw them to the floor.

"All right then!" he shouted, unloved, bereft. His mind shouted silently, Look at what beauty's won from truth, the way it always is! One of the girls, who was sitting before Clive, who was not even seeing Clive, stood quickly, awkward with courage. Deliberately, with less drama than she intended, she pulled her own button from its place above her left nipple, and threw it too, across the room to Joseph's feet. She rubbed the snag the pin had made on her terrible turquoise sweater and stumbled to him, Joseph staring, horrified, at the face, greasy with hope; and at the eyes, popping behind the thick glasses, that were coming to join him. Before she could reach him, Joseph had gathered his own buttons back safely into his hands, his mind shouting, And see what truth always wins! and he was gone from the apartment, leaving the door to sail to of its own accord. The girl caught it with her hand before it could slam.

Clive turned Noel Coward over; he rummaged in his desk. He stood among his audience and read, from the papers in his hand, "Sacco and Vanzetti: A Death Without a Cause." The girl who had wanted Joseph leaned over the punch bowl and drank, over and over again, from the ladle.

"Tell me, tell me," said Gary Spoon, wriggling on his tucked-up heels. "I love stories of the Old South. I could tell you stories about *me* and the Old South that would curl your straight hair!" Saradove was being wrapped in the petals of Gary Spoon's rose; the sun of his attention was making her bloom. That great man! A cold glass, again, nudged into her hand.

The blue curtains clattered on their rings hard against the wall. The singer's suède pumps gouged with fast, short steps into the carpet. Clive sang out from the floor, "The best mezzo-soprano in town is going. . . ." The suède heels kicked at Clive; he dodged. "Going!" Clive warbled. The doorknob split through the wall's plaster as the door smashed open. "Gone!" shouted Clive. The singer had left a trace of her perfume, almost like the scent of Gary Spoon, in the air behind her. The door crashed shut.

Saradove felt, an inch away from the back of her head, the stare from L.E.'s eyes. She turned, facing it, screaming, "What does she mean to you?"

L.E. caught her lower lip between her teeth, made it pink as a rose; she smiled into Saradove's face. They gathered in each other's hands.

"Hanky-panky! Hanky-panky!" Gary Spoon called.

L.E. said, "Give me a kiss, Saradove, and tell him about the time your father tried to get into bed with you. That's South!"

Saradove kissed her; she would never stop. "Did he?" said Saradove.

"He did?" said Gary Spoon. "He did? That's not South, my dears, that's literature; that's Nobel stuff! What I want is to hear about your handsome beaux!"

"Don't listen to him," L.E. whispered. "Listen to me. Didn't you tell me about playing house? That's only half of it. Listen to me, Saradove."

"That girl's the very devil," said Gary Spoon. "Why doesn't she go back behind the curtains?"

Saradove thought, Did my father try to go to bed with me? She could not see her father; she could see nothing then but the mossed, cool bricks of the First Presbyterian Church, and herself, splendid and good inside its architecture.

"I am thinking of a place." She smiled at Gary Spoon. "It was designed from plans by Christopher Wren." Her glass was empty, but it still felt cold; then it was full and at her lips again.

Clive said, "And death by such injustice . . ." And he flipped Noel Coward over again, one more time.

"In the name of God!" Gary Spoon screamed, ripping his rose to shreds. "One would imagine you'd *had* Noel Coward the way you *do* go on!"

The peace marchers clung to Clive's last word. "Injustice," murmured a girl.

Clive folded his arms across his chest. He froze; his voice, too. "And what," he said, "may I play for you, Mr. Spoon? Please, Mr. Spoon, you are my honored guest. What is your pleasure?"

Gary Spoon stretched out full length, imagining himself a slim, attractive snake; he folded his hands over his round belly. The boys on the coffee table straightened their spines, like suddenly alert rabbits.

"Let's have some Stones," Gary Spoon snickered. "Let's have some pachanga. Let's have some rock *and* roll!"

Clive dropped the needle. Noel Coward gulped. "The party is over," said Clive. "Now the party is over!"

The peace marchers went limp and fell full-length over the rosy carpet. "Oh, no," they moaned. "Oh, no, Clive, sir! Oh, sir, you haven't finished Sacco and Vanzetti yet!" Clive held his hands out to them and gave Gary Spoon a look to make him disappear.

"Since you're all so young," said Clive, "and desperately need to know . . ." The peace marchers sat up straight again. "The day dawned," said Clive.

"I remember," said Saradove, "that it always seemed like

Easter morning in that place; like spring." L.E.'s mouth pressed against her hair.

"The place you lived in, where you were born, suckled by a black mammy, raised to be a lady, right?" said Gary Spoon.

"Oh, yes. The honeysuckle, for instance, grew in tangles all up the walk to the little chapel."

"The house," said Gary Spoon.

"The house," said Saradove. "My first memory is of walking . . . yes, with my black mammy . . . yes, riding my pony . . . yes, in my silk dress from France . . . yes, in my gold locket . . . to smell the big, thick blossoms of rhododendron—they were white, with pink hearts—that grew by the gate, yes . . ."

"What do the flowers remind you of?" said L.E., into her ear.

"Stop interrupting," said Gary Spoon. "Get back behind the curtain. Big, thick blossom, all white, pink at the center. How fleshly! We all know what it means. Get back behind the curtain, girl!"

"What do the flowers remind you of?" L.E. whispered.

"My daddy was so handsome and gentle, but ruined, disappointed . . ."

"The Depression," said Gary Spoon, "the war."

"Yes, but somehow he managed to keep us all in this beautiful place, inside the thick, cool walls; and he had an organ . . ."

"Well, yes," said Gary Spoon, "if he tried to get into . . ."

"That he played Bach on, to while away his last years." Saradove closed her eyes. "I hear the roar of the 'Toccata and Fugue' coming through me still, hear the chandelier ring with his music . . . I sat beside him while he played . . . listen to me." Her back ached; she leaned against L.E., and L.E. crossed her arms around Saradove. After a while, she could hear Gary Spoon talking.

179

"And that was a particularly marvelous part about how they had to keep your mad auntie locked up in the attic. Dreadful trauma for a sensitive beauty like you to have to tote up her collard greens every evening. Surprised it didn't turn you queer. . . ." Gary Spoon was giggling.

Saradove opened her eyes. The room tilted. Gary Spoon was no longer on the couch. The coffee table was empty of boys. Beneath her eyelids she saw herself, drawn in heavy, black outline, filled in with bright, primary colors. She was Elmer Fudd being lured over the cliff by Bugs Bunny. She was running through thin air. She was above the clouds. Like Elmer Fudd, she was safe from falling as long as she did not look down. She could flash through thin air for miles, as long as she did not look down. She opened her eyes: miles below, the party was being shuttered out. The sound of slamming doors rang in her head. She fell.

A window opened, and a breeze as blue as the curtains it fell through spread over her.

"I opened my eyes and looked down," said Saradove. "Who do I love?"

"Not me, not me." Clive's answer came through the rattling of glasses in a sink. "You're not afraid of the dark, are you, Saralove? I'm going to turn out the lights now; go to sleep. Let's neither of us cry over anything."

Clive was kneeling in the window seat, smoking one small stick of marijuana, reading the day's lesson from the Book of Common Prayer.

"Go to sleep, Saradove. You find patterns to get through these things. Eventually you find patterns, and you get through them. Go to sleep."

In the dark, beneath the sound of Clive's prayers, Saradove clamped her hand over her mouth so that she would not scream or speak up in her sleep; and she shut her eyes.

jail

The window seat was empty. The blue curtains still sailed with air, but weakly, in and out. The sun would follow the curtains inside, then be pushed urgently out again. It rained through the sunshine, a thick, lethargic rain that, even inside the city, smelled of overripe roses, of full-grown grass.

Saradove's eyes went over the room from corner to corner: it was morning, the party was missing. The carpet flowers were indented with the vanished prone shapes of the peace marchers. Clive's essay on Sacco and Vanzetti lay dog-eared and fanned out like a deck of cards. Bathroom water went gurgling and rolling against the thumpings of the rain. The clock ticked at noon. Then Clive was with her, his hair turned from gold to brass, and matted; his eyes were red. He stuck his arm deep inside a Chinese jar on his desk and pulled out very dark glasses; they made huge black holes in his face.

Saradove sat up. "Where is everybody?"

"Everybody has gone to Los Angeles. Evelyn finally put my butter knife away and took everybody to the plane. L.E. is gone."

"Gone?" Saradove began crying, her tears thumping hard as rain against her hands.

"Yes," Clive answered. "One thing that sticks with me from Miss LeBontemps . . ."

"And what is that?" said Saradove, crying.

"Be hard core. Always be hard core."

"And what is that?" said Saradove, thinking that whatever it was, it could be no substitute for being broken by L.E.

"Intrepid. It means be intrepid. And that means, she always said, support and celebrate Number One through thick and thin. This is the thin, as you must know."

"Clive, where are your eyes?"

"In my head, Saradove. Everything is there in my head, the world as I make it. The mask I wear in front of it doesn't matter, but the mask is quite as important as the real thing. It makes the real thing what it is; it's part of it, and just as true. For instance, never try to feel passion without first pretending to feel it. The false makes the real; perhaps, in the end, it becomes the real." Clive took off the glasses.

"Put them back on, Clive."

"Yes," he said, and did. "Now, support yourself by spreading marmalade on the toast and eating it. Celebrate yourself by combing out your hair, fixing your face. If you pretend to be glorious, you will be. Proceed, Saradove."

With one hand, Saradove ate; with the other, she pulled off the long black stockings. With its thick, callused hand the heat grabbed her, sticking the corduroy jumper to her skin like a wet bathing suit. Her legs blanched at their exposure to light. The stench of old rum came humid as the weather from the empty punch bowl, still on the table; and the crumbs from their breakfast toast fell through the petal-shaped holes of the lace tablecloth.

Clive ate happily, spooning soft egg onto the bread and swallowing it as greedily as the patient who gets the wonder drug at the eleventh hour of his illness. He stirred Ovaltine into his glass of milk.

He sighed when he had swallowed it all. "I think now that my stomach will not contract too viciously at the sight of the police."

"The police?" Saradove began drinking Clive's coffee; her own cup stank of rum.

"They're always there to get us when we go to City Hall to demonstrate against the Bomb. You know, I told you. And don't carry old LeB.'s principles quite so far, Saradove—give me back my coffee." Clive drank more milk. Saradove drank his coffee, and he gave her a cigarette.

"Am I invited?" She spooned up the remains of Clive's egg. "How can I get to be a demonstrator against the Bomb?"

Clive stood up, flicking crumbs away, closing his eyes, lifting his arms. He began performing the dance movements of Isadora Duncan. She was, Clive always said, the only dancer of the century. She could have been, Clive always said, another Nijinsky if she'd tried hard enough. He stretched, and leapt.

"Don't worry," he called from the air, "you are one. It requires only a heart in the right place and a realistic fear of death." Clive bent his knees, lifted his face, arms and a stage smile to the place above his roof where the sun might be shining. He twirled, paying homage to the goodness of the god who had made him and Isadora beautiful. He stretched out his arms, pushing them against two imaginary Greek pillars.

"And it's not a tea party," he added. "One is not invited. One demonstrates from a sense of dedication to the untrammeled human spirit and from a realistic fear of death."

Saradove finished both cups of coffee. Clive tossed away his imaginary Isadora draperies and sat back down. A sense of dedication, thought Saradove, might well replace a sense of love. She searched herself for a fear of death. Perhaps it would come when the monstrous policeman pointed his revolver at her and broke her arm when he slung her in the cell. Perhaps she would go to jail, after all.

"Are you afraid to die, Clive?"

"I *said*," he repeated, pretending huge patience, "a *realistic* fear of death. The Bomb means being smashed and burned to a crisp in the second balcony of a Forty-second Street movie. Among people who are not one's peers. Among popcorn and Hollywood."

"Do you want to die alone?" she asked, but knowing there was not a chance of being alone for anything.

"Not alone. That isn't the way it's done. Everybody, including the second balcony, deserves a clean bed and a warning illness that doesn't tamper too harshly with one's facial expressions. And the hand of a lover in one's own, and a literate priest chanting in the background; a decent doctor who has packed up and gone after doing the best he can. And, especially, a dear, lifelong friend who is listening for the last words. I have a book recording the last words of one thousand famous people." Clive offered another cigarette. "Do you know why Christ died?"

"Do you believe in him?" She could not see Clive pasting the gold stars on the picture of Our Lady.

"One doesn't have to believe in what is simply *there*. He was the original demonstrator. Buddha, however, had more of an aesthetic sense. Christ's bit of action was to die so that every last one of us has a right to his seven last words. Before ascending into heaven. Or going into a reincarnation—whichever; take your choice. I've had my last words picked out for a long time. I hope you'll be there to hear them. Promise!"

He spun out on his toes for a necktie. Saradove went to the kitchen and began washing above the cluster of dirty punch cups. Before a piece of mirror propped in the window, she began arranging her face into different expressions to show lost love and a sense of dedication. If Clive was right, she would soon feel what her face showed. She put lipstick on it and combed the hair around it. She held her hands against the face, wishing she could paralyze the expression, wishing she could lock the skin around it, like a door into an empty, dusty room.

Clive was waiting for her, wearing clothes suitable for an afternoon at the Russian Tea Room. "It's too bad," he said, "that there isn't time for you to go home and change." He tried not to look at the wrinkled corduroy. "I believe in going to these affairs looking as upper class as possible. It confuses the police when one has neither beard nor Levis."

Saradove took his hand. "I have neither beard nor Levis," she said.

"Come on," said Clive.

having Johnson

In the last of the summer's heat, Saradove stood in front of the bar where Johnson had told her to meet him. She stood still and listened, baking between the sun and the sidewalk, to a girl who had run to catch up with her two blocks away, to a girl she had once hated very much at a party.

"Lorraine," said Saradove, "I have to go in here now."

"Take my advice," said Lorraine. "Johnson is a wonderful lover—I ought to know, I was the first woman he had when he hit New York from Iowa. But he'll make a terrible husband and father." Lorraine pushed at the heads of three stocky little children who were chewing on lollipops and wiping their brows against her dress. Lorraine was like a fourth stocky child, but with protuberances and thick red hair that hung low down her back, for the sake of sexiness, even in the heat.

Beside her, Saradove felt cool and thin. Her encumbrances were not flesh and children, but only the tiny yellow flowers that bloomed over her new dress. Clive had cropped her hair until it curled around her ears. She could see that Lorraine had not lost her stomach from her last pregnancy.

"You should know, shouldn't you?" said Saradove. The red juice from a lollipop began slithering, along with the sweat, down Lorraine's leg.

"Because I've had a husband and know? Certainly."

"No, because you've had Johnson." Lorraine lifted one eyebrow, badly penciled before breakfast, bad now from wear and tear. She lifted one eyebrow, sexily.

"You're in love with Johnson, aren't you?"

"Yes." Saradove was pleased to be praised so directly.

"Take my advice," said Lorraine. "You only want a husband because you've never had one before. But if you have to do it, go find one in advertising or public relations or—whatever—a librarian." She named the things most distant from her own life. "Don't pick a man just out of jail who's just aching to be a hero for humanity and do it all over again."

Saradove thought of jail, cold and comfortable with its regular lock-ups, regular exercise; its narrow cot meant for one.

"He says he's never going to jail again. He says they treat murderers better than peace demonstrators in the Tombs. He says advertising is what we're fighting against, that Madison Avenue is the Bomb. How can you say that? You took your children to the demonstration—I saw you!" She stopped, breathless, amazed at all the answers the sense of dedication could give. When had love ever answered?

187

"You'll see what I mean," said Lorraine, thinking, really, of the same thing. Her children began pulling her toward a Good Humor wagon that was jingling at them through the waves of heat. Lorraine had to slap each square little face; she had to yell to be heard over the screams, over the relentless bells of the ice-cream man.

"Johnson wants to do time inside a baby and a television and a meatloaf jail now. The marriage jail. But just his time, and no more. You'll see." She screamed at the jumping children, "I said NO!" The Good Humor man waited patiently. "Didn't you see? At the demonstration it took four cops to haul him up and throw him in that paddy wagon. Didn't you see him loving every minute of it? Before, of course, you got the hell out of there with Clive."

The Good Humor man lighted a cigarette and listened and waited. Lorraine's children moaned, and hugged his wagon.

"Yes," said Saradove. "But I did not run off; I did not get the hell out. I had to get Clive out—he can't get arrested—jail would crucify him."

"Forget Clive. Just look at Johnson; just look at my husband. He was a draft dodger here . . ."

"A conscientious objector . . ."

". . . and now he's a draft dodger some place else. The only difference is my husband usually needs a fifth cop to carry his *guitar*. The cops have been very careful with that guitar over the years." Lorraine kicked at the children, who were trying to open her pocketbook. "You'll see! That will be Johnson for the rest of his life, one way or another; and you'll be like me—and just look at me!"

Saradove looked instead at the Good Humor man, catching him in the midst of his fantasy: he was sailing first class on a gigantic luxury ocean liner, and suddenly the ship was ramming into an iceberg. Some fool was yelling, "Women and children first!" and the ice-cream man, wearing his beautiful dinner jacket and smoking a thick cigar, was grabbing the **very** first lifeboat all for himself; and he was sailing off alone into the dark seas, with a picnic hamper of champagne and roast turkey, and he was clubbing all the women and children who were trying to climb in with him, sending them down to drown. He was drifting happily through the dark—no bells, no snotty kids, no bitching mothers; no goddamned ice cream.

Saradove opened her pocketbook and gave each of the children a dime.

"What in hell did you do that for?" Lorraine cried. "I never have money to give them, not with a shiftless draft-dodging husband; and now they'll want dimes all the time!" She dipped her fingers in her mouth and tried to bathe the lollipop smear from her legs. The children pushed the ice cream into their mouths. The Good Humor man pushed his wagon, off for the playground.

"I'm sorry." Saradove was swimming for the ice-cream man's lifeboat; her mermaid tail was swishing, and diamonds glittered in her hair, and he held his arms out, welcoming her aboard.

"I'm sorry too!" Lorraine pointed through the window of the bar where something like the reflection of a ghost bent over the wavering mahogany, bent and leaned and drank and let the street cast its heated, moving images over it. "Look," Lorraine said, "you can see him inside, acting like a goddamned cowboy, bragging about jail. Good-bye."

Inside the bar, it was dark; it was cool with an air that transposed itself into sounds of ice clinking against glass. Saradove is a wraith, she told herself, a wraith dressed in white and flowers, coming here to become real.

Johnson looked over his shoulder, made her materialize, and jerked his hips to the tables at the rear, leading the way, stomping the floor, jingling the boot buckles like spurs. She followed, past the thin, late-afternoon group of drinkers who were comfortably treating the bar like their own front parlors. Painters tired of painting drank; painters with their success behind them drank and talked. Some lady residents of the Village sat and sipped alone, propped up and dignified by hats and gloves and cocktail napkins; soon they would leave quarters on the bar and leave for supper in the drugstore.

They faced each other in a booth very deep and dark. It was like hibernating through summer, in a cave until winter, hibernating with someone who might or might not be another bear.

Johnson's bottom teeth let go of his mustache. "I'm glad, *violently* glad, you didn't get arrested at the demonstration," he said.

"I'm ashamed. I got caught up in the people running away. I meant to get to jail, but Clive dragged me off."

"You already told me that. I said I'm glad you didn't go. I don't want you in jail." It meant that he wanted her someplace, at least; but no one ever would let her share his jail. Johnson looked back into his marvelous past, grabbed his beer bottle by the neck and swigged to kill the pain.

"Clive grabbed you last night too."

"When?"

"You know, to get you out of Lorraine's party, away from me. I heard him say it, plain as day, in that prancy, phony voice of his, 'Oh, Johnson's just fine for her to have an affair with, but he'll want to catch her and marry her and get her all middle-class bohemian with diapers and babies and beer on the Lower East Side! Disaster for Saradarlingdove!' I heard him say it! Stupid pansy, and he's absolutely wrong. That's the thing about faggots, and that's Clive all over—they can't stand to have their special chicks, their *show* chicks, like

190

show niggers at an all-white party, get to be somebody's *real* chick. Hell with him." Johnson smiled hard at Saradove.

An affair with Johnson? Marry Johnson? Me, a chick? Saradove couldn't smile back.

"Am I a real . . . ?" she asked.

"Chick," Johnson finished. Saradove blushed; over what, she was not sure, and she drank her beer. It tasted, she imagined, of salvation. Any minute now, thought Saradove, Saradove might turn into a chick and walk like that in broad daylight, for anyone to see, down Eighth Street. She felt like calling her mother up.

Johnson shook his hips down, very easily, shimmying, until he sat on the base of his spine. He was like a grimy old two-by-four someone had tried to saw on and then had left propped in the booth. He kept his eyes on a patch of his belly that sprouted much black hair; then his shoulders moved, and his shirt slid up completely free from his Levis. Suddenly, his navel was showing. Saradove wondered when they would get married. His mustache shook, as though a breeze was getting in it.

"What?" she asked.

He scowled at his navel. "I said," he muttered angrily, "that I like what you said about the lantern being like the moon."

Saradove, confused by the navel, answered, "What? What lantern?" He seemed so angry that she could barely light her cigarette. The flame furled through their cave, like the coming of sunset to their cave.

Johnson jerked himself upright, hiding his belly. He stared hard into the palms of his folded hands, counting his calluses, figuring that another week and he would have as many as the print shop's foreman.

"The damned Japanese lantern hanging from Lorraine's

ceiling at the party last night," he shouted. "That's what!"

"The one you were dancing with Lorraine under, I know. And she was kissing you all over your prison pallor. I heard her doing it." Along with her beer, Saradove swallowed her guilt over the ice-cream dimes. But what if her children wanted more ice cream tomorrow? The answer was to love Lorraine. Johnson shouted some more.

"You were just sitting there on Clive's lap, like a scaredy-cat baby or something—what would you know? And *what* prison pallor? I was only in for a week!" Johnson rubbed his face. Only a week in jail—it wasn't much to show, and Joseph had a scar that anyone any time could look at. But, of course, Joseph hadn't gone in this time—getting yellow, probably.

"And you could hear her too; of course you could," said Saradove. "She was kissing you all over it. She kissed the others who got out too." Johnson studied the halftones in a sporting print on the wall. It was, he thought, a shit job.

In agony, he said, "Yeah. And I spent the night with her."

"That's all right," said Saradove. She considered smiling through the tears.

Johnson banged his fist on the table; their beer glasses touched and rang out. "No! It's not! You were so great, you don't know how great! Just getting up off Clive like that and walking right up to us and saying the lantern looked like a moon—and you were smiling through your tears! There's proof I'm a bastard! I take you to the party and then you were so great pointing to the lantern in front of Lorraine and then I have to go and sleep with her! A bastard!" Johnson straightened his shoulders and held his head high.

"It's all right," she said, wondering if Lorraine was great.

The waiter, a slim and lovely ex-Venetian, arrived and cocked his head at Johnson. He pointed to the glasses. He knew the English only for "beer" and "double Martini" and made a good living. Johnson counted out his last money. They sat, quiet, while the Venetian returned with two more wet bottles.

Saradove, she told herself, you are married to Johnson; you are buying stainless steel and eating off plates from potters' wheels, but you would just as soon eat off the sidewalk: Spode or nothing for old Saradove. Can you eat off Spode and still be a fearless demonstrator and learn to love your neighbor, even Lorraine; be peaceful and dedicated? Naturally, you are going to marry him; Clive held your hand in City Hall park and introduced you to him, nearly bowing, terribly formal, making a wedding of an introduction; and Clive's gold stickpin gleamed over the two of you, gleamed over the rear ends of paddy wagons jutting into the park, the demonstrators, the cops, everything impassive and yearning for action. Clive let his stickpin gleam over all and then he put your hand into Johnson's, and all your body, except for the hand that held Johnson's, shook all over; and Johnson was looking everywhere at everything but you. And the last warning siren whined and you ran, as trippingly as possible, as though you were playing scales with your feet, your hand again in Clive's, to safety from law and order.

From a window in the League of Liberators' offices, she had watched Johnson's humiliation. Below her, he was having to beg for arrest. He had fallen like a stone at the feet of the police; and, instead, they had taken a woman breast-feeding her baby; the police spat on him and chose anything but him. He had wandered, going limp before all the law he could find; and one time he had had to roll beneath a park bench to save himself from a falling fat man. Up above it all, Saradove watched it as though it were a moving, flickering film, like one she remembered, *Forbidden Games:* Parisians are fleeing

Paris; the Germans have entered the city. Over a country road, filled with hurrying refugees, German planes begin strafing. There is a woman out in the open because she is looking for her strayed child. She falls flat below the bullets coming from the sky; one enters her body, she shakes, and is instantly dead.

On City Hall park, nothing fell but sunshine and blue-bodied pigeons; Saradove heard no sounds that were not efficient: pacifists shouting last-minute instructions to each other, police bellowing through their horns, the wagons clanging as they pulled their loads away, one after another. But Johnson had stayed a very long time beneath his bench before they had taken him, seeming to give in to him, like a weary mother to a spoiled child. He must have seen something coming from the sky besides birds and sun; he had watched the sky too long, too hard to have seen nothing coming.

She had to gulp her beer to catch up with him. She watched him staring down into his empty bottle, seeing in the brown below a great vision of himself leading a great tradition of bastards, who were, after all, real men who had to have it. He was tearing the wet label from his bottle; and Saradove was seeing her own smile floating in her beer's foam, the smile on a girl who didn't show a single wiggle to real men, who ran around in little-girl dresses, holding hands with fags, making remarks to Japanese lanterns in order to trap a husband.

"I walked all night," Johnson mumbled.

"When?"

"After I left Lorraine. And I left her pretty fast. Thinking about what you said and looking at the real moon."

No, thought Saradove, there was no moon that night at all, just rain and clouds and smoky air. She felt adored. She had driven him to the streets to bay at a moon that wasn't there. And she had used the least of her weapons.

"You shouldn't walk around all night, ever! You could be mugged and killed." Genuine fear caught her, surprised her in her throat. She could see the assassin's knife flash through the moonlight that wasn't there, reaching for a heart that adored Saradove.

Johnson closed his eyes to show her nothing like that mattered; and to hide from the Venetian, who hovered.

"*How* fast did you leave Lorraine?" Just how fast is it done, she wondered; just how is it done, and how quickly?

Johnson slapped his palm against the wet table, treating it like a face wet with nagging tears. "That doesn't matter any more, not to me, not to you!" He turned sideways and challenged the Venetian with a look. The waiter lifted his eyebrows at someone else.

It matters to me, thought Saradove; just how fast; and how?

He was putting a small white box on the table between them. *Simon's 14th Street Jewelers* it said. Inside the box, she knew, Saradove was solved, her knotty self unraveled and coiled and tamed forever. Johnson looked up from the box, up at Saradove, lifting his smooth, thick eyebrows. Will his eyebrows, she wondered, be thick and bushy like Bertrand Russell's when he's an old man? Will the same sort of hair that grows on his belly grow from his nostrils?

"Open it!" Johnson cried, beaming at his solution to everything. She pulled at the lid of the box, watching him square his shoulders against the booth, seeing his head go clanging off like a wagon with a bell, ringing solutions to the whole city, seeing herself trapped in his joy, beneath him already, surrounded by his babies.

The pasteboard box split beneath her nails, and the two brass rings clattered to the table. She held his rings and opened his mind the way she had opened the box, split it like pasteboard, and saw exactly what he was making of her,

195

that she was an enchantress, a witch, wrapping him in virgin spells, making him wallow in her net, making a future for him safe from lonely bars and humiliating fucks with women too experienced for him. She watched him canceling out that other business, his notions of a couple of females: they read a lot of poetry together and occasionally sleep in long nightgowns in the same bed. Those girls he had seen her with were becoming, over the brass rings and the cold, beer-slopped table, simple figments of his imagination. Those girls! In his mind, she watched them become little old stories or something she'd made him dream about. He had trapped her; she could forget everything now. He took the rings up and slipped the smaller one on her finger. In his world, he murdered ceremonies; she would not nag for a wedding.

The brass cut into Saradove's finger, and she felt it. One day she had wrestled to pull the diamond ring from Olympia's finger, to put it on her own hand, one boring summer day. Exhausted from the heat and bother, Olympia had slapped her to make her stop. That diamond was her wedding ring; and Saradove had tried to kiss her on the mouth. There was no telling the real thing, the brass that weighed her hand down now or the diamond that sparkled, like a lake she longed to swim, on her mother's hand. For an instant, in one swift, cold image, she felt L.E.'s body; and Johnson's hand against her own went up like vapor against that memory. She pulled Johnson's hand to her mouth, and pushed L.E. back to her heart where she belonged. She touched Johnson's fingers with her tongue, and they were warm. What did it matter if she were only imagining them? If she called her mother, would she be home; and would it matter? She knew, suddenly, that mother, Johnson, L.E., all who had loved her, were reality and that Saradove was the only lie, the only fantasy; and she was trapped in the real, remaking it, every moment making it more real through the lie of herself.

"You're taking me to dinner too?" she asked, laughing. He would take what sat before him, Saradove, to dinner and fill her with reality.

They were going to step into the warm, glistening dark outside; the wolves were baying like revenge at her heels, calling the names of all who had loved her, and the curses they were sending her; and she hummed with happiness. Johnson and Saradove stepped into the street together and began to walk. At each step she counted, one by one, the people who had loved her. Father, mother, grandmother, lover, lover—and how many friends? She drank in, along with the sweet polluted air of the evening, their curses and felt strong. Ten thousand times ten thousand, a hymn began; the love cursing her from her cradle to the street where she walked with Johnson was as stiff with rules as a religion. It was a myth elaborate with generations of gods, ten thousand times ten thousand, approaching her with every night, their dark, imperative faces bending to her, impregnating her with demigods whom she aborted; setting her tasks that she slid from when their backs were turned; coming to her in furious dreams and leaving her to wake into fantasies they had devised to look like the real world.

Saradove looked up at Johnson's sleek nose, twitching slightly with every breath he took, and disliked it. The pressure of his hand made her shudder and seem to walk above the street. In a moment, in just a moment, she would go back into the god's make-believe of reality, would become sane, solid true; would again love Johnson.

Inside a drugstore window someone had propped a narrow mirror; and they began to approach it. The mirror was not

197

alone. It was surrounded by curly-tailed birds made of paper; purple, dinosaur-sized roses of tissue; orange and pink streamers of ribbon tied in bows. Its edges reflected the ornaments and paints of both beautiful and ugly women—white and gold boxes of powder, huge puffs of down that floated, could barely touch bottom; tiny, enameled cases of color that shaded indistinctly from one hue to another; little brushes, little tubes, little pencils, all poised and ready to leap on one great canvas of a face that would receive and blend them all with favor, and startle the beholder's eye into loathing nature and adoring art. But most of the mirror was empty. Saradove stopped and put herself in front of it and saw that it was placed so that its top caught a section of the evening's late, dark-blue sky. Saradove looked at herself suspended from heaven, legless; her hands, through the mirror's grace, were caressing and gathering the tubes and puffs and ribbons and paper beasts. She was royal and divine, with heaven on her head.

Johnson's hand pulled her away. The mirror rejected her. They hurried to Washington Square and then walked slowly, promenading in an old-fashioned way around the great circle of the fountain. They began a fourth circle but had to stop to kiss, to clasp each other, to pant into each other's mouths. The night was refusing darkness; drenched in royal blue, it stayed that way, spotted all over with stars. Saradove had emptied herself into the fountain until, at the first kiss, there was nothing left of Saradove for Johnson to kiss; there was nothing, in the dark, but a female body against a man's. Another kiss, and her eyes turned around, to see back through her mind, not thought, but another night of this identical color and identical sweetness; and herself and Olympia. In her bed, she was waking to find Olympia asleep beside her.

The moonlight was crashing through the windows and making a precious thing there, a skating pond, something she had never seen before, across her floor. A genuine winter lay on her bedroom floor, and Olympia had run, this one and only night, from Duncan's drunkenness, to sleep beside her. She was here, pressed against Johnson, feeling him hard as rock, seeing him monstrous against the light sky; she was there, slithering from her bed, careful to leave Olympia sleeping. She was dancing and leaping across the skating pond, slipping, describing a figure eight, clasping her hands behind her back and twirling. Ecstatic with the color of the night, she went back to bed, trembling, sweating; and heard Olympia's eyes closing.

Johnson turned her to him. Olympia's open eyes were watching her from the bed. Johnson whispered in her ear. Saradove began to laugh, to chatter, imitating girlish ways, and broke from him to run in circles. She came back, ready to fall into his arms, and he was gone. Before her teeth could chatter, he had returned, pacing in the path of a huge tree's shadow. Above his head, he bore a wreath of dead flowers. Florist's wires stuck from it like nails, and a rain-faded ribbon fluttered against his face. She waited, her head and shoulders bent for him. Without gentleness, efficiently, Johnson forced the wreath over her head, pushed it to her shoulders. The wires scratched her cheek, and she hoped for blood.

Johnson stepped back, his head cocked, smiling in the starlight, his face clear as day. "Smile and look proud," he said. "Garibaldi won't mind. With all those pigeons on his head, with all the shit on his face, he doesn't need anniversary wreaths to keep him company. Look at his statue, Saradove! He was a good wop; he'd love for the bride to have flowers. Especially since she won't get her pasta tonight!"

Saradove lifted her face from the stench of the dead flowers and looked up at the lighted, laughing man. "You're not going to give me dinner?"

His voice was slow and coarse. "You don't really want dinner."

They began leaving the square, clamped together by their arms; but when they were inside the deep shadow of the huge arch, she made him stop. The square lay before them, as brilliant beyond their darkness as a rollicking music hall. And her animals were there in that light, as poised, as deeply etched into the blaze as friezes on a temple wall. Saradove raised her hand, beckoning for them to begin their chase, but they only watched her, unmoving as stone, still as painted marble. Saradove let go of Johnson, raised both hands to them. But the Tiger, the swiftest, who could follow Saradove like an arrow, would not turn from her own reflection that she watched in the glass ball at her feet. She nuzzled the ball, licked at her own distorted face that she thought was her cub. She would not look up and see her true child being stolen away under the arm of the hunter.

The Wolf stared at her, with eyes brighter, more lurid than the stars. Saradove thought she was calling to him, Come and eat me up! But he would not move, and Johnson, hearing nothing, stroked her hair; and it was like an aphrodisiac to him. It was like wolf's hair. Johnson was trying to pull her home, but she pulled back to the beasts, desperate to try some more. Her fingers rattled against the bare, hard blue moonlight. The Lions, the curly-maned and the straight-maned, would not hear. Both seemed to sleep, their heads upon their paws; but the hearts of both beat with courage that was awake, that ignored Saradove. When they awoke and began a hunt, it would not be for Saradove. They waited for a girl they could catch, devour, save. She called to the Fox, who must never leave her, not until she was dead and carried off to hell. But the Fox lay alone beneath the darkest tree, and the moon shone on fur that was caked and covered with red mud. The Fox lay on his back, played dead, waited for a worthy victim.

Not a growl or a footpad came to her. Even the summer birds had closed their throats, waiting for a new sunrise to sing. Saradove had been too crafty, too hard to catch; but a man had caught her and she was no longer fit for the beasts.

Saradove caught her breath and went on with what she had left, with him. He pulled her, running, behind him. When she made him stop again, it was to beg him never to leave her, in a voice that begged him to let her go. But Johnson ran on, did not hear, laughed; the smell of her hair was in his nostrils.

Frédéric Chopin

On their backs, they watched the glow from the street lamp enter the room and turn it hotter. She listened, on her back, to the breaths she took rattle like ice down her throat. She read Johnson's wonder through his sweating skin: is she a woman now or just another girl still, pretending womanhood, pretending delight in him, Johnson the magician? She felt dissatisfaction join with the room's heat and enter him like a pain.

I know, thought Saradove, I've taken another one, a new kind. She touched her own skin, to feel its heat; but the ice had melted through her throat and turned her body cold as painted marble statues. Johnson, in an effort toward tenderness, began to rub her belly and cool his palm.

"It's never any good the first time," he said. He had planned what he would say.

"For you?" she said to the ceiling.

"No." Impatiently, meanly, he pinched her. "For girls; for *you*."

Now that there are no paths left for me to run down, she decided, I will stay here. And she turned again to him. Johnson took her. He swelled with pride, leaving desire far behind. He held her down beneath him, making a duty of her salvation in the arms of a good, kind man. She felt him grow into a good, kind man; she felt desire leave him, and she had him.

Outside, the street was covering itself in snow. At the window, Saradove watched the tenement doors open like sores for the tenants to dribble out, stagger through the slush for a piece of meat, some sugar, some smelly Puerto Rican fish. She sat still, stroking the bulge in her belly where the baby lived, to keep from stroking the head lying below the baby in her lap. Her boredom was immense. She was captured in a cold room, stilled by a baby, pinned beneath a head that did not move her heart.

In a corner of the room, they had cleared and swept a place for a Christmas tree. They were waiting for a friend to come with his car to take them to the woods to cut it down. From the corner of her eye, Saradove could see three Hassidic Jewish boys, their heads and forelocks bent to the street, march past in a tight row. The boys looked at nothing but their own feet; only their huge, oversized overcoats seemed to move, propelling them after their father, who strode, black-hatted, black-bearded, ahead, watching only the spaces in front of him. The boys' overcoats would have fit their father; but the father's coat fitted him neatly as a uniform.

The pregnant maiden, thought Saradove, remembering the Saradove who had sat in Johnson's hot kitchen, trapping him. Johnson the unicorn, who put his head in her lap, waited for his chain of flowers. The trouble with life, she thought, is that it moves. The maiden's perfect moment, trapping the fabulous beast, is over the instant its head lies in her skirt. Pinned beneath the head, she is no longer the maiden; and the beast has trapped her.

Today, she must gather Christmas trees, not chains of flowers. Johnson held and squeezed her legs.

"I don't know how to say this," he said.

"Try," said Saradove, and said it for him. "You want to leave me, don't you?"

"Yes," he said, squeezing his eyes together to keep out the sight of her. Saradove stroked his head then, to thank him. It was over, she was complete; and now it could all disappear, and it all did. She concentrated on the vacancy spreading over her, and she shared it with Johnson, to comfort him. It was the vacancy that belonged to a house, abandoned, rejected by its tenants. The vacancy felt like luxury; she was wrapped in it, the only one home.

Until she heard Duncan turn their car into another street, she sat as paralyzed into place as the furniture around her, as though she meant to gather dust, like the furniture around her. When there was not a sound from the streets, she turned off all the lights but one—just enough to keep the winter dark away—and squatted on her heels in his chair, fitting her own head into the grease spot his head had made. When she had completely replaced him, she got up and struck one note from the piano. The tone was like the noise of a brass band beneath her finger. She lifted her hand quickly. If she were careless, the sound would travel through the walls, across the row of green bushes and into the neighbors' ears, like an alarm. She ran the same finger down the rough green surface of the hymnal, propped open eternally on the music rack. Secretly, and by heart, she knew all the tunes and words to the hymns. If she wanted to, she could sit down now, pound them out, sing them, stretching her lungs to their fullest with their messages of lambs and heaven and hell and ghosts. She opened the book, crinkled and bent the slippery pages in her haste to find "There Is a Fountain Filled with Blood." She played it through, her fingers barely striking the cold keys. She whispered the words and ignored all of them except for those that meant, over and over, there is a fountain filled with blood. Redeemers were not her meat. "Flows from the Redeemer's side" was a lie. The fountains filled with blood were not the Redeemer's; they were Saradove's and Olympia's.

The small lamp on the marble-top table cut through more and more of the hasty darkness. Outside there was winter afternoon, a cold pretension of daylight; but in the cramped, overfilled living room, it could have been midnight and Sara-dove herself, the witching hour. She slid her thumbnail down the keyboard, feeling it click; then folded her hands and watched the music. Only the year before, she remembered, she had spent nearly all her time dreaming herself into the body of Frédéric Chopin. She had curved her shoulders forward to remind herself of his enchanting consumption; she had pretended to hack blood all over the ivories. Through the summer, she had demanded rain from the hymnal's Lamb of God so that she could play "The Raindrop Prelude" and cough and long for the sound of the carriage that would bring George Sand home to her. She had read all the Chopin storybooks she could find. Saradove giggled; she slapped the hymnal shut. Her stomach sank with a load of remembered embarrassment: the nonsense of pretending to be Chopin! Being Chopin had landed her in a ruffled dress beating out "In a Faery's Garden" in the church parlor, a big girl with something like breasts and shaved armpits playing a baby piece and bringing shame down on her head. She hadn't had to play first, with the first-grade babies—it was not that bad—but a girl five years younger had played last, played genuine music, something hard and loud by Anna Magdalena Bach, and had sent the audience home full of sweet dispositions and chitchat about the genius in their own town.

Saradove slammed the piano lid shut, tight on top of the Faery's Garden, on top of Anna Magdalena Bach; she went behind the fireplace fan and got out her stale and hidden pack of cigarettes. She lay on the couch and smoked and considered the horror of being sixteen, and the horror of being sixteen and becoming the duplicate of Olympia. She saw it all going on forever: both of them batting around a mean, contrary man who gave the mockingbirds that sang in the front yard names like Pete and Sam and got mad as hell when the two bleeding fountains in his house didn't go out on the front porch and listen to them, Pete and Sam, with him. She flicked ashes behind the couch. It was clear that there had never been any real hope of slicing off Olympia's breasts that grew bigger each passing year on her own chest, or of healing the wound inside her that made blood spout every month, that made her helpless in the company of the boys in geometry class. She had planned other ways, but the great leap from "In a Faery's Garden" to performing something hard and long in New York City was possible only in her head before she went to sleep at night; and the visiting art teacher had got rich from her paintings of flattened-out persimmons, vicious-looking irises, before he had packed up and left town.

Saradove rubbed the cigarette out on the sole of her shoe, shoved the butt behind a cushion. She began counting the folds in the organdy curtains, then went back and counted all the shadows between the folds. What am I going to be? What is me? she had nagged at her mother when the art lessons were over. Olympia had smiled, her face beaming in a rare expression of security. "Why just like me!" she had answered. "You'll be a mother and look just like me; that's why you don't need no art lessons, just to be like me."

Between the mattress and the springs of her bed lay the George Sand outfit, untouched for a whole year, and imprinted with all the little squares and circles that had come from the pressure of Saradove's sleep. When she had the clothes on, she broke into a sweat of fear—but it was not the car coming home, only the roar of the hall heater starting up. She watched herself through the long mirror on her door, imagining that the Levis from Sears Roebuck were black velvet pants, loose in the crotch, skintight in the legs. Duncan's white shirt that scratched her neck was really silk, the color of eggshell, and Byronic. She tied a pink sash beneath the collar and it became a black scarf knotted to flow freely. She pushed her hair behind her ears and pulled up her long white socks to make riding boots. She clenched a cigarette between her teeth and spoke to the mirror.

"Stop sniveling, Freedrik. Get up off your knees before I slap you one! You knew I would come home, sooner or later, and now . . . ah! You force me to! Slap-slap. Ah no! Poor *mon enfant!* Ah no, never . . . nevair!" Saradove held an imaginary head cupped in her hands. Chopin knelt before her, his tears beating like raindrops down her own cheeks.

"Listen to you, just listen to you, *mon* Freedrik!" Saradove snorted from the cigarette smoke. "You sit up all night in the drafty ballroom at the piano, and it's me that's got to break my neck nursing you." Saradove dropped Chopin's head and stepped through the consumptive lungs, closer to the mirror. She squeezed tears from her own eyes. I sound just like her, she thought. Mama says, All right for you, Saradove Racepath, it's not you that's got to sit up all night trying to get you on your feet again after you run around without a coat or sit up all night long straining your eyes in a cold house. It's not you, it's me! Now listen to me, it's me driving Chopin crazy, just like her!

Saradove dropped to her knees and put her arms around Chopin.

"Oh, listen, listen, *mon cher!* Did you really write that beautiful music just for me, because you were sitting here so agonized about me getting home last night? Oh, *mon cher, mon cher*, I love you so much and am so grateful, you wonderful genius Freedrik! Come on in here to the ballroom and play it again for me. I can't get enough of it!"

Saradove sat blindly back down at the piano and started pounding through the music. She longed to shut her eyes and rear her head back the way José Iturbi did it in the movies, but it was hard enough getting the notes right with her eyes open. But just the same, wrong notes and all, a summer sun was rising inside her; and George Sand's arm was around her shoulder (thin, bony shoulder); and George Sand was whispering, through the dreadful coughing, Oh, you're so wonderful, you're so special, unlike other girls! I could just eat you up! Oh, I'm taking you this very minute to a place fit for you, away from here where nobody appreciates how different, how wonderful you are! My big car, my enormous car, is going to drive right up to the front door for you,

it and jam Mrs. Bagley's face into the pine cones, scratch out her eyes, stick pine straw up her nose.

"Huh?" said Mrs. Bagley. "You still playing dress-up at your age?" She followed Madeline inside. Mrs. Bagley was square and tall, the shape of a fat, blown-up car if it were stood up on its rear wheels.

"You want to come in, sit down? They ought to be back any minute." But Mrs. Bagley had already sat down, on the couch, next to Madeline. And Madeline had already found the cigarette butt. She was holding it up in her fingers, looking hard from it to Saradove, acting like she'd just found a dollar in the street. Madeline stood and started wandering around the furniture, the cigarette butt an inch from her nose.

"I'm only going to stay a minute. You must be hot with that housecoat on, on top of all that." Mrs. Bagley giggled. Saradove, laughing heartily, rolled her eyes at the two naked maidens above the mantel. Who would save her now? She yanked at the pink sash, nearly choked pulling it off.

"If you don't sit down this minute, Madeline Bagley, I'm going to have a fit. You sit down, Saradove, then maybe she will." Madeline put the butt in her pocket and sat. Saradove fell into Duncan's chair.

Sitting, Mrs. Bagley was all mashed together in the white uniform she wore to work in at the Sweet Time Bakery. Next to her, Madeline was not her mother's daughter, was thin and undersized, would not eat, had long strong fingers that were beyond her age, that played Anna Magdalena Bach. Madeline began kicking the coffee table leg in time to "Alexander's Ragtime Band"; and she sang it, loudly.

"What?" Saradove yelled. "I can't hear you."

"I said," said Mrs. Bagley, "that your mama is a good woman."

"Why? I mean . . . what?"

Mrs. Bagley's face, concerned, was like pinched, fluted pastry crust. It meant, A good daughter of a good woman wouldn't have asked, What? Mrs. Bagley rolled to one side of her uniform, pulled out a Lucky Strike and lighted it. Saradove gasped, trying to suck in some of the smoke from across the room.

"Well, Saradove, who else would've come in and waxed my kitchen floor after they had to take poor Desmond away? And bring a chocolate layer cake with her? That's why I'm here. Madeline Bagley, where's the cake plate?"

"Come on and hear!" *Thump, thump.* "Come on and hear!" *Thump, thump!* Madeline kept on shouting and thumping with her foot. "Oh. What, Mama? Oh. Don't cry, Mama." Madeline said it twice, quickly, automatically, the way she said her prayer every night.

Mrs. Bagley swung her arm and cuffed her on the shoulder.

"That's all over now, Madeline," she said. "When are you going to learn some sense? I'm not crying any more. I said, where's the cake plate? That's what we're here for."

Madeline shook her head; the permanent frizz stayed perfectly still.

"I don't know," she said. "I left it on the front porch when I had to go back to the bathroom."

Mrs. Bagley closed her eyes tight and smoked. "You don't know about trials yet, Saradove," she said, "but the Lord Jesus Christ willing, some day you will."

Madeline said, "Don't cry, Mama!"

Mrs. Bagley hit her on the shoulder again.

"Then go and get it!" she yelled.

Madeline ran out, banging the door behind her; and the room did not give off the slightest quiver. Saradove felt the sweat soak deeper through her father's shirt. She started pulling the housecoat off, but remembered the front zipper of the Levis just in time. She gritted her teeth.

"How's Mr. Bagley, Mrs. Bagley?" Just as the room had been filling up with the beautiful smell of Lucky Strike, Madeline had had to open the door and let it out. Mrs. Bagley snuffed out her cigarette and buried her face in one especially clean hand.

"No change, no change, and there never will be. He just sits there all the time and laughs. He don't take no notice of anything, didn't your mama tell you? And after we make that long trip to Raleigh every Sunday after Sunday school, he just sits there and laughs at us. We can't even stay for church any more, because we got that long trip ahead of us just to sit there and see Desmond laugh at us!" Mrs. Bagley lifted her face and sighed in the direction of her own house.

Saradove felt like crossing herself, the way she did so freely and frequently in front of the sisters at the Catholic school. "Well, I'm glad he's so happy, even if you do have to go to Raleigh all the time. I was always crazy about the way Mr. Bagley laughed!"

Mrs. Bagley came up out of her sigh. "That's not happy by a long shot, Saradove," she said sharply. "You ought to know what's happy and what's not by this time, and I've known you since you were a baby. You ought to hear about some of the things poor Desmond does when he's not laughing! What the doctor tells me about, to my shame! Then you wouldn't think he was so happy!"

Saradove forgot the pack of Luckies. "What?" she asked quickly. "What things does he do?"

"Oh, now, well." Mrs. Bagley took out another Lucky. "I can't think why I'm sitting here jawing on when I've got enough work for a mule over there." She smiled and blew smoke through her nose, like a dragon. "A little bird's going

213

around telling about how New Oriental isn't good enough for you, how you're going to go *North* any old time, New York City, and break your mama and daddy's heart. It's not for me to say, I know your mama's said it enough times already til she's blue in the face, but you don't appreciate what a good mama and daddy are until they're dead and laid out in their coffins. Then you know, but then it's too late. Besides, you don't have to leave town. Let me tell you, just look at me, it don't take being beautiful to get married. You don't have to worry about that in the long run. There's other things."

Saradove fixed an idiot grin on her face and thought about sticking lighted Lucky Strikes up Mrs. Bagley's nose, then setting the rest of the pack on fire and shoving it up between her fat legs.

"I'm not going to get married. Besides, I have to go to college before going North."

Mrs. Bagley smoked and smiled, knowing better. Her answer came out in a long stream of smoke. "Well, I wouldn't know about all that. Jones Business College was good enough for me, and I'd like to see Madeline Bagley in some nice-looking insurance office or something before she settles down like I did."

Saradove felt herself turning into a lunatic from the heat of all her clothing: God's punishment for pretending to be George Sand or Chopin, one.

Mrs. Bagley went and opened the door, letting in the cool November air. The skirt of her uniform, because she wasn't wearing any underpants, got stuck in the cleft of her buttocks. She called, "Hoo hoo, Madeline! Hoo hoo!" and pulled gently at her skirt, trying to release it without notice. Madeline didn't answer, and the skirt did not free itself. Mrs. Bagley looked hard up at the pine tree and used two fingers, before Saradove's eyes, to reach in and yank the skirt free. Saradove grew hotter, from shame, from her layers of clothes, from sheer wonder at the ways of women when they are alone with other women; and she asked the Lamb of God to hurry her mother home. It was exactly the sort of thing grown women were always doing in front of one another, and laughing about it. If Olympia were here, she and Mrs. Bagley would be laughing about it.

Saradove wrapped the housecoat tighter. Give me Desmond any day! He's the only person in this whole town I'll send a postcard to when I get *North*, to New York City.

"Madeline!" Mrs. Bagley shouted across the yard. "You answer me this minute!"

I have adored Desmond since that August Sunday, last year, when it was so bad the heat swirled in and out of your brain, and you couldn't move because your brain was sweating too hard to let you. Desmond came strolling out of his house, his hands in his pockets, just his undershirt on, and smiling, to watch his wife and daughter come home from church. Madeline was rummaging in the back seat of the car, Mrs. Bagley in the front, getting out their gloves and pocketbooks and Sunday-school lessons. They had already set the big bag of two dozen cream puffs they always picked up at the bakery after church, on the steps, up there with Desmond. The altar flowers that were going to Mrs. Bagley's daddy's grave that afternoon leaned against the bag. Desmond, still smiling at them, sat down on the steps and let his left leg crush all the baby's breath; and he opened the bag, delicately picking it open, smiling down inside it. I wondered how he could stand eating on a day like that. But Desmond couldn't eat. He opened the bag wide, stood up, unzipped his fly, and pissed lengthily and with perfect aim straight into the cream puffs. They caught him before he could run around the house. He was too little to be a match for his big, puffed wife and his strong-fingered daughter. They got him inside through the kitchen door, but it was all day before anybody got back outside to move the bag and wash the steps. The flowers were all wilted by that time.

I told my mother about it, but she said I must have dreamed it all and for Lord's sake, don't talk like that on Sunday. That night, I did dream about Desmond running around and around his house, stuffing himself all the while with disgusting cream puffs; and waving to me every time he circled the front. It must have been a nightmare, I think.

"Here comes Madeline now," said Mrs. Bagley. "What I meant about Desmond is you'll have to get your mama to tell you after you're a grown married woman."

Saradove stood up to see Madeline shoot into the front yard with the cake plate. Zaaaap! whispered Saradove. I have paralyzed you with my ray gun, Madeline Bagley, so you can't run another inch until she tells me what it is about Desmond.

"I know the nurses are Christian women with crosses to bear just like me, but I wear my skirts longer. And there are some things I could tell you about the colored boys, the help, up there and poor Desmond that I didn't even *know* about ahead of time!"

Madeline rushed up the front steps.

"I could tell you too!" she said breathlessly. "Don't cry, Mama. Here's the cake plate."

"Here's the cake plate, Saradove; I can't wait any longer. Tell your mama I said thank you. I could just hit you, Madeline Bagley, for the things you say!"

Saradove held the big green plate up in front of her face and watched them leave her yard, Madeline sailing and leaping, Mrs. Bagley rocking her flesh apart with every step.

Through a glass, darkly, said Saradove's mouth against the

plate. Through a glass, greenly, Saradove rolled through the town, beyond big and little Bagley, losing one relative after another, shaking the rest off her ankles; prizing one friend only at a time, shaking the rest off her ankles. She marched, ten years old, in the Confederacy Day Parade, wearing a skimpy girl-scout uniform, enclosed by withered, tattered, tatty old ladies uniformed in purple and hats, all of them behind the Mayor, who rode like a beauty queen on the back of a convertible. She sneaked, at twelve years old, the dirtiest book she could find in the library to a friend waiting beneath the library window: "Oh honey," the book panted, "Doris panted, do it, do it, DO IT, go on do it hard, and they wallowed in her black lace underwear, he tearing and biting, she sucking on his tongue, twirling her thighs, First, you bitch, he said, when he had her where he wanted her, Why did you go with Jimmy last night? Oh, honey, Doris moaned," the book moaned. Saradove posed, seven years old, on the front porch across the street, on Desmond's porch, with five other little girls (no boys born on that street since the Depression, the funniest thing), all in pink or blue or white, skirts stuck out with starch; the sun, the world, the termites beneath the house, all pausing dead still to hear the happy birthday song from five little girls' mouths, all waiting for little Madeline Bagley to blow out her candles. And the six mamas, round in the hips, round in the chest, round in the arms that crossed and hugged the chests, stood in the yard, frowning or smiling at it all— don't pick your nose, stop holding yourself, do you have to go to the bathroom? Don't Madeline look pretty (wobbly, bald Madeline), just like a little girl—the strong odor of mothers rising up in a mushroom cloud above their daughters' world, stinking, or sweeter than roses, one; the smell each little girl learned and nestled to. The mamas, they didn't want to do a single thing but get on home after the cake and ice cream and

217

shell them butter beans, set the food on the table and eat last of all, with the sun falling down behind the back porch; and get to bed, last of all, after the socks were washed out, the shoes polished, his shirt ironed and hung on the icebox handle. They didn't want to do a single thing but get up mornings in their torn nightgowns and love their little girls: You'll be just like me, you'll see, you're mine, aren't you? And the mamas, they didn't want to do a single thing but wait, wait all day, running the washing machine, sweeping the porch, digging around the rosebushes, tying up the broken branches that someone coming home had crushed down. And: Let's go down street on the bus and see about new patent leathers for you; let's dig up those bushes before they choke up the bathroom plumbing; let's hear you say yes ma'am and no ma'am, and get your feet off that coffee table. . . . One day, a week before the bleeding started, Saradove got up with the sun and took over the house, moving a broom over rugs, under rugs, squeezing Duncan's undershirt, oil-soaked, against the carved legs of all the tables, getting wild-eyed at the sight of dust-curls in organdy ruffles, throwing Old Dutch with a free hand into the sinks. She'd never lifted a hand before, content to give a puff of her breath to the piano lid before she opened it, enjoying the feel of toast crumbs beneath her bare feet on the kitchen floor. Olympia watched her that day, moving silently from room to room, always one room ahead of Saradove's frantic cleaning, sucking on a fingernail, chewing the skin around her thumbs, waiting to see the end. Even then she did not tell her why. It was hard to wait, to suffer for poor Saradove. It was so hard to be a mother and be shy about things. It turned a mother gray; the poor little thing.

Saradove lowered the green plate. Big Bagley and little Bagley were holding hands at the street's edge, trying to decide if anything was coming. All of a sudden, something was coming! A green Ford, the Racepath Ford! Saradove saw it, spinning slowly down the hill, traveling a curving line; and at the wheel, there was Olympia, deliberately twisting the steering wheel extreme right, then extreme left. Two dogs chased the crazy car, barking with delight: this time they'd get it! Mrs. Bagley ran too, and chased it. She was a big ball bouncing. She hit the pavement and went back up, straight for heaven. By the time she got hold of the Ford's door handle, Olympia had already braked in Desmond's front yard. Desmond's azalea bush was directly beneath the right rear wheel, as though he had planted it, planned it that way.

Saradove stood stock-still and raised the green glass to quiver before her face again. Through the blackened screen door, through the glass, the entire scene across the street convulsed into a jumble of fat fishes and thin fishes, swimming and playing it all out beneath something like green swimming-pool water. And Saradove was catching them all with a net, a green glass net woven into a pattern of roses.

She slid the glass plate behind her into Duncan's chair and went out on the porch. The car had not moved from Desmond's azalea bush; the flowers that bloomed in its spring were over for good. Mrs. Bagley was leaning through one car window; Madeline through another. Olympia was going home, crossing the street with her shoulders thrown back as stiff as broom handles, looking thin. In one hand, she carried a box of face powder; in the other, a lipstick.

"Sit down there on that doorstep, Saradove," she said. "I know this is going to hit you like a thunderbolt, but you got to take the bitter with the sweet. Just a minute." With enormous care, as though she were lifting a newborn, she opened the powder and lipstick and began to make herself up, copying, so it seemed in the white winter light, some memory she had of the face of Gloria Swanson. Saradove could not look at her. Something remained in the front seat of the Ford, something she hadn't seen yet, not through the green glass, not through her own wide eyes. The Bagleys were looking at it; and Duncan was not here at home with them. Was this the way she planned to go on shelling butter beans and worrying about the porch light attracting bugs in summer? Like this? Looking like Gloria Swanson?

"That's better," Olympia said to her little mirror; and she snapped her powder box shut. She sat, grasped her knees, and began rocking back and forth on her spine like a little girl sitting there on the step. She tilted her long nose up, she held her mouth down in a smile. "How do I look?"

Saradove looked. "Like Gloria Swanson," she answered. It was almost true. There were old movie magazine photographs of Gloria Swanson pasted into a dime-store scrapbook that Olympia kept on her bedside table, along with the Bible.

"About time." Olympia took a deep breath and stretched her arms, as though she were relishing the cold weather. "That's all right for you, missy. Right after we left the hospital, he pulled over and said, you take the wheel, and so I started driving, and then before you could say Jack Rabbit, he just keeled over in the seat and dropped dead. And that's the way I got him home, dead. There's a lot to be said for me, Saradove."

Olympia rocked; the Bagleys went in their house to telephone. Saradove closed her eyes and touched their lids with her fingers; the lids were hot and dry and sore; beneath them, the eyes fluttered sightless, but wild, and made her finger tips tremble. She said, "Oh Mama, it'll be no time before I go away North!"

Olympia rocked and rocked, her spine creaking like an old door in a draft. Death crawled through the brown November yard, through the sky pumping out little gray clouds, into the body where the organs were straining to grow up, to grow old, before death could get at them, could make them shudder to a stop. Saradove watched her own hands rise with purple veins, grow chalky and dry in the skin. Her hair began to crinkle and gray against her skull; her heart faltered, needed medicine; her legs trembled, needing wheelchairs.

Olympia stood up, smoothing her legs, straightening her stockings.

"Are the seams correct, Saradove? Listen to me, are the seams correct?" Her voice was the soft, romantic whisper that swept from a thousand movie screens, a whisper that thousands could sit and hear and sigh to; could take for their very own.

Saradove's voice, cracked with old age, asked, "What are you going to do with him? You can't leave him over there. . . ." She shrieked, "Desmond might come home!"

Some neighbor women started coming from their houses, their arms crossed over their breasts. Already, one of them carried a covered dish. They were all going straight for the Bagleys', without a look at the silent Ford. Their side glances saw what was happening across the street. When would the ambulance come?

Saradove stood beside her mother; and her hand reached for an invisible, not-born baby's hand, and her eyes hunted for lost toys and socks, and she wondered with her whole mind where the money for a baby's new shoes would come from.

"Things get taken care of," said Olympia. "That's one thing I've learned in this vale of woe. Your fancy notions you can just take with you to that biggity old North you want so much, but I'll see you off at the train if I have the time. You take your part of the insurance money and go on off to school if that's what you want so much; and I'll take my part and go I don't know where. Now it don't matter, not a speck, about big sister Lady and all her big house and rich husband and those girls of hers with natural curly hair. A thing or two. We'll show her a thing or two. Sit up straight now, Saradove, and try to see without your glasses. You can if you try. This is the last time I'm telling you. The very last time. Now, are my seams correct?"

The ambulance came clanging down the street, in a big hurry over nothing. Madeline Bagley stood in the middle of the street waving her arms at it. Then she sat up on the Ford's back fender and sucked at a Coca-Cola. She rolled her eyes at the two very black boys who jumped out with a stretcher and started wrestling with something in the front seat of the Ford. One boy rolled his eyes back at Madeline; then he had Duncan by the arms.

Duncan seemed to sag with an awful weight beneath his drape of white tablecloth. Two polished brown shoes, two navy blue socks stuck out from beneath the white sheet—it was not, at second glance, a tablecloth. Who in the world would set an old felt hat in the center of a white *tablecloth?* Working as neatly as two mules, the black boys got him in the ambulance, and, without looking back at anyone or anything, or at each other, they sprinted into the front seats and clanged away, in a big hurry over nothing.

Olympia stood on her porch and watched them go. Her arms, for the first time, stretched out in a gesture which she, like all mothers, could use to welcome onto her body a child running. The child was not there, but Olympia held out her arms for it, and looked for it, across her yard, across her street, across and into her past where, at that very moment, the poor orphan child from the County Home was being revealed to the world as a changeling princess. Her white face glistened above her pink dress and sweater and turned her into some big rose caught by the early frost.

In easy, straggling lines, the neighbor women began to

come into the yard carrying the suppers meant for their own families. They went straight for Olympia's wide-open arms, saluting death with well-cooked food.

Hunched inside herself like a jackknife, Saradove sat on her bottom step and spoke to a stray worm that coiled out of the harsh-colored winter grass and around her shoe. You brute, I am the wicked fairy—brute, brute! I was the uninvited guest at her wedding. Her long sleep, her wrong life is all my fault. Where can I find her again and start all over? Where can I be good?

north

The doorbell whistled; it was broken and would not ring. Johnson got off his knees and began smoothing his shirt tail into his pants with long, caressing motions.

"I should have waited," he said. "I should have waited until we had the Christmas tree and all, until we had . . ." He looked at her belly.

"Oh, no," said Saradove. "You shouldn't have waited; there's nothing to wait for, and you're not cut out for it, are you?" The baby inside her was much too young to move: what was there to wait for?

"That's it! That's it!" said Johnson, breaking into gigantic relief and smiles. "You have it right on the nose. You have always had me so *exactly*, the right word for me!"

Saradove smiled back at him. "That's the trouble," she said.

"What?"

"The trouble is having had you so exactly. Go on and have yourself now."

Johnson took long, masculine strides to the door; strides so long, so masculine, that they nearly toppled him over on his face. At last he was free of women, could live like a man. He opened the door, presenting his face to his friend, his back to Saradove.

Saradove considered her open, empty hands with disgust. It is typical, she thought, that my fingers, at this perfect moment, do not clutch a long and daggery knife. With my knife, with the perfect aim that the gods would send me, I could have him sagging into the arms of his friend, the knife quivering between his shoulder blades.

Johnson, still alive, clasped his friend by the shoulders with a richness of loving feeling that could never have passed from man to woman, from Johnson to Saradove. They smiled at each other, declaring the masculine secret society of love.

Saradove sat and stretched out her fingers to grasp the invisible edge of an invisible white tablecloth. After I've thrown the knife, she thought, I will snap the tablecloth over their heads, their dying heads, and eat my meal off their covered bodies. The Jewish boys will run in from the streets, drop the cold delicatessen at my feet, and run out again into the snow. I will lay the curiously lumped tablecloth with my best silver and eat what the neighbors bring me.

She smiled up at Johnson's friend. "Will you come in and sit with me? Or . . . shall we go?"

"I brought you a letter," said the friend. His breath continued puffing frost even inside the apartment. It was cold, but the friend was colder, seemed frozen beyond any work of the weather. His eyes, close up, were clouded with something, perhaps frost, like his breath. Even his overcoat radiated cold. His hair was too young to be white, but it was silver; it curled around his pointed ears like a pair of hands cupping the ears to overhear every whisper in the world. His nose was always waiting to smell something else. He delivered the letter.

"Full of life, Saradove?" His fingernails were too long and clawed the ridges of her corduroy dress as he felt her belly. Johnson laughed, made them laugh with him, to show they loved him. He started for the kitchen, at each step pausing for his friend to follow, pausing for a friend to go with him, not a wife.

"A beer?" Johnson called to him. "A beer? Let's us have a beer while she reads. Come on!" In his jingling boots, Johnson stomped; but his friend, even though he seemed to glide, even though his feet seemed not to touch the floor, made a louder noise across the uneven boards. Each of his footsteps was a crash, something trying to tear their house down. They went away and left her to read. Saradove shivered in the poor, unheated apartment; and the walls chattered with the running feet of rats. She wondered why the pink envelope resisted being opened; but she did not bother to wonder why Johnson's friend made the room seem colder with his presence, or where he had come from, or why he was a friend. He was simply, she decided, the freezing North; and there was nothing dangerous about cold. She read the pink page that came from the pink envelope.

Hi Hon! This will tell you what's what (and show you, see enclosed snap) in sunny Fla. House sold at last to New Oriental dealer and am really ready to get around to enjoying myself down here where it's warm and *full of life*, really!

226

(See enclosed snap.) Now you're married and all (just don't let me hear tell of you making me a grandma too soon). Too young (me) and if I've learned one thing in this vale of woe save time to enjoy yourself while you're young. Can't do that with younguns, you know, no offense intended. Why don't you and John come on down here where it's *warm* and see me, maybe next year or so. Brrrr! Couldn't stand it up North. Must be awful, would be death of me! Like it hot! Write soon. Love, Mama. *P.S.* My *friend* in the snap is Farley. Yankee, just like you.

Saradove saw the enclosed snap. The cold air of her room seemed to smart and withdraw from its loud, heated-up colors. Olympia filled nearly all the photograph. She seemed so large that certain parts of her body were ready, Saradove felt, to overhang the snapshot's rippled edges. The unnatural colors of the drugstore print brought Olympia's huge smile out in orange, made her tanned face look black. Her eyes glared out as bright as sky or water, were unflinching in the unshadowed noonday of her new hot world. She was wearing a black bathing suit with a little pleated skirt attached to it; it made Olympia look straight and slim and uniformed, like a woman warrior. She was cocking an arm on a hip, an arm that looked made out of nutcracker steel. She was ready to use her arm for an embrace, a conquering embrace. Above the strong arm, a little white squirrel face, distorted behind thick bifocals, peered out, as though from the branch of an oak.

Farley, thought Saradove. Farley's bare skull was made for a lifetime of reflecting the glory of Olympia's new pale lavender permanent wave. It was nothing like the hair that had dampened and curled over a steaming kitchen sink. Farley's skull was radiant in its color; and just below Olympia's cocked arm, Farley's stomach bulged in a small and perfectly proportioned spare tire.

227

Saradove held the photograph close to her eyes, hunting for some kind of sickness or desperation Olympia would want her to cure; some need for love from Saradove. But Olympia's face asked for nothing; it bloomed through its garish colors with self-sufficiency, pleasure, beaming triumph.

Saradove let the picture drop to her lap. She had held it so tightly that her thumbs were going to leave prints over the lavender hair.

"Give us a kiss," she asked the orange mouth. The woman in the picture smiled only at the photographer; her lips did not move.

Johnson and his friend were standing in the doorway, shoulder to shoulder, tilting their beer bottles. Through the heat that pulsed from the letter, the picture, and enclosed the room, Johnson's friend was suddenly a man without a skin, without a use for blood to keep him warm. The friend, suddenly, was a see-through plastic man, a neat case of motionless organs, with wipe-off clothes. She saw a heart painted red, a stomach in light green; the beer poured through him in a clear golden stream, untainted by juices or acids, into the stomach. The stomach was clicking, faintly whining, and passing the beer on into a clear little tube; presently the beer would fill the pale-blue kidneys. Her mother's letter was turning a man into a god or a demon or into something that she and Johnson were imagining; and it was turning cold weather hot.

Saradove pushed the letter to the floor, burning her fingers on it. If Olympia's face and words were a warning, an omen, a promise, she could not bear it: she needed a climate that sparkled with ice; she needed to see Johnson's friend become cold, manlike, and friendly again. She looked at him; she ground the letter into the floor with her shoe. He breathed; he had a skin like anyone else. His overcoat was open, and his white shirt was dirty at the collar. Five ballpoint pens were clipped in his pocket. The friend was looking hard at Johnson, pouring his look into him, between swigs of beer. And the friend's face was not a plastic mask; it was a face looking hard at Johnson.

Burned by the look, Johnson's eyes were spurting tears; and the tears were gathering to make a river. His friend had done something, with a look, to Johnson's eyes. He was making Johnson see a masterpiece; and Johnson was a man worshiping a thing, invaluable and beautiful, that he had ruined and lost through innocence. The friend's look had turned Johnson's face into something twisting with knowledge and wisdom about the thing he adored and was suddenly suffering for.

Saradove, motionless, thought, What does Johnson adore? What is his friend forcing him to see? The look turned on Saradove, and then Saradove saw it too. It was herself, sitting in a red wing chair in the only space of sunlight the apartment windows allowed. Her legs were stretched out like black branches in their stockings, the world's only straight and perfect branches out of the world's only perfect tree, herself, shining like autumn out of her golden dress. Her hand dropped through the air, straining sun through her fingers; her hair draped her cheeks, black and straight and like a velvet curtain around a painting. The light was blurring her face with radiance; and she could not move. Johnson's friend had made her and would not let her go. If Johnson could talk now, she thought, he would say, Give it to me, it's mine now, I love it now! Now I want it! But Johnson's tongue had been smashed into silence; and he could do nothing but stand still and adore magic.

The friend, as remarkable as the magic he had made, as remarkable as Saradove, could have made it last forever. But he snapped his fingers, and the wind came whistling through the windows and blew Saradove into a corner of Johnson's eye; and there magic would make her stay with him, like dust or a cinder, forever. The friend laughed and let them shiver and feel their imperfect, mortal blood run again. Johnson threw the beer bottles into the clean Christmas tree corner; and they put on their coats.

Easily, without slipping on ice or becoming snarled in traffic, they left the city fitted inside the friend's car. Saradove curled, resented curling, then languished, alone, in the back seat. Johnson slumped and propped his knees on the dashboard and tunelessly, without success, tried to sing the song his friend was singing as he drove them north. The car horn was blaring, at nothing, and they were being driven through banks of snow and trees that grew more intimate and bare as they went along, farther to the north.

Saradove began to sleep; and the song the friend was singing rolled thunder through her sleep and regulated her dreams.

> "O Good lord judge, and sweet lord judge, peace for
> a little while, methinks I see my own father
> come riding by the stile! O father, O father,
> a little of your gold and likewise of your fee
> to keep my body from yonder grave and my neck
> from the gallows tree."

The friend sang; he blew his horn between the words of the song at nothing, at the bare highway, at skis passing them on the tops of Volkswagens. Johnson's attempt at the song, in a voice like the sound of hands crushing paper, grew softer, quieted for longer intervals, until he too slept; and the singing of the friend controlled all the sleep in their bodies.

Saradove, in her sleep, was not going north. She was nestling in clear blue water between her mother's legs. They were sitting in the shallows and staring together up at the Florida sun. "Oh, my little girl," her mother was saying; and her mother's hand was making a funnel of itself and dribbling a ribbon of sand over her thighs. Her mother's hand was rubbing her salt-stiffened hair, was cupping her chin; and her mother's voice was saying over and over, "Oh, I love you, give your mother a kiss"; and Saradove was turning around in the water, her arms and lips ready for the lovely woman. But only the sun was where the woman should be, and only light, too much of it, was embracing Saradove. Heat was swallowing her up; but she kept reaching until the water grew cold.

The voice and the song were returning, splashing through her dream like warm salt water and then freezing the dream into ice.

"For I am come to see you hanged, and hanged you shall be.
O, good lord judge, and sweet lord judge,
peace for a little while,
methinks I see my own mother come riding by the stile!"

Johnson's head throbbed gently against the windowpane as he slept, safe and outside the voice.

The friend turned from his driving and grinned at Saradove. "Past Albany now," he said.

"For a Christmas tree!" Panic shook her upright. He had taken them too far; and how much farther would they have to go? Her hands snatched at his throat, to throttle him, to turn him around and point him to the south; but she caught only a loose coat collar and a pair of shoulders shaking with laughter.

"The best trees in the world are where we're going. I promise you'll be merry this Christmas, Saradove." He blared his horn again. The highway's silence froze the noise, and they left it far behind.

231

"Go back to sleep, Saradove," the friend said. His laughter lapsed into short chuckles. "You need sleep to be a mother."

Saradove lay back down. The rhythm of the wheels was closing her eyes again and making a heat that burned her like the words of her mother's letter: he is a god or a demon or Clive's Mephistopheles mask come to life; Johnson says he is his friend. "Where do you come from?" she asked.

He said, "Go to sleep. I come from where I'm taking you." He hummed the tune until he was sure she was asleep again; and then he whispered, "And then the mother said:

> "None of my gold now shall you have
> nor likewise of my fee,
> for I am come to see you hanged
> and hanged you shall be."

He sang loudly. The car heater was like a blanket, but everything outside their car slept and grew stiffer with cold. Nothing was awake but the song Johnson's friend sang.

Everything stopped. Saradove moved her foot and felt it press against the handle of the friend's ax.

"Wake up, dear. Dear, wake up!" Johnson was buttoning his coat. It was his friend who was calling her dear, calling her to wake up. At his command, she opened her eyes. She looked out the window. In contrast to what she saw there, she was a blackamoor. There was no earth left. They were stopped in the middle of a field of snow, snow so thick, so white in the last short glare of day that it seemed to wrap them up inside a white rubber ball. They were the jingly bell inside the ball that made it amusing for babies or cats. At the horizon, the sky and the snow tried to touch to make all suffocating and pure; but the trees interrupted their union. In a thick, nearly perfect circle, far blacker than they should be, the trees enclosed the field, a long distance from the car.

232

The trees, or their driver, had trapped them in a circle, centering them inside cold, setting them up for someone's marksmanship.

With the same thought, Saradove and Johnson began turning their heads, following the circle of trees, hunting everywhere for that gap through which the friend had driven. They did not find it. And when their eyes met, they stopped looking. The friend had got out, was standing in the snow, bending to it, rubbing his face and hands in it, laughing in it, swallowing it. "Ah!" they heard him call, "My beautiful home again, at last!"

"Johnson," she whispered, "who is he? Where did you find him? What kind of friend is he?"

Johnson laughed at her. "You're a worry-wart! I don't exactly know, but who the hell cares? I met him on the street late one night, and after that, I seemed to run into him everywhere . . . he buys me drinks in bars, gives me rides home in taxis. The damndest thing . . . I woke up one night and thought I saw him flying over our bed, circling above us like an airplane or an angel and singing that song of his . . . it was a hell of a dream; I thought he was trying to kill me and carry you off."

She held him to his seat. "His *name!*"

"He says anything we want to call him is all right with him. He says call him the woman's home companion, the lady's friendly avenger . . . he's funny as hell sometimes. He says he's an actor and can impersonate anything in nature. I saw him do it one night . . . first he was a mountain, then a tree, then a field of clover, then a snowfall. You should have seen it! He's wild! I'm crazy about him, so stop being a bitch, Saradove."

Saradove let him go. He got out and began stamping his feet, loosening himself up, pretending, she thought, that all

233

was as normal as a cold football game on a Saturday afternoon. She looked for anything to look at besides white snow and black trees. When she found it, it was red. Blooming through the snow as easily as roses from sandy soil, were long pale stalks with bulbs of growth at their tops like red velvet. There were clumps of them all over the snow. Beyond them, one tree, with a gesture of reassurance, shook and showed her the green needles of its branches.

The friend was dropping an arm over the front seat and dragging up his ax, moving it slowly up against Saradove's leg. His face leaned over her like a frozen lake. "And you ought to see me do impersonations of nature's animals, Saradove," he grinned. "The lion, the tiger, the wolf, the fox, the tiger's cub! You really should!"

Johnson caught his words. "Where are we?" His voice was frantic, tearful.

His friend began his song again. He had a voice like a bird's.

"Where are we?" Johnson's voice was full of terror. The singing stopped, and the friend looked like any man again.

"Why, you know, outside of Albany somewhere . . . Christmas-tree country!" The friend made a fist and jabbed Johnson in the shoulder. "Man, it's what you asked for, isn't it?" And he started laughing and hugging Johnson. Johnson laughed too, full of relief.

Saradove drew her legs together.

"Wait here in the car, baby," Johnson called. "My pal and I are off to the woods."

"Yes, dear," his friend answered, answering for Saradove, mimicking her. His eyes had lost their frost; and, for a moment before he swung away, they turned warm and golden on Saradove, too bright for eyes to be.

They walked out into the snow, the ax gleaming dully,

then brightly, from the friend's shoulder. Johnson had his hands in his pockets, with nothing to carry.

Before they entered the trees, Saradove rolled down the window and called after them. "Will you hurry? What if it gets dark?"

The friend stopped and answered her. "It will," he called. His mouth seemed close to her ear.

Johnson went first into the trees. His friend did not walk well through snow; he seemed to hobble, like a cripple or like a goat on hind legs. Saradove tested the knobs on the dashboard. No radio, and the heater had gone off with the motor. She slid beneath the wheel, pretending to be the driver, humming the driver's song, twisting the wheel right and left, stamping her boots against the pedals. When she remembered the red stalks outside, she got out. She sank in and out of the snow, her shadow turning violet before her. The red bulbs were more like wool than velvet in her fingers; and their stalks came up from the snow without resistance. She was her grandmother lopping the heads of white roses off into a basket, smiling, squinting at the sun.

The image was colder than the weather, and it sickened her. The cold was forcing her mind to swim for a safe shore; and it swam, lifting its arms, slicing its legs through the green surf, pushing the drowning water away, finally to lie panting and rocking in the safe foam, relaxing against sharp rocks and broken stone, feeling a shell cup one shoulder blade.

Olympia, wrapped and belted in white terrycloth, was sitting on the beach shaking her head, chewing on her thumb. At sixteen, what girl lies flat in the shallows, spreading out her arms and legs, letting small boys jump over her, drip white ice cream on her?

Saradove knelt in the snow to pull the red-flowered stalk up by its roots.

235

Saradove rolled over and knelt in the hard, wet sand. A boy dropped his ice-cream stick. With it, using long strokes, she made the outline of a woman in the sand. She crawled on her hands and knees from the head to the foot of her drawing, forcing the curves of the body and legs to become perfect. The woman drawing was larger than life. If Saradove had stretched herself on it, head meeting head, her toes would have reached only to the sand-woman's thighs. She molded the woman, shaping breasts, quarreling with the sand over the size of the waist, heaping and rubbing until a small belly bulged; rounding the thighs, shaping ten toes. The sand-woman's hands rested on her hips. Her eyes were two little pits; her mouth a razor shell.

When Saradove became too hot to draw another breath, she raised her head from the woman to see the crowds of bare legs and pointing fingers surrounding her. Olympia was saying, I'm not leaving the beach; she's part yours, you do it. She's not like anybody I ever knew. And for the next hour, she sat in the front seat of the car with her father and listened to him drink gin from a bottle; and watched him hold tightly to the steering wheel. Long before Duncan died, long before that November, the sand-woman had been washed clear away to China.

Her fingers were too cold to hold the red blossom. It disappeared into the dark night below her knees; and the night was rising all the way up her body. She threw the flowers, in wide arcs, back to the snow; there was no way of seeing where they had landed. She ran to get back to the car before the dark hid it. She started the motor and the heater, switched on the headlights, and shook until the warmth began soothing her.

Get them back, she said, get them back *now* while I can still see that one branch yonder, and I will never love anybody

236

wrong again. The blackness hung over the trees for an instant, then ate them up. The branch was gone. Soundlessness crept into her and took her apart. Her head rang with silence. It was the death of all life that could make noise which made her shake: noise that could crunch through snow, could whistle, slap a face, roar a subway; it was *no noise* that grew arms, took her by neck and shook her until the lower lip fluttered against the top teeth and the knees knocked and stuck together with sweat.

Out of her head, or out of the invisible trees, the shrill note of panic whistled; and soon she danced to the music. It was the replacement of sound; it was wilderness. The foreign traveler would be made wild too. Saradove held to the steering wheel; Saradove screamed the names of everyone she remembered to come and save her. She said, The trees begin and end where the sky begins and ends. In a moment, the music will become a big fist that will slug me into the snow that is no longer snow but a black void that will catch me, push me forever into cold, while I scream in my sleep. She beat the horn with her fist and shouted into the blackness.

Down in her body the baby moved for the first time. She spread herself over the front seat, legs apart, ready to have it. She looked up through the windshield and saw the stars too spread themselves.

After they are cut down, she said, the branches will be flat against the barks. Some will be stuck over with ice. But when we drive home through the city streets, the warm fumes from the trucks will melt the ice; and in the house, the heat from the fire I will start with her letter will shake the branches down, open, spread them apart for candy, glass balls, and tinsel that will rub out the smell of wild dark woods. I will never let my tree come back here to its stump again.

Hours from now, she said, the dark will lift, and I'll walk

into the trees and find the path they made. And when I've stumbled in several wrong directions, I'll finally see them there, frozen into the ropes around their necks, stiff, knocking against each other with loud cracks when the wind blows. There's a madman waiting in the woods who got them. Something got them and is trying to get me outside to get me. Or else the madman will come to the car, smash the window and drag me through. I will say, she said, look at me, I'm a mother; who can kill somebody's mother? It will need milk and blankets and toys before you can kill me.

She pressed her hand hard against each window, testing its strength, watching for the face that would soon come and freeze its laughs against the glass. And the laughs would shatter the glass, and the hand would drag her to death in the dark.

Saradove went to sleep. She dreamed, with many colors, much light, herself and Johnson back into the apartment. Johnson was holding their baby in his arms, laughing into its face. Saradove was vomiting and holding her thin belly, but the two of them, father and child, would not get out of her sight and ease her sickness. The baby's diaper was stinking; its skin hung from the bones, leper-white, marked with dirt. Its head was flat, like a bent penny; and its one eye was peering at its mother through a face made of thin, raw dough. A dough mask of a face that kept slipping from its bones and covering, then uncovering, the one eye that winked at its mother. "Don't you love it?" its father was saying. "Don't you just love our little baby? Look at the new present for it from our friend." Johnson was rattling the present at her. It was a small tin globe, painted in purples and greens. Johnson was shaking it in the baby's face; and the baby was laughing. Its mask was falling apart from its laughter. And the tin world was stretching like a rubber balloon, blowing itself up in short quick gasps until it was enormous and filling their tiny house. But it was made of tin and would not burst. Pressed into a corner Saradove was waking with a taste of metal geography in her mouth; and inside the giant sphere Johnson and the baby floated gravity-free, their heels and heads knocking gently against the tin circle. Saradove could hear them kissing each other good-bye, and good-bye again.

She opened her eyes. The smacking sound grew louder: it was the suck of feet bounding in and out of snow. For a moment, her head quivered on its neck, shaking from the effort of sitting up, shaking like a red wool blossom on a thin stalk, or the last of the August roses. She held her throat, her head grew still. She saw what was coming for her.

Into the car's headlights, the friend came leaping, like a deer crossing a road, closer with every bound to Saradove's speeding heart. In one hand he carried Johnson's head; and as he came nearer, his delighted smile grew wider. Just in front of the car he stopped still, dazzling in the dazzling snow. He began to jump up from the lights into the overhead dark, and then back down pointed and twirling like a diver or a dancer. The head, Johnson's head, was balanced on the tips of his fingers, spinning too, pouring all around the friend a loose umbrella of blood. The blood, like rain, was soaking and carving little pits into the snow. The friend's naked body, drenched, warmed, pleased, bowed to Saradove; and, afterward, like a minor dancer, the head bowed too, tilted from the friend's gracious fingers. The dance was over, and the head was falling into the snow, its eyes glaring into the light.

When the friend was settled comfortably inside his car, he took Saradove beneath his arm and caused her to lay her head on his wet shoulder.

"I won't kill you too," he said.

"I will," answered Saradove. But she was warm against him, and the sight of the trees lighting up against the sky was exhausting her. They sat quietly before the sun's rise, tired, companionable.

"The kind of day," he said, "when I always go hunting, then back to my fire feeling tired and good and happy to sing my song. It took all my strength to save you, Saradove."

"Yes," yawned Saradove. The baby was making her sleepy and hungry all the time. But the friend was pouring refreshment over and through her. Still the head gleamed, open-eyed and gory in the headlights.

"The dawn's up. You can turn off the lights now," she said. He did. The snow swallowed the head.

"We will be going now," he said. "And what are you going to do now, now that I've finished all your fears, Saradove?"

"I don't know," she said, thinking only of the long sleep she would have on the ride home. "You tell me."

He turned to her with a kiss that sank through her like pleasure. He said, "Why, go and love her, Saradove."

"Where will I find her?"

"First in yourself. Then in the heat and in the cold. Then in your mother, then in your daughter, then in your future. Go and catch her, Saradove."

And Saradove did.